NON SANS DROICT.

William Shakespeare

HENRY VI, PART ONE

Edited by Lawrence V. Ryan

The Signet Classic Shakespeare
GENERAL EDITOR: SYLVAN BARNET

Revised and Updated Bibliography

A MENTOR BOOK
NEW AMERICAN LIBRARY

TIMES MIRROR
NEW YORK AND SCARBOROUGH, ONTARIO
THE NEW ENGLISH LIBRARY LIMITED, LONDON

Library of Congress Catalog Card Number: 67–18405

SIGNET CLASSIC TRADEMARK REG. U.S. PAT. OFF. AND FOREIGN COUNTRIES
REGISTERED TRADEMARK——MARCA REGISTRADA
HECHO EN CHICAGO, U.S.A.

SIGNET, SIGNET CLASSICS, MENTOR, PLUME
and MERIDIAN BOOKS
are published *in the United States* by
The New American Library, Inc.,
1301 Avenue of the Americas, New York, New York 10019,
in Canada by The New American Library of Canada Limited,
81 Mack Avenue, Scarborough, 704, Ontario,
in the United Kingdom by The New English Library Limited,
Barnard's Inn, Holborn, London E.C. 1, England

First Signet Classic Printing, March, 1967

3 4 5 6 7 8 9 10 11

PRINTED IN THE UNITED STATES OF AMERICA

Contents

Shakespeare: Prefatory Remarks

Between the record of his baptism in Stratford on 26 April 1564 and the record of his burial in Stratford on 25 April 1616, some forty documents name Shakespeare, and many others name his parents, his children, and his grandchildren. More facts are known about William Shakespeare than about any other playwright of the period except Ben Jonson. The facts should, however, be distinguished from the legends. The latter, inevitably more engaging and better known, tell us that the Stratford boy killed a calf in high style, poached deer and rabbits, and was forced to flee to London, where he held horses outside a playhouse. These traditions are only traditions; they may be true, but no evidence supports them, and it is well to stick to the facts.

Mary Arden, the dramatist's mother, was the daughter of a substantial landowner; about 1557 she married John Shakespeare, who was a glove-maker and trader in various farm commodities. In 1557 John Shakespeare was a member of the Council (the governing body of Stratford), in 1558 a constable of the borough, in 1561 one of the two town chamberlains, in 1565 an alderman (entitling him to the appellation "Mr."), in 1568 high bailiff—the town's highest political office, equivalent to mayor. After 1577, for an unknown reason he drops out of local politics. The birthday of William Shakespeare, the eldest son of this locally prominent man, is unrecorded; but the Stratford parish register records that the infant was baptized on 26 April 1564. (It is quite possible that he was born on 23 April, but this date has probably been assigned by tradition because it is the date on which, fifty-two years later, he died.) The attendance records of the Stratford grammar school of the period are not extant, but it is reasonable to assume that the son of a local official attended the school and received substantial training in Latin. The masters of the school from Shakespeare's seventh to fifteenth years held Oxford degrees; the Elizabethan curriculum excluded mathematics and the natural sciences but taught a good deal of Latin rhetoric, logic, and literature. On 27 November 1582 a marriage license was issued to Shakespeare and Anne Hathaway, eight years his senior. The couple had a child in May, 1583. Perhaps the marriage was necessary, but perhaps the couple had earlier engaged in a formal "troth plight" which would render their children legitimate even if no further ceremony were performed. In 1585 Anne Hathaway bore Shakespeare twins.

That Shakespeare was born is excellent; that he married and had children is pleasant; but that we know nothing about his departure from Stratford to London, or about the beginning of his theatrical career, is lamentable and must be admitted. We would gladly sacrifice details about his children's baptism for details about his earliest days on the stage. Perhaps the poaching episode is true (but it is first reported almost a century after Shakespeare's death), or perhaps he first left Stratford to be a schoolteacher, as another tradition holds; perhaps he was moved by

> Such winds as scatters young men through the world,
> To seek their fortunes further than at home
> Where small experience grows.

In 1592, thanks to the cantankerousness of Robert Greene, a rival playwright and a pamphleteer, we have our first reference, a snarling one, to Shakespeare as an actor and playwright. Greene warns those of his own educated friends who wrote for the theater against an actor who has presumed to turn playwright:

> There is an upstart crow, beautified with our feathers, that with his *tiger's heart wrapped in a player's hide* sup-

poses he is as well able to bombast out a blank verse as
the best of you, and being an absolute Johannes-factotum
is in his own conceit the only Shake-scene in a country.

The reference to the player, as well as the allusion to
Aesop's crow (who strutted in borrowed plumage, as an
actor struts in fine words not his own), makes it clear
that by this date Shakespeare had both acted and written.
That Shakespeare is meant is indicated not only by
"Shake-scene" but by the parody of a line from one of
Shakespeare's plays, *3 Henry VI:* "O, tiger's heart
wrapped in a woman's hide." If Shakespeare in 1592 was
prominent enough to be attacked by an envious dramatist,
he probably had served an apprenticeship in the theater
for at least a few years.

In any case, by 1592 Shakespeare had acted and written, and there are a number of subsequent references to
him as an actor: documents indicate that in 1598 he is
a "principal comedian," in 1603 a "principal tragedian,"
in 1608 he is one of the "men players." The profession
of actor was not for a gentleman, and it occasionally
drew the scorn of university men who resented writing
speeches for persons less educated than themselves, but
it was respectable enough: players, if prosperous, were
in effect members of the bourgeoisie, and there is nothing
to suggest that Stratford considered William Shakespeare
less than a solid citizen. When, in 1596, the Shake-
speares were granted a coat of arms, the grant was made
to Shakespeare's father, but probably William Shakespeare
(who the next year bought the second-largest house in
town) had arranged the matter on his own behalf. In
subsequent transactions he is occasionally styled a gentleman.

Although in 1593 and 1594 Shakespeare published two
narrative poems dedicated to the Earl of Southampton,
Venus and Adonis and *The Rape of Lucrece,* and may
well have written most or all of his sonnets in the middle
nineties, Shakespeare's literary activity seems to have
been almost entirely devoted to the theater. (It may be
significant that the two narrative poems were written in

years when the plague closed the theaters for several months.) In 1594 he was a charter member of a theatrical company called the Chamberlain's Men (which in 1603 changed its name to the King's Men); until he retired to Stratford (about 1611, apparently), he was with this remarkably stable company. From 1599 the company acted primarily at the Globe Theatre, in which Shakespeare held a one-tenth interest. Other Elizabethan dramatists are known to have acted, but no other is known also to have been entitled to a share in the profits of the playhouse.

Shakespeare's first eight published plays did not have his name on them, but this is not remarkable; the most popular play of the sixteenth century, Thomas Kyd's *The Spanish Tragedy*, went through many editions without naming Kyd, and Kyd's authorship is known only because a book on the profession of acting happens to quote (and attribute to Kyd) some lines on the interest of Roman emperors in the drama. What is remarkable is that after 1598 Shakespeare's name commonly appears on printed plays—some of which are not his. Another indication of his popularity comes from Francis Meres, author of *Palladis Tamia: Wit's Treasury* (1598): in this anthology of snippets accompanied by an essay on literature, many playwrights are mentioned, but Shakespeare's name occurs more often than any other, and Shakespeare is the only playwright whose plays are listed.

From his acting, playwriting, and share in a theater, Shakespeare seems to have made considerable money. He put it to work, making substantial investments in Stratford real estate. When he made his will (less than a month before he died), he sought to leave his property intact to his descendants. Of small bequests to relatives and to friends (including three actors, Richard Burbage, John Heminges, and Henry Condell), that to his wife of the second-best bed has provoked the most comment; perhaps it was the bed the couple had slept in, the best being reserved for visitors. In any case, had Shakespeare not excepted it, the bed would have gone (with the rest of his household possessions) to his daughter and her husband. On 25 April 1616 he was buried within the chancel of the church at Stratford. An unattractive monument to his memory, placed on a wall near the grave, says he died on 23 April. Over the grave itself are the lines, perhaps by Shakespeare, that (more than his literary fame) have kept his bones undisturbed in the crowded burial ground where old bones were often dislodged to make way for new:

> Good friend, for Jesus' sake forbear
> To dig the dust enclosèd here.
> Blessed be the man that spares these stones
> And cursed be he that moves my bones.

Thirty-seven plays, as well as some nondramatic poems, are held to constitute the Shakespeare canon. The dates of composition of most of the works are highly uncertain, but there is often evidence of a *terminus a quo* (starting point) and/or a *terminus ad quem* (terminal point) that provides a framework for intelligent guessing. For example, *Richard II* cannot be earlier than 1595, the publication date of some material to which it is indebted; *The Merchant of Venice* cannot be later than 1598, the year Francis Meres mentioned it. Sometimes arguments for a date hang on an alleged topical allusion, such as the lines about the unseasonable weather in *A Midsummer Night's Dream,* II.i.81–117, but such an allusion (if indeed it is an allusion) can be variously interpreted, and in any case there is always the possibility that a topical allusion was inserted during a revision, years after the composition of a play. Dates are often attributed on the basis of style, and although conjectures about style usually rest on other conjectures, sooner or later one must rely on one's literary sense. There is no real proof, for example, that *Othello* is not as early as *Romeo and Juliet,* but one feels *Othello* is later, and because the first record of its performance is 1604, one is glad enough to set its composition at that date and not push it back into Shakespeare's early years. The following chronology, then, is as much indebted to informed guesswork and sensitivity as it is to fact. The dates, necessarily imprecise, indicate something like a scholarly consensus.

PLAYS

1588–93	The Comedy of Errors
1588–94	Love's Labor's Lost
1590–91	2 Henry VI
1590–91	3 Henry VI
1591–92	1 Henry VI
1592–93	Richard III
1592–94	Titus Andronicus
1593–94	The Taming of the Shrew
1593–95	The Two Gentlemen of Verona
1594–96	Romeo and Juliet
1595	Richard II
1594–96	A Midsummer Night's Dream
1596–97	King John
1596–97	The Merchant of Venice
1597	1 Henry IV
1597–98	2 Henry IV
1598–1600	Much Ado About Nothing
1598–99	Henry V
1599	Julius Caesar
1599–1600	As You Like It
1599–1600	Twelfth Night
1600–01	Hamlet
1597–1601	The Merry Wives of Windsor
1601–02	Troilus and Cressida
1602–04	All's Well That Ends Well
1603–04	Othello
1604	Measure for Measure
1605–06	King Lear
1605–06	Macbeth
1606–07	Antony and Cleopatra
1605–08	Timon of Athens
1607–09	Coriolanus
1608–09	Pericles
1609–10	Cymbeline
1610–11	The Winter's Tale

| 1611 | *The Tempest* |
| 1612–13 | *Henry VIII* |

POEMS

1592	*Venus and Adonis*
1593–95	*The Rape of Lucrece*
1593–1600	*Sonnets*
1600–01	*The Phoenix and Turtle*

Shakespeare's Theater

In Shakespeare's infancy, Elizabethan actors performed wherever they could—in great halls, at court, in the courtyards of inns. The innyards must have made rather unsatisfactory theaters: on some days they were unavailable because carters bringing goods to London used them as depots; when available, they had to be rented from the innkeeper; perhaps most important, London inns were subject to the Common Council of London, which was not well disposed toward theatricals. In 1574 the Common Council required that plays and playing places in London be licensed. It asserted that

> sundry great disorders and inconveniences have been found to ensue to this city by the inordinate haunting of great multitudes of people, specially youth, to plays, interludes, and shows, namely occasion of frays and quarrels, evil practices of incontinency in great inns having chambers and secret places adjoining to their open stages and galleries,

and ordered that innkeepers who wished licenses to hold performances put up a bond and make contributions to the poor.

The requirement that plays and innyard theaters be licensed, along with the other drawbacks of playing at inns, probably drove James Burbage (a carpenter-turned-actor) to rent in 1576 a plot of land northeast of the city walls and to build here—on property outside the jurisdiction of the city—England's first permanent construction designed for plays. He called it simply the Theatre. About all that is known of its construction is that it was wood. It soon had imitators, the most famous being the Globe (1599), built across the Thames (again outside the city's jurisdiction), out of timbers of the Theatre, which had been dismantled when Burbage's lease ran out.

There are three important sources of information about the structure of Elizabethan playhouses—drawings, a contract, and stage directions in plays. Of drawings, only the so-called De Witt drawing (c. 1596) of the Swan—really a friend's copy of De Witt's drawing—is of much significance. It shows a building of three tiers, with a stage jutting from a wall into the yard or center of the building. The tiers are roofed, and part of the stage is covered by a roof that projects from the rear and is supported at its front on two posts, but the groundlings, who paid a penny to stand in front of the stage, were exposed to the sky. (Performances in such a playhouse were held only in the daytime; artificial illumination was not used.) At the rear of the stage are two doors; above the stage is a gallery. The second major source of information, the contract for the Fortune, specifies that although the Globe is to be the model, the Fortune is to be square, eighty feet outside and fifty-five inside. The stage is to be forty-three feet broad, and is to extend into the middle of the yard (i.e., it is tweny-seven and a half feet deep). For patrons willing to pay more than the general admission charged of the groundlings, there were to be three galleries provided with seats. From the third chief source, stage directions, one learns that entrance to the stage was by doors, presumably spaced widely apart at the rear ("Enter one citizen at one door, and another at the other"), and that in addition to the platform stage there was occasionally some sort of curtained booth or alcove allowing for "discovery" scenes, and some sort of playing space "aloft" or "above" to represent (for example) the top of a city's walls or a room above the street. Doubtless each theater had its own peculiarities, but perhaps we can talk about a "typical" Elizabethan theater if we realize that no theater need exactly have fit the description, just as no father is the typical father with 3.7 children. This hypothetical theater is wooden, round or polygonal (in *Henry V* Shakespeare calls it a "wooden *O*"), capable of holding some eight hundred spectators standing in the yard around the projecting elevated stage and some fifteen hundred additional spectators seated in the three roofed galleries. The stage, protected by a "shadow" or "heavens" or roof, is entered by two doors; behind the doors is the "tiring house" (attiring house, i.e., dressing room), and above the doors is some sort of gallery that may sometimes hold spectators but that can be used (for example) as the bedroom from which Romeo—according to a stage direction in one text—"goeth down." Some evidence suggests that a throne can be lowered onto the platform stage, perhaps from the "shadow"; certainly characters can descend from the stage through a trap or traps into the cellar or "hell." Sometimes this space beneath the platform accommodates a sound-effects man or musician (in *Antony and Cleopatra* "music of the hautboys is under the stage") or an actor (in *Hamlet* the "Ghost cries under the stage"). Most characters simply walk on and off, but because there is no curtain in front of the platform, corpses will have to be carried off (Hamlet must lug Polonius' guts into the neighbor room), or will have to fall at the rear, where the curtain on the alcove or booth can be drawn to conceal them.

Such may have been the so-called "public theater." Another kind of theater, called the "private theater" because its much greater admission charge limited its audience to the wealthy or the prodigal, must be briefly mentioned. The private theater was basically a large room, entirely roofed and therefore artificially illuminated, with a stage at one end. In 1576 one such theater was established in Blackfriars, a Dominican priory in London that had been suppressed in 1538 and confiscated by the Crown and thus was not under the city's jurisdiction. All the actors in the Blackfriars theater were boys about eight to thirteen years old (in the public theaters similar boys played female parts; a boy Lady Macbeth played to a man Macbeth). This private theater had a precarious existence, and ceased operations in 1584. In 1596 James Burbage, who had already made theatrical history by building the Theatre, began to construct a second Blackfriars theater. He died in 1597, and for several years this second Blackfriars theater was used by a troupe of boys, but in 1608 two of Burbage's sons and five other actors (including Shakespeare) became joint operators of the theater, using it in the winter when the open-air Globe was unsuitable. Perhaps such a smaller theater, roofed, artificially illuminated, and with a tradition of a courtly audience, exerted an influence on Shakespeare's late plays.

Performances in the private theaters may well have had intermissions during which music was played, but in the public theaters the action was probably uninterrupted, flowing from scene to scene almost without a break. Actors would enter, speak, exit, and others would immediately enter and establish (if necessary) the new locale by a few properties and by words and gestures. Here are some samples of Shakespeare's scene painting:

> This is Illyria, lady.

> Well, this is the Forest of Arden.

> This castle hath a pleasant seat; the air
> Nimbly and sweetly recommends itself
> Unto our gentle senses.

On the other hand, it is a mistake to conceive of the Elizabethan stage as bare. Although Shakespeare's Chorus in *Henry V* calls the stage an "unworthy scaffold" and urges the spectators to "eke out our performance with your mind," there was considerable spectacle. The last act of *Macbeth,* for example, has five stage directions calling for "drum and colors," and another sort of appeal to the eye is indicated by the stage direction "Enter Macduff, with Macbeth's head." Some scenery and properties may have been substantial; doubtless a throne was used, and in one play of the period we encounter this direction:

"Hector takes up a great piece of rock and casts at Ajax, who tears up a young tree by the roots and assails Hector." The matter is of some importance, and will be glanced at again in the next section.

The Texts of Shakespeare

Though eighteen of his plays were published during his lifetime, Shakespeare seems never to have supervised their publication. There is nothing unusual here; when a playwright sold a play to a theatrical company he surrendered his ownership of it. Normally a company would not publish the play, because to publish it meant to allow competitors to acquire the piece. Some plays, however, did get published: apparently treacherous actors sometimes pieced together a play for a publisher, sometimes a company in need of money sold a play, and sometimes a company allowed a play to be published that no longer drew audiences. That Shakespeare did not concern himself with publication, then, is scarcely remarkable; of his contemporaries only Ben Jonson carefully supervised the publication of his own plays. In 1623, seven years after Shakespeare's death, John Heminges and Henry Condell (two senior members of Shakespeare's company, who had performed with him for about twenty years) collected his plays—published and unpublished—into a large volume, commonly called the First Folio. (A folio is a volume consisting of sheets that have been folded once, each sheet thus making two leaves, or four pages. The eighteen plays published during Shakespeare's lifetime had been issued one play per volume in small books called quartos. Each sheet in a quarto has been folded twice, making four leaves, or eight pages.) The First Folio contains thirty-six plays; a thirty-seventh, *Pericles,* though not in the Folio is regarded as canonical. Heminges and Condell suggest in an address "To the great variety of readers" that the republished plays are presented in better form than in the quartos: "Before you were abused with diverse stolen and surreptitious copies, maimed and deformed by the frauds and stealths of injurious impostors that exposed them; even those, are now offered to your view cured and perfect of their limbs, and all the rest absolute in their numbers, as he [i.e., Shakespeare] conceived them."

Whoever was assigned to prepare the texts for publication in the First Folio seems to have taken his job seriously and yet not to have performed it with uniform care. The sources of the texts seem to have been, in general, good unpublished copies or the best published copies. The first play in the collection, *The Tempest,* is divided into acts and scenes, has unusually full stage directions and descriptions of spectacle, and concludes with a list of the characters, but the editor was not able (or willing) to present all of the succeeding texts so fully dressed. Later texts occasionally show signs of carelessness: in one scene of *Much Ado About Nothing* the names of actors, instead of characters, appear as speech prefixes, as they had in the quarto, which the Folio reprints; proofreading throughout the Folio is spotty and apparently was done without reference to the printer's copy; the pagination of *Hamlet* jumps from 156 to 257.

A modern editor of Shakespeare must first select his copy; no problem if the play exists only in the Folio, but a considerable problem if the relationship between a quarto and the Folio—or an early quarto and a later one —is unclear. When an editor has chosen what seems to him to be the most authoritative text or texts for his copy, he has not done with making decisions. First of all, he must reckon with Elizabethan spelling. If he is not producing a facsimile, he probably modernizes it, but ought he to preserve the old form of words that apparently were pronounced quite unlike their modern forms —"lanthorn," "alablaster"? If he preserves these forms, is he really preserving Shakespeare's forms or perhaps those of a compositor in the printing house? What is one to do when one finds "lanthorn" and "lantern" in adjacent lines? (The editors of this series in general, but not invariably, assume that words should be spelled in their modern form.) Elizabethan punctuation, too, presents problems. For example in the First Folio, the only text for the play, Macbeth rejects his wife's idea that he can wash the blood from his hand:

> no: this my Hand will rather
> The multitudinous Seas incarnardine,
> Making the Greene one, Red.

Obviously an editor will remove the superfluous capitals, and he will probably alter the spelling to "incarnadine," but will he leave the comma before "red," letting Macbeth speak of the sea as "the green one," or will he (like most modern editors) remove the comma and thus have Macbeth say that his hand will make the ocean *uniformly* red?

An editor will sometimes have to change more than spelling or punctuation. Macbeth says to his wife:

> I dare do all that may become a man,
> Who dares no more, is none.

For two centuries editors have agreed that the second line is unsatisfactory, and have emended "no" to "do": "Who dares do more is none." But when in the same play Ross says that fearful persons

> floate vpon a wilde and violent Sea
> Each way, and moue,

need "move" be emended to "none," as it often is, on the hunch that the compositor misread the manuscript? The editors of the Signet Classic Shakespeare have restrained themselves from making abundant emendations. In their minds they hear Dr. Johnson on the dangers of emending: "I have adopted the Roman sentiment, that it is more honorable to save a citizen than to kill an enemy." Some departures (in addition to spelling, punctuation, and lineation) from the copy text have of course been made, but the original readings are listed in a note following the play, so that the reader can evaluate them for himself.

The editors of the Signet Classic Shakespeare, following tradition, have added line numbers and in many cases act and scene divisions as well as indications of locale at the beginning of scenes. The Folio divided most of the plays into acts and some into scenes. Early eighteenth-century editors increased the divisions. These divisions, which provide a convenient way of referring to passages in the plays, have been retained, but when not in the text chosen as the basis for the Signet Classic text they are enclosed in square brackets [   ] to indicate that they are editorial additions. Similarly, although no play of Shakespeare's published during his lifetime was equipped with indications of locale at the heads of scene divisions, locales have here been added in square brackets for the convenience of the reader, who lacks the information afforded to spectators by costumes, properties, and gestures. The spectator can tell at a glance he is in the throne room, but without an editorial indication the reader may be puzzled for a while. It should be mentioned, incidentally, that there are a few authentic stage directions —perhaps Shakespeare's, perhaps a prompter's—that suggest locales: for example, "Enter Brutus in his orchard," and "They go up into the Senate house." It is hoped that the bracketed additions provide the reader with the sort of help provided in these two authentic directions, but it is equally hoped that the reader will remember that the stage was not loaded with scenery.

No editor during the course of his work can fail to recollect some words Heminges and Condell prefixed to the Folio:

It had been a thing, we confess, worthy to have been wished, that the author himself had lived to have set forth and overseen his own writings. But since it hath been ordained otherwise, and he by death departed from that right, we pray you do not envy his friends the office of their care and pain to have collected and published them.

Nor can an editor, after he has done his best, forget Heminges and Condell's final words: "And so we leave you to other of his friends, whom if you need can be

your guides. If you need them not, you can lead yourselves, and others. And such readers we wish him."

SYLVAN BARNET
Tufts University

Introduction

The First Part of Henry the Sixth is a play with many imperfections, so many, indeed, that editors and critics have often been reluctant to attribute the greater part of it to Shakespeare. "That Drum-and-trumpet Thing," the eighteenth-century critic Maurice Morgann called it in his essay on Sir John Falstaff, "written doubtless, or rather exhibited, long before *Shakespeare* was born, tho' afterwards repaired, I think, and furbished up by him with here and there a little sentiment and diction."

Such reluctance of ascription has led to the expenditure of much scholarly energy on attempts to isolate as undeniably Shakespearean a few scenes, in particular the finely managed quarrel of the Yorkists and Lancastrians in the Temple Garden (II.iv), and to assign the bulk of the work to various teams of collaborators, among them Christopher Marlowe, George Peele, Thomas Nashe, and Robert Greene. Another consequence has been an exceptional tentativeness in much of the critical speculation about *1 Henry VI,* though several fine studies have been made of its significance in Shakespeare's evolution from prentice playwright to master dramatist.

Arguments against Shakespeare's authorship, or primacy within a group of collaborators, have focused mainly upon resemblances in the text to patterns of diction and versification characteristic of other Elizabethan playwrights. The evidence amassed has been considerable, though sometimes contradictory; at times impressive, but never conclusive. For it is likely enough that a Shakespeare who was just setting out on his literary career would have tended to imitate the stylistic mannerisms of already established dramatists. Even Allison Gaw, among the champions of multiple authorship one of the most sensitive to the potential and actual virtues of the play, failed to associate the unusual effort to integrate historical theme and dramatic structure in a theatrically meaningful way with the designing hand of Shakespeare.

Against the collaborationist theory, however, have stood a number of commentators, among them Charles Knight and Hermann Ulrici in the nineteenth century and Peter Alexander, J. P. Brockbank, Leo Kirschbaum, Hereward Price, and E. M. W. Tillyard in our own time. These critics perceive the three dramas on the reign of Henry VI as of one piece, and regard the case for denying the Shakespearean authorship of any part as not proved. It would be rash to assert categorically that *1 Henry VI* as printed in the Folio of 1623 is entirely by Shakespeare, or that no version involving extensive collaboration with others ever did exist. But an approach to the play through the relationship between theme and dramatic design, rather than through its stylistic echoes of various contemporary writers, does considerably strengthen the argument that Shakespeare played the major, if not an exclusive, role in its composition.

Any reader or spectator coming to *1 Henry VI* after exposure to the chronicle plays of other Elizabethan authors is suddenly aware that here he is being asked not simply to observe the pageant of history, but to ponder the meaning of man's role in history. Most other works of the period in this dramatic kind are, even more evidently than the civic and national chronicles upon which they are based, mere strings of episodes in sequence of time, governed, if by any sense of theme at all, by the notion of the capriciousness of the goddess Fortune. Very few are concerned with seeking any other guiding principle in history or with the dramatic interaction of personalities within the pattern of historical events. Very few are concerned with the meaning of history at all, their authors often preferring instead, like a certain kind of modern historical novelist, to invent romantic situations involving historical personages within a bare framework of actual events.

The theme that runs throughout the tetralogy of plays composed by Shakespeare on the reigns of Henry VI and Richard III, and in fact throughout all of his dramatizations of English history, is the individual's, and a people's, response to the continuing alternations of order and disorder allowed by divine providence in the political life of a nation. A strong and heroic king whose regime brings glory and harmony to the commonwealth is succeeded by a monarch lacking, through extreme youth or defect of character, in the virtues necessary for unifying all the diverse constituents of society. The ineptitude or negligence of the sovereign looses the restraints on ambitious and unscrupulous subjects, whose schemes and counterschemes for self-aggrandizement promote faction, public disorder, and eventually civil war. As Tillyard points out in the selection printed later in this volume, in the struggle for domination degree, or acknowledgment of one's proper place in the hierarchically constituted political, and even cosmic, order, is forgotten. "Vaulting ambition" causes men to o'erleap themselves and drag the rest of society with them to the brink of chaos. Finally, when a ruler appears who is powerful and virtuous enough to triumph over the contending parties and restore degree and order, the hallmarks to the Elizabethan mind of good political economy, the wheel comes full circle.

Like the sixteenth-century chronicler Edward Hall, Shakespeare seems, officially at least, to have regarded the larger cycle of order emerging from disorder as having come round fully with the rise of the Tudor dynasty. Hall, whose book is entitled *The Union of the Two Noble and Illustre Families of Lancaster and York,* believed that the cause of the civil warfare which plagued England intermittently throughout the fifteenth century had been removed by the coronation of Henry VIII, whose father was connected with the Lancastrian, or Red-Rose, branch of the royal family, and whose mother was the daughter and heir of the Yorkist, or White-Rose, King Edward IV. For Shakespeare and his contemporaries, the full benefit of this restoration of harmony and degree after the near-anarchy of the Wars of the Roses was manifest in the long and prosperous reign of their virgin queen. "This royal infant," prophesies Archbishop Cranmer of the just-christened Elizabeth in the final scene of *Henry the Eighth,*

> Though in her cradle, yet now promises
> Upon this land a thousand thousand blessings
> Which time shall bring to ripeness. (V.v.18–21)

Nor will the maiden queen's death, continues Cranmer (how unprophetic the playwright here becomes of later Stuart history!) set the old cycle in motion again, because phoenix-like her "blessedness" will be reborn in her successor.

But Shakespeare was more concerned with presenting the ill effects of disrupted order than with depicting the glories of successful monarchs. Of all his plays on British historical or pseudohistorical subjects, only one, *Henry V,* concentrates on the personality of an all-prosperous ruler and an undeniably glorious moment in England's past. Despite the good fortune of the kingdom during most of Elizabeth's reign, he apparently brooded about the possibility that the cycle might recur, especially if men should ignore the lessons taught by history. Within the larger cycle described by Hall and accepted as complete by many writers of his age, Shakespeare saw smaller cycles or undulations of order and chaos that should have reminded men how precarious any state of equilibrium is in their moral and political lives.

This is not to suggest that in his earliest years as a playwright he had already blocked out in his mind a whole series of dramas to illustrate the pattern and point the historical lessons for his audiences. The order of composition of his various "chronicle histories" should dispel any such assumption. The later-written tetralogy on the troubled history of England toward the end of the Middle Ages—*Richard II, Henry IV: Parts I and II,* and *Henry V*—deals with events that antedate those of the three *Henry VI* plays and *Richard III*. There also exists some possibility that the second and third parts of *Henry VI* were composed before and provided suggestions for the first. Even the earlier tetralogy, therefore, hints at a gradually emerging and changing conception in Shakespeare's mind of what his subject signified and how that significance might be rendered in dramatic terms.

The breakdown of good order, manifest in the undermining of ancient chivalric ideals that had earlier held society together, has its origins for Shakespeare in the events leading to the deposition of King Richard II at the close of the fourteenth century. Richard, a minor at his accession and as an adult deficient in the private and public virtues requisite in a king, is forced to abdicate by his cousin Henry Bolingbroke, whom he has wronged. Bolingbroke, reigning as King Henry IV, is haunted by the rebellions consequent upon Richard's death; his own success in violating degree has ironically given rise to ambition in others. His son Henry V, however, brings to the throne a clearer conscience and the qualities needed for effective rule. His triumphant kingship marks the close of one of the smaller historical cycles, and is epitomized in his ability to control the anarchical forces in society and weld its different elements into the efficient little army that defeats the French at Agincourt (1415).

Yet this brief period of glory is only an interval in the larger pattern. The hero-king has scotched, not killed, "civil dissension," the "viperous worm / That gnaws the bowels of the commonwealth" (*1 Henry VI*, III.i.72–73). The opening scene of *1 Henry VI* is shrewdly designed to give warning of the impending disorder. At the funeral of Henry V the four speeches by the king's brothers and uncles convey an awesome sense of cosmic upheaval and heavy finality. Their foreboding is immediately justified, for within less than three dozen lines the lamentations dissolve into a quarrel between the Duke of Gloucester and the Bishop of Winchester. This altercation symbolizes the release of disruptive forces within a society deprived of its main source of unity. Bedford, the new king's uncle, in fact responds to the quarrel with a desperate invocation, asking Henry V's spirit, as his living presence had done, to

> Prosper this realm, keep it from civil broils,
> Combat with adverse planets in the heavens!

Nor does the playwright waste any further time before showing how disastrous has been the untimely death of this "king of so much worth." Bedford's prayer is interrupted by the entrance of a courier, who rushes in unceremoniously with news of English reversals in France. He is succeeded by two others, each arriving with worse tidings, worst of all being the account of Lord Talbot's capture. The remarkable economy of the scene is evident from the impact made by this trio of messengers. Their accounts project to the audience the importance for England's success in France of the efforts of such leaders as Salisbury, Talbot, and Bedford, who reacts to the news by preparing to go immediately to the aid of the others. Through this sequence of speeches the dramatist focuses attention on the three warriors, who stand for the ideals that have caused English arms until now to prosper. Yet all three worthy nobles are represented as advanced in years and fated to die later in the play. They carry with them to their graves not only the hopes of England's monarchs for possessing the crown of France, but also the chivalric ideals of a more innocent and masculine era. Their kind will be displaced, at least temporarily, by a self-seeking breed of new "risers," the Winchesters, the Suffolks, and the Yorks.

In spite of Bedford's resolve, there can be no doubt as the scene concludes that all coherence is already gone, that the downturn in England's fortunes has begun. With a real instinct for symmetrical design, the author concludes the scene by repeating the pattern of its opening. The royal brothers and uncles take their leave in precisely the order in which they have been introduced as speakers. As each goes his way to carry out his separate function in governing the realm, there is a momentary feeling that if they can work to one end, all may yet be well. Lest the audience presume, however, that shared grief and determination to act will lead to an effective coalition, the sense of division, of a pilotless ship of state, is emphasized by the words and pageantry of the departures. When all the rest are gone, there remains the unscrupulous politician Winchester, whose earlier altercation with Gloucester has already struck the note of discord, and who regards his nephew's death as an opportunity for him to seize control "And sit at chiefest stern of public weal."

The masterful construction of this introductory scene is more evident in theatrical performance than from silent reading. For it wants, as does the play on the whole, that poetic fire one is accustomed to look for in the work of Shakespeare. But as has often been remarked about his career, he seems to have developed a keen feeling for construction and for what is theatrically right before he evolved a poetic style that can thrill the auditor with its justness for the occasion or discriminate for the sensitive ear subtle differences of mood and character.

Symmetry and purposefulness of design, unlike the formlessness of most Elizabethan chronicle plays, are indeed the keynotes of this work, and of the Lancaster-York tetralogy as a whole. If later—beginning with *Richard II* and *Henry IV* and at length most impressively in *King Lear* and *Macbeth*—Shakespeare learned to portray characters helping to shape as well as enduring history or growing in perception and self-knowledge from their interaction with events, in *1 Henry VI* he is not yet ready for such an achievement. Here the problem of man's role in history is reduced to simpler terms: a dramatic personage responds in a particular way to events and to other persons involved in the action because he has a fixed character, rather than the possibility of an evolving one. This simple consistency is, in a way, true even of the heroicomical portrayal of Joan of Arc. Although she gives an impression at the outset of being admirably eloquent, efficient, and patriotic, and then of degenerating into wantonness and diabolism, the unsavory side of her character is hinted at in her very first scene. If we are disturbed by the seemingly inconsistent and finally un-chivalrous treatment of the Maid of Orleans, we should remind ourselves that in Shakespeare's day she had not yet been canonized or become the subject of more sympathetic characterizations by dramatists like Schiller, Shaw, and Anouilh. Character in Shakespeare's play is conceived broadly, flatly; the peculiar quality of every personage is unequivocally represented.

The solution for him, consequently, was to develop his dramatic theme mainly through formal structure; that is, through symbolically parallel and contrasting episodes, and through confrontations between characters representing sharply defined ethical and political values.

The first clue to this intention is the extremely cavalier handling of chronology, a disruption of time-sequence far beyond that in any of Shakespeare's other plays based on chronicles. Rather than demonstrating an ignorance of history or indifference to order, the rearrangement of events indicates a sense on the author's part that dramatic logic and the historical lesson are better served by recreating than by retelling what happened in the past. Thus, while *1 Henry VI* is grounded upon chronicle materials, it employs them so freely that one is not always certain how much indebted to the sources a given scene may be, or even, except in manifest instances, whether the principal inspiration is the work of Edward Hall or that of Raphael Holinshed.

The play also includes totally fictional scenes, among them the dispute in the Temple Garden and Talbot's encounter with the Countess of Auvergne. Unlike the arbitrarily invented episodes common in other history plays of the age, those in *1 Henry VI* serve to clarify the meaning of actual events, far more effectively than anything available to the author in his historical sources. The disjointing of time, moreover, enables him to achieve striking dramatic and didactic effects. The episodes cover a period of more than thirty years, from the beginning of Henry VI's reign in 1422 to the death of the Talbots near Bordeaux in 1453, but from the opening lines incidents are juxtaposed that were in actuality separated by a number of years. Thus, the siege of Orleans (1428–29) is already taking place during the funeral of Henry V seven years earlier. The dramaturgical reason is evident: to introduce immediately the main conflict, between Joan of France and Talbot of England. In Act Five, the capture of Joan (1430) is succeeded directly and without even a scene division by Suffolk's fictitious capture and wooing of Margaret of Anjou, though the negotiations for the king's marriage did not actually take place until 1444. Finally, the death of the Talbots, chronologically the last in the long series of events here dramatized, precedes these other carefully paired episodes. Apparently this dislocation was made in order to maintain as long as possible the symbolical conflict between the mirror of English chivalry and the diabolically assisted Joan, and also to imply that Margaret is about to arise from Joan's ashes to carry on the scourging of England in the remainder of the trilogy.

Divine providence allows England to be plagued by infernal as well as political enemies because her people have sinned. How the nation might have remained true to itself is signified by the words and deeds of Talbot. What she is in danger of becoming is signified in the shortcomings of the French, failings that crop up increasingly among Englishmen as the action of the play proceeds. The dissension that breaks out at home in the opening lines begins immediately to sap the English strength abroad, for it is accompanied by the decay of feudal loyalties and forgetfulness of degree. Also manifest are an English decline toward French effeminacy and the beginnings of reliance on fraud and cunning rather than manly courage and straightforward knightly virtue.

In the second scene, which shifts to Orleans, the playwright quickly sketches in the defective moral character of Frenchmen, as epitomized in the behavior of the Dauphin. A braggart like his counterpart in Shakespeare's *Henry V*, he begins a sortie against the English with the cry to his followers,

Him I forgive my death that killeth me
When he sees me go back one foot or fly. (I.ii.20–21)

Some moments later, his forces are beaten back, and he excuses his retreat in words a Talbot or a Salisbury would have died rather than utter:

> I would ne'er have fled,
> But that they left me 'midst my enemies. (I.ii.23–24)

Nothing they can do as men, it is apparent from the ensuing conversation among the French leaders, can overcome these dogged Englishmen.

At this point Joan comes onstage, and the Dauphin's conversation with her brings out two grave defects of Frenchmen that also begin gradually to taint the characters of Englishmen in the play. After bowing to her in single combat, Charles woos Joan in the language not of her royal prince, but of the fashionable courtly lover, asking to be her "servant and not sovereign," and imploring her "mercy" (that is, the favor of her love) as her "prostrate thrall." Such domination by the female is obviously scorned by an audience of Tudor Englishmen; it confirms their prejudices against Gallic dandyism and effeminacy. For in spite of Joan's high-sounding claims and self-assertive dash, one's admiration of her must stop far short of the Dauphin's; she is, after all, no more than a shepherd's daughter from Lorraine. The comedy of the scene is also obvious. From the number of double entendres in the Ovidian tradition of lovemaking as armed combat, the audience can scarcely be expected to take seriously Joan's claims to divine inspiration and vow to maintain her virginity while Englishmen remain on her country's soil.

All doubt about the tenor of the scene is dispelled by Charles's final ecstatic response to her messianic claims:

> Was Mahomet inspirèd with a dove?
> Thou with an eagle art inspirèd then.
> Helen, the mother of great Constantine,
> Nor yet Saint Philip's daughters, were like thee.

Bright star of Venus, fall'n down on the earth,
How may I reverently worship thee enough?
                                        (I.ii.140–45)

Not only are the allusions to other lofty examples of
divine inspiration too characteristic of the Dauphin's lack
of moderation to be taken seriously, but their very ex-
travagance is a strong hint that Joan's pretensions are
false. When Charles climaxes his apostrophe with the
words "Bright star of Venus," the imagery of courtly
wooing and the bawdy overtones of the earlier part of
the scene intrude themselves again. Besides, "star of
Venus, fall'n down on the earth," calls to mind not only
the goddess of profane love, but also Lucifer, that brightest of angelic stars tumbled out of the heavens for his
aspiration to divinity. Feminine wiles are thus linked by
the epithet with diabolical fraud and deception. Charles
is blameworthy for allowing himself to be dominated by
a woman—a peasant girl at that!—and for resorting to
preternatural aid in his efforts to rid his country of the
English. "Coward of France!" exclaims Bedford,

> how much he wrongs his fame,
> Despairing of his own arm's fortitude,
> To join with witches and the help of hell. (II.i.16–18)

The rest of the scenes in France are fashioned to contrast the reprehensible behavior of Joan and the Dauphin,
as well as of Englishmen whose characters become similarly stained as the moral fiber of their leaderless country
weakens, with that of the upright Talbot. These contrasts
are effectively brought out through patterns, as Ernest
Talbert calls them, of "intensified repetition." One such
pattern is the strategic paralleling of episodes either to
heighten the opposition between worthy and reprehensible
forms of behavior or to point up symbolical relationships
between apparently unconnected incidents. The playwright is also fond of grouping characters and episodes
in climactic triads to underscore several of the main
themes of the play.

Thus, since Talbot is the standard by which the measure of the other characters is taken, his first meeting with Henry VI is presented as an idealized interview between an unselfishly devoted vassal and his sovereign. For his loyal service and recovery in France of

> fifty fortresses,
> Twelve cities, and seven wallèd towns of strength,
> Beside five hundred prisoners of esteem,
>
> (III.iv.6–8)

Talbot is created Earl of Shrewsbury. But the episode distinctly recalls the first scene of the same act, where the already scheming Plantagenet is made Duke of York without having done anything to merit his elevation and pledges his fealty to the king with a hollow heart. Again, in the opening scene of Act Four Talbot tears the Garter from Falstaff's* leg for cowardice in battle and delivers a speech on what it means to bear "the sacred name of knight." His action is a clear example of how noblemen, in helping the monarch to maintain true order and degree, should deal with the presumptions of their subordinates.

As soon as Talbot departs, however, Vernon and Basset disrupt the coronation scene with their demands for trial by combat in behalf of their respective masters, York and Somerset. In order to further their own ambitions, Henry's nobles are obviously willing to let faction breed rather than suppress their contentious retainers. Toward the end of the scene York even appears to be on the point of exclaiming to Warwick (line 180) that he would prefer to have the king himself take sides against him since he might then turn it to his own advantage. This is but one of several scenes in which Talbot's conduct is sharply contrasted with that of other characters. The dramatist's intentions are unmistakable: Talbot is the ideal, the centripetal force of order that gradually gives

---

* Not the famous fat knight of *Henry IV*, whose death is described in *Henry V*, but rather a character based on the historical Sir John Fastolfe (*c.* 1378–1459), a prominent retainer of the Duke of Bedford and, according to the chronicles, one of the most valiant captains in the regent's armies.

way to the centrifugal forces of chaos represented by York and others of the rising new breed.

Dramatic triads appear in many places in *1 Henry VI* from the opening scene onward: the sense of climactic urgency in the arrival of the three messengers hot on one another's heels; the trio of ambitious nobles—Winchester, York, Suffolk; the focusing on the three stout but aging generals—Salisbury, Bedford, and Talbot—each of whose deaths is a more discouraging blow, the last the final blow, to English dynastic ambitions in France. Talbot opposes the French and their sorceress champion on all three of these occasions: at Orleans, where Salisbury is shot; at Rouen, where Bedford dies; and finally near Bordeaux, where he and his son meet their heroic end.

In each incident, fraud at first succeeds, not force of arms, and the placing of blame in each indicates progressive deterioration on the English side. At Orleans, Salisbury is killed by chance and Talbot is temporarily set back, to his complete bewilderment, by Joan's "art and baleful sorcery." His martial enterprise and trust in God, however, in contrast with the Frenchmen's lax discipline and reliance on "the help of hell," win the day for him when he returns to the attack. At Rouen (III.ii) Joan gains entrance by means of a stratagem historically employed by the English on another occasion, according to Holinshed, and transferred in the play to the French as an instance of their treachery. Eventually, Talbot overcomes again, while Bedford watches the struggle from "his litter sick." But now it is not only the French who are cowardly, who, as Talbot complains,

> keep the walls
> And dare not take up arms like gentlemen. (III.ii.69–70)

Just before the victory is assured and Bedford dies content, Falstaff again shows the white feather, this time on stage instead of in a messenger's report, and runs like a Frenchman from the battle scene. It is this defection that provides the occasion for Talbot later to tear the badge of the Order of the Garter from his leg at Henry's coronation in Paris.

At Bordeaux, where the audience might expect a final confrontation between Talbot and Joan, none is provided, nor does Joan make use of any cunning device to gain advantage over the English. The dramatist's reasons are clear enough. They are placed in the mouth of Sir William Lucy as he vainly begs York and Somerset to come to Talbot's relief. It is "the vulture of sedition" and "Sleeping neglection" that are causing the loss of Henry V's conquests:

> The fraud of England, not the force of France,
> Hath now entrapped the noble-minded Talbot.
> (IV.iv.36–37)

Malice and cunning deceit are beginning to corrupt even the highest English nobility, and Talbot is the sacrifice to their dissension. Yet even against the forces of hell and the wily allurements of womankind, England might have stood fast, if only all her noblemen had been like her stoutest champion. But when men place their self-interest ahead of the common good, the old ideals are readily forgotten. Joan's cunning becomes no longer necessary; the English are now their own worst enemies, having succumbed to the vices of the French.

This eroding of English virtue is nowhere more skillfully depicted than in the triad of scenes involving the first appearances of each of the three evil-designing Frenchwomen (interestingly enough, the only feminine characters in the play!). The scenes in question are Joan's introduction to the Dauphin, Talbot's reception by the Countess of Auvergne (II.iii), and Suffolk's wooing of Margaret of Anjou (V.iii). All three women represent a threat to English fortunes; the manner in which the three men respond to them neatly dramatizes the lesson.

Earlier it was pointed out that not only the Dauphin's accepting the demoniacally inspired assistance of Joan but also his self-debasement to servant-lover of a peasant girl, is conduct inexcusable in a prince. And even if his behavior were not a burlesque of courtly traditions, it runs counter to the ruggedly heroic ideal represented by

Talbot. Not that Talbot is a boor: he does know how to treat a lady as becomes a worthy English chevalier. The Dauphin's involvement with Joan is a breaking of degree and serves, moreover, to unhinge her judgment of herself even beyond what traffic with fiends has done. When she is finally on her way to the stake, this peasant maiden who has been graced with sovereignty over her infatuated monarch pretends to "noble birth" and "gentler blood" than that of her shepherd father. Even the phrase with which she rejects the old man—"Decrepit miser!"—accentuates her disdain for her lowly origins; *miser* is the worst term of opprobrium in the vocabulary of the courtly tradition.

But the true measure of the Dauphin's folly is the scene between Talbot and the fictional Countess. This lady too plots evil to the English through her ruse for capturing "the terror of the French." There is even a suggestion that she, like Joan, may have resorted to witchcraft by practicing sympathetic magic on her guest's portrait:

> Long time thy shadow hath been thrall to me,
> For in my gallery thy picture hangs.
> But now the substance shall endure the like.
>
> (II.iii.36–38)

The resourceful Talbot, however, outwits her by a simple counterstratagem and, refusing like a true and valiant gentleman to avenge himself on so weak an adversary, asks only honest entertainment for himself and his men before they take their leave.

Obviously if all of Talbot's compatriots had been thus immune to the allure of scheming Frenchwomen, all might have remained well enough for England. But the third encounter of this kind, that between Suffolk and Reignier's daughter Margaret, shows that Englishmen no longer are men of true honor, who, in contrast with the French, place their country's interests above their own selfish desires. Suffolk is dazzled, almost bewitched, by Margaret's beauty when he first gazes on her. And while he is the active, she almost entirely the passive, agent in this scene, from the course taken by the remaining action there can be little doubt that this woman will supplant Joan as the punishment for the sins of faction and ambition among Englishmen. Having Joan's and Margaret's captures occur in the same scene, in another of those symbolically meaningful parallelings of seemingly unconnected episodes, is theatrically most effective. And even though Joan's final scenes are far different in tone from Margaret's entry into the action, they serve a twofold function in helping to knit up the events of *1 Henry VI* and to anticipate the subsequent development of the trilogy.

In defiance of historical fact, but with excellent dramatic sense, York is made to be Joan's captor and judge. But even as he is mercilessly taunting his prisoner about her past affairs with the Dauphin and his nobles, another game of man and woman is being played that will prove his undoing. The parting curses of Joan are not the impotent ragings of a "fell banning hag"; they are prophecies of ambitious York's own downfall and of the miserable years for England that are being engendered in the dalliance of Suffolk with Margaret of Anjou.

Suffolk would enjoy this lady's love and use her to further his own ends at the sacrifice of English interests in France. Worse still, his "wondrous rare description" of Margaret's beauty serves to corrupt King Henry's mind and causes him to break his pre-contract of marriage with the daughter of the Earl of Armagnac. That the choice is both impolitic and immoral is clear from the king's own inner turmoil in the last moments of the play: the "sharp dissension" that he feels within makes him "sick with working of my thoughts," and he finally departs in a state of "grief" rather than expectant elation at "This sudden execution of my will."

The threat latent in Henry's impending marriage to Margaret, with whose arrival in England the second part of the trilogy opens, is brilliantly suggested by a pair of images in the last scene of Part One. The king compares his infatuation to a tempest, driving his soul against its more settled inclinations like a ship against the tide:

So am I driven by breath of her renown
Either to suffer shipwreck or arrive
Where I may have fruition of her love. (V.v.7–9)

The sudden intrusion here of the conventional figure of the lover as a vessel in danger of shipwreck on the stormy seas of passion calls to mind the dangers that Petrarch ("*Passa la nave mia colma d'oblio*") and his imitator Sir Thomas Wyatt ("My galley chargèd with forgetfulness") lamented as besetting the soul of the man tossed by sexual desire. For a king to make such an admission, and then to overrule good counsel and follow the inclination of his will rather than reasons of state, is a most unregal kind of behavior.

Most disturbing of all, however, are the verses with which the drama concludes. If restoration of order were to be implied at the end of the action, according to the usual Shakespearean closing formula there would be a speech explicitly saying so. But here the final words, coming after the king's confused withdrawal, are left for Suffolk, who exults in his success and departs for Anjou

As did the youthful Paris once to Greece,
With hope to find the like event in love,
But prosper better than the Trojan did. (V.v.104–106)

The image could hardly be lost on an Elizabethan audience, whose own mythmaking historians traced the ancestry of the British race to Troy. French Margaret will bring disaster to England as certainly as Spartan Helen brought ruin to "the topless towers of Ilium."

The remainder of the trilogy portrays Margaret, though she is in neither play the solely dominating figure, as an evil influence in England's domestic affairs. In Part Two it is she and her lover Suffolk, along with the malevolent Winchester, who engineer the downfall of the Duke of Gloucester. In Part Three, her monstrous treatment of her archrival York is the climax of her role as England's scourge. Eventually, in *Richard III,* this figure of nemesis who for long has borne a "tiger's heart wrapped in a woman's hide," becomes inactive though not silent, an unheeded Cassandra warning the now-dominant House of York of its own impending doom.

Though not a great poetic drama, *1 Henry VI* is by no means a failure as a play for theatrical performance. It exhibits a thoughtful design through which important themes are vigorously, if somewhat crudely, realized in the completed action. Nor is the affair of Margaret and Suffolk, as some critics would have it, only an afterthought. Strange as the final act and scene divisions in the Folio may be, the matter of these last episodes is not something inexpertly tacked onto what was originally conceived as an independent tragedy of Talbot simply because the author, or reviser, needed a way to patch together a trilogy. All that previously transpires is too carefully articulated with the concluding scenes for that. Act Five is the logical conclusion to the events set in motion at the play's beginning, and at the same time an effective opening-out to the even greater disorder and calamities of Parts Two and Three. The close is nearly symmetrical with the opening, and far more ominous though more restrained and economical in its language. A nation that is leaderless because its king is an infant as the play begins, is still leaderless, or subject to dangerous misguidance, as the action ends because its now-grown king has succumbed to a destructive passion. And the unscrupulous new risers have now found an instrument for gaining the illicit power to which they aspire.

The bad news from Orleans that marked the downturn of England's fortunes in France is superseded by bad news from Angiers that will lead to misery on England's soil itself. All this the maker of *1 Henry VI* was capable of rendering theatrically effective. By 1592 Shakespeare may not yet have been a supreme dramatic craftsman, but neither was he a mere botcher of other men's work, a snapper-up of other playwrights' unconsidered trifles.

LAWRENCE V. RYAN
Stanford University

The First Part of Henry the Sixth

THE HOUSES OF LANCASTER AND YORK
(Simplified)

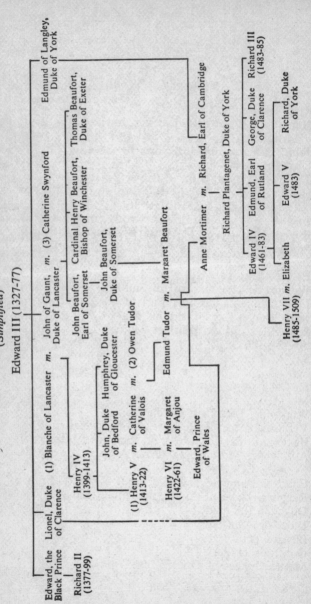

Edward III (1327-77)

Edward, the Black Prince   Lionel, Duke of Clarence   John of Gaunt, m. (3) Catherine Swynford   Edmund of Langley, Duke of Lancaster   Duke of York

Richard II (1377-99)

(1) Blanche of Lancaster   m.   John of Gaunt, Duke of Lancaster

Henry IV (1399-1413)

John Beaufort, Earl of Somerset   Cardinal Henry Beaufort, Bishop of Winchester   Thomas Beaufort, Duke of Exeter

John, Duke of Bedford   Humphrey, Duke of Gloucester

John Beaufort, Duke of Somerset

(1) Henry V (1413-22)   m.   Catherine of Valois   m. (2)   Owen Tudor

Margaret Beaufort

Henry VI (1422-61)   m.   Margaret of Anjou

Edmund Tudor   m.   Margaret Beaufort

Edward, Prince of Wales

Anne Mortimer   m.   Richard, Earl of Cambridge

Richard Plantagenet, Duke of York

Edward IV (1461-83)   Edmund, Earl of Rutland   George, Duke of Clarence   Richard III (1483-85)   Richard, Duke of York

Edward V (1483)

Henry VII (1485-1509)   m.   Elizabeth

[Dramatis Personae

King Henry the Sixth
Humphrey, Duke of Gloucester, uncle to the King, and Protector
John, Duke of Bedford, uncle to the King, and Regent of France
Thomas Beaufort, Duke of Exeter, great-uncle to the King
Henry Beaufort, Bishop of Winchester, and afterwards Cardinal, great-uncle to the King
John Beaufort, Earl, afterwards Duke, of Somerset
Richard Plantagenet, afterwards Duke of York, son of Richard, late Earl of Cambridge
Earl of Warwick
Earl of Salisbury
William de la Pole, Earl of Suffolk
Lord Talbot, afterwards Earl of Shrewsbury
John Talbot, Lord Lisle, his son
Edmund Mortimer, Earl of March
Sir John Falstaff*
Sir William Lucy
Sir William Glansdale
Sir Thomas Gargrave
Mayor of London
Woodville, Lieutenant of the Tower
Vernon, of the White-Rose or York faction
Basset, of the Red-Rose or Lancaster faction
A Lawyer. Mortimer's Jailers. A papal Legate

Charles, Dauphin, and afterwards King, of France
Reignier, Duke of Anjou, and titular King of Naples
Duke of Burgundy
Duke of Alençon
Bastard of Orleans
Governor of Paris
Master-Gunner of Orleans, and his Son

* See note, Introduction, p. xxxiv.

General of the French forces in Bordeaux
A French Sergeant. A Porter
An old Shepherd, father to Joan la Pucelle

Margaret, daughter to Reignier, afterwards married to
King Henry
Countess of Auvergne
Joan la Pucelle, commonly called Joan of Arc

Lords, Ambassadors, Warders of the Tower, Heralds,
Officers, Soldiers, Messengers, Attendants

Fiends appearing to La Pucelle

Scene: England; France]

The First Part of Henry the Sixth

ACT I

Scene I. [*Westminster Abbey.*]

Dead March.°1 *Enter the Funeral of King Henry the Fifth, attended on by the Duke of Bedford, Regent of France; the Duke of Gloucester, Protector; the Duke of Exeter, Warwick, the Bishop of Winchester, and the Duke of Somerset, [with Attendants].*

Bedford. Hung be the heavens with black,° yield day
    to night!
  Comets, importing change of times and states,°
  Brandish your crystal° tresses in the sky,
  And with them scourge the bad revolting stars
  That have consented unto° Henry's death!   5
  King Henry the Fifth, too famous to live long!
  England ne'er lost a king of so much worth.

---

1 The degree sign (°) indicates a footnote, which is keyed to the text by line number. Text references are printed in **boldface** type; the annotation follows in roman type.
I.i.s.d. **Dead March** a solemn piece of music for a funeral procession 1 **black** i.e., as a stage was draped in black for a tragedy 2 **Comets . . . states** i.e., the appearance of comets portending some misfortune 3 **crystal** bright 5 **consented unto** conspired to bring about

Gloucester. England ne'er had a king until his time.
　　Virtue he had, deserving to command;
　　His brandished sword did blind men with his°
10　　beams;
　　His arms spread wider than a dragon's wings;
　　His sparkling eyes, replete with wrathful fire,
　　More dazzled and drove back his enemies
　　Than midday sun fierce bent against their faces.
15　　What should I say? His deeds exceed all speech:
　　He ne'er lift° up his hand but conquerèd.

Exeter. We mourn in black; why mourn we not in
　　blood?°
　　Henry is dead and never shall revive.
　　Upon a wooden° coffin we attend,
20　　And death's dishonorable victory
　　We with our stately presence glorify,
　　Like captives bound to a triumphant car.°
　　What! shall we curse the planets of mishap°
　　That plotted thus our glory's overthrow?
25　　Or shall we think the subtle-witted French
　　Conjurers and sorcerers that, afraid of him,
　　By magic verses have contrived his end?

Winchester. He was a king blessed of the King of
　　Kings.
　　Unto the French the dreadful judgment day
30　　So dreadful will not be as was his sight.
　　The battles of the Lord of Hosts he fought;
　　The church's prayers made him so prosperous.

Gloucester. The church! Where is it? Had not church-
　　men prayed,
　　His thread of life had not so soon decayed.
35　　None do you like but an effeminate prince,
　　Whom, like a schoolboy, you may overawe.

10 **his** its　16 **lift** lifted　17 **in blood** i.e., by shedding blood, probably of the French in order to avenge the king's death (see lines
25–27)　19 **wooden** unfeeling　22 **car** chariot　23 **of mishap** causing misfortune

Winchester. Gloucester, whate'er we like, thou art
    Protector°
  And lookest° to command the prince and realm.
  Thy wife is proud; she holdeth thee in awe
  More than God or religious churchmen may.　　　　40

Gloucester. Name not religion, for thou lov'st the
    flesh,
  And ne'er throughout the year to church thou go'st
  Except it be to pray against thy foes.

Bedford. Cease, cease these jars° and rest your minds
    in peace;
  Let's to the altar. Heralds, wait on us.　　　　45
  Instead of gold, we'll offer up our arms,°
  Since arms avail not now that Henry's dead.
  Posterity, await for wretched years,
  When at their mothers' moistened eyes babes shall
    suck,
  Our isle be made a nourish° of salt tears,　　　　50
  And none but women left to wail the dead.
  Henry the Fifth, thy ghost I invocate:
  Prosper this realm, keep it from civil broils,°
  Combat with adverse planets in the heavens!
  A far more glorious star thy soul will make　　　　5.
  Than Julius Caesar° or bright—

        Enter a Messenger.

Messenger. My honorable lords, health to you all!
  Sad tidings bring I to you out of France,
  Of loss, of slaughter, and discomfiture:
  Guienne, Champagne, Rheims, Orleans,　　　　(
  Paris, Guysors, Poictiers, are all quite lost.

Bedford. What say'st thou, man, before dead Henry's
    corse?°

---

37 **Protector** governor of the realm during the king's minority　38
lookest expect　44 **jars** quarrels　46 **arms** weapons　50 **nourish**
nurse　53 **broils** disorders　56 **Julius Caesar** (whose soul, according to Ovid, *Metamorphoses*, xv. 843–51, became a star in the
heavens after his assassination)　62 **corse** corpse

Speak softly, or the loss of those great towns
Will make him burst his lead° and rise from death.

65 *Gloucester*. Is Paris lost? Is Rouen yielded up?
If Henry were recalled to life again,
These° news would cause him once more yield the
ghost.

Exeter. How were they lost? What treachery was
used?

Messenger. No treachery, but want of men and
money.
70 Amongst the soldiers this is mutterèd,
That here you maintain several factions,°
And whilst a field should be dispatched and fought,
You are disputing of your generals:
One would have ling'ring wars with little cost;
75 Another would fly swift, but wanteth wings;
A third thinks, without expense at all,
By guileful fair words peace may be obtained.
Awake, awake, English nobility!
Let not sloth dim your honors new begot;°
80 Cropped are the flower-de-luces° in your arms;
Of England's coat° one half is cut away.

Exeter. Were our tears wanting° to this funeral,
These tidings would call forth her° flowing tides.

Bedford. Me they concern; Regent° I am of France.
85 Give me my steelèd coat; I'll fight for France.
Away with these disgraceful wailing robes!
Wounds will I lend the French, instead of eyes,
To weep their intermissive° miseries.

---

64 **lead** lining of the coffin   67 **These** (since *news* was originally
plural)   71 **factions** (trisyllabic; the endings *-ion* and *-ions* are
often pronounced as two syllables in Shakespeare)   79 **new begot**
recently obtained   80 **flower-de-luces** fleur-de-lis, or lilies of France
(heraldic symbol of the French monarchs)   81 **coat** coat of arms
(the English royal family, as a sign of its pretensions to the throne
of France, included the fleur-de-lis in its coat of arms from the
fourteenth through the eighteenth centuries)   82 **wanting** lacking
83 **her** i.e., England's   84 **Regent** ruler in the king's absence   88
intermissive coming at intervals

Enter to them another Messenger.

Second Messenger. Lords, view these letters full of
　　bad mischance.
　　France is revolted from the English quite,　　　90
　　Except some petty towns of no import.°
　　The Dolphin° Charles is crownèd king in Rheims;
　　The Bastard of Orleans with him is joined;
　　Reignier, Duke of Anjou, doth take his part;
　　The Duke of Alençon flieth to his side.　　*Exit.*　95

Exeter. The Dolphin crownèd king? All fly to him?
　　O, whither shall we fly from this reproach?°

Gloucester. We will not fly, but to our enemies'
　　throats.
　　Bedford, if thou be slack, I'll fight it out.

Bedford. Gloucester, why doubt'st thou of my for-
　　wardness?　　　　　　　　　　　　　　　　100
　　An army have I mustered in my thoughts,
　　Wherewith already France is overrun.

Enter another Messenger.

Third Messenger. My gracious lords, to add to your
　　laments,
　　Wherewith you now bedew° King Henry's hearse,
　　I must inform you of a dismal fight　　　　　　105
　　Betwixt the stout Lord Talbot and the French.

Winchester. What? Wherein Talbot overcame, is't so?

Third Messenger. O no, wherein Lord Talbot was
　　o'erthrown.
　　The circumstance I'll tell you more at large.°
　　The tenth of August last, this dreadful lord,　　110
　　Retiring from the siege of Orleans,
　　Having full° scarce six thousand in his troop,

91 **import** importance　92 **Dolphin** Dauphin, title of the heir to
the French throne　97 **reproach** disgrace　104 **bedew** moisten
109 **The circumstance . . . large** I shall tell you the details at greater
length　112 **full** all told (?)

By three and twenty thousand of the French
Was round encompassèd and set upon.
115 No leisure had he to enrank° his men;
He wanted pikes° to set before his archers;
Instead whereof, sharp stakes plucked out of hedges
They pitchèd in the ground confusedly,
To keep the horsemen off° from breaking in.
120 More than three hours the fight continuèd;
Where valiant Talbot, above human thought,
Enacted wonders with his sword and lance.
Hundreds he sent to hell, and none durst stand him;
Here, there, and everywhere, enraged he slew.
125 The French exclaimed the devil was in arms;
All the whole army stood agazed° on him.
His soldiers, spying his undaunted spirit,
"A Talbot! a Talbot!" cried out amain,°
And rushed into the bowels of the battle.
130 Here had the conquest fully been sealed up,
If Sir John Falstaff had not played the coward.
He, being in the vanward,° placed behind
With purpose to relieve and follow them,
Cowardly fled, not having struck one stroke.
135 Hence grew the general wrack and massacre:
Enclosèd were they with their enemies.
A base Walloon,° to win the Dolphin's grace,
Thrust Talbot with a spear into the back,
Whom all France, with their chief assembled
     strength,
140 Durst not presume to look once in the face.

Bedford. Is Talbot slain then? I will slay myself
For living idly here in pomp and ease
Whilst such a worthy leader, wanting aid,
Unto his dastard foemen is betrayed.

---

115 **enrank** set in ranks   116 **pikes** stakes with sharpened iron
points, set in the ground to impale the enemy's horses if the
mounted troops charged the archers   119 **off** (apparently redun-
dant, and inserted for metrical purposes)   126 **agazed** astounded
(probably a variant of aghast)   128 **amain** with all their might
132 **vanward** vanguard   137 **Walloon** inhabitant of the region
between northeastern France and the Netherlands

Third Messenger. O no, he lives, but is took prisoner, *145*
  And Lord Scales with him and Lord Hungerford;
  Most of the rest slaughtered or took likewise.

Bedford. His ransom there is none but I shall pay.
  I'll hale the Dolphin headlong from his throne;
  His crown shall be the ransom of my friend; *150*
  Four of their lords I'll change for one of ours.
  Farewell, my masters, to my task will I;
  Bonfires in France forthwith I am to make
  To keep our great Saint George's feast° withal.°
  Ten thousand soldiers with me I will take, *155*
  Whose bloody deeds shall make all Europe quake.

Third Messenger. So you had need, for Orleans is be-
    sieged;
  The English army is grown weak and faint;
  The Earl of Salisbury craveth supply
  And hardly keeps his men from mutiny *160*
  Since they, so few, watch such a multitude.

Exeter. Remember, lords, your oaths to Henry sworn:
  Either to quell° the Dolphin utterly
  Or bring him in obedience to your yoke.

Bedford. I do remember it and here take my leave *165*
  To go about my preparation.°   *Exit Bedford.*

Gloucester. I'll to the Tower° with all the haste I can
  To view th' artillery and munition,
  And then I will proclaim young Henry king.
                    Exit Gloucester.

Exeter. To Eltham will I, where the young king is, *170*
  Being ordained his special governor,
  And for his safety there I'll best devise.   *Exit.*

Winchester. Each hath his place and function to at-
    tend;
  I am left out; for me nothing remains.

---

154 **Saint George's feast** April 23   154 **withal** with   163 **quell** destroy   166 **preparation** (five syllables)   167 **Tower** Tower of London

175   But long I will not be Jack out of office.°
     The king from Eltham I intend to send
     And sit at chiefest stern of public weal.°

Exit [with Attendants].

[Scene II. *France. Before Orleans.*]

*Sound a Flourish.° Enter Charles [the Dauphin],
Alençon, and Reignier, marching with Drum and
Soldiers.*

Dauphin. Mars his° true moving, even as in the
     heavens,
     So in the earth, to this day is not known.
     Late did he shine upon the English side;
     Now we are victors; upon us he smiles.
5   What towns of any moment° but we have?
     At pleasure here we lie near Orleans;
     Otherwhiles° the famished English, like pale ghosts,
     Faintly besiege us one hour in a month.

Alençon. They want their porridge and their fat bull-
     beeves:°
10   Either they must be dieted° like mules
     And have their provender° tied to their mouths,
     Or piteous they will look, like drownèd mice.

Reignier. Let's raise the siege; why live we idly here?
     Talbot is taken, whom we wont° to fear;
15   Remaineth none but mad-brained Salisbury,

---

175 **Jack out of office** a person deprived of official function   177
And . . . weal and maintain control of the government   I.ii.s.d.
Flourish fanfare of trumpets   1 **Mars his** Mars's   5 **moment** importance   7 **Otherwhiles** at times   9 **bull-beeves** (eating of bull-
beef was believed to give one courage)   10 **dieted** fed   11 **pro-
vender** food   14 **wont** were accustomed

And he may well in fretting spend his gall;°
Nor° men nor money hath he to make war.

Dauphin. Sound, sound alarum!° we will rush on
    them.
Now for the honor of the forlorn French!
Him I forgive my death that killeth me   20
When he sees me go back one foot or fly.   *Exeunt.*

*Here alarum; they are beaten back by the English with
great loss. Enter Charles [the Dauphin], Alençon,
and Reignier.*

Dauphin. Who ever saw the like? What men have I?
Dogs! cowards! dastards! I would ne'er have fled,
But that they left me 'midst my enemies.

Reignier. Salisbury is a desperate homicide;   25
He fighteth as one weary of his life.
The other lords, like lions wanting food,
Do rush upon us as their hungry prey.°

Alençon. Froissart,° a countryman of ours, records
England all Olivers and Rowlands° bred   30
During the time Edward the Third did reign.
More truly now may this be verified,
For none but Samsons and Goliases°
It sendeth forth to skirmish. One to ten!
Lean raw-boned rascals!° who would e'er suppose   35
They had such courage and audacity?

Dauphin. Let's leave this town, for they are
    hare-brained slaves,
And hunger will enforce° them to be more eager.°
Of old I know them; rather with their teeth
The walls they'll tear down than forsake the siege.   40

16 **gall** bitterness of spirit   17 **Nor** neither   18 **alarum** call to arms
28 **their hungry prey** prey for which they hunger   29 **Froissart** chronicler of fourteenth-century French, English, and Spanish affairs   30
Olivers and Rowlands heroes of the French medieval epic, *La Chan-
son de Roland*   33 **Goliases** Goliaths   35 **rascals** lean, inferior deer
38 **enforce** compel   38 **eager** (1) hungry (2) fierce

Reignier. I think, by some odd gimmors° or device
    Their arms are set, like clocks, still to strike on;
    Else ne'er could they hold out so as they do.
    By my consent, we'll even let them alone.

45 *Alençon.* Be it so.

Enter the Bastard of Orleans.

Bastard. Where's the Prince Dolphin? I have news
    for him.

Dauphin. Bastard of Orleans, thrice welcome to us.

Bastard. Methinks your looks are sad, your cheer
    appaled.°
    Hath the late overthrow wrought this offense?
50 Be not dismayed, for succor is at hand:
    A holy maid hither with me I bring,
    Which by a vision sent to her from heaven
    Ordainèd is to raise this tedious siege
    And drive the English forth° the bounds of France.
55 The spirit of deep prophecy she hath,
    Exceeding the nine sibyls° of old Rome:
    What's past and what's to come she can descry.
    Speak, shall I call her in? Believe my words,
    For they are certain and unfallible.°

Dauphin. Go, call her in. [*Exit Bastard.*] But first, to
60   try her skill,
    Reignier, stand thou as Dolphin in my place;
    Question her proudly; let thy looks be stern:
    By this means shall we sound° what skill she hath.

Enter [*the Bastard of Orleans, with*] *Joan* [*la*]
    Pucelle.°

Reignier. Fair maid, is't thou wilt do these wondrous
    feats?

41 **gimmors** (variant of *gimmals*) connecting parts for transmitting
motion   48 **cheer appaled** countenance pale with fear   54 **forth**
beyond   56 **nine sibyls** nine books of prophetic utterances offered
to King Tarquin of Rome by the sibyl at Cumae   59 **unfallible**
infallible   63 **sound** test   63s.d. **la Pucelle** the virgin

Pucelle. Reignier, is't thou that thinkest to beguile me?   65
  Where is the Dolphin? Come, come from behind;
  I know thee well, though never seen before.
  Be not amazed, there's nothing hid from me;
  In private will I talk with thee apart.
  Stand back, you lords, and give us leave awhile.   70

Reignier. She takes upon her bravely at first dash.°

Pucelle. Dolphin, I am by birth a shepherd's daughter,
  My wit° untrained in any kind of art.
  Heaven and our Lady° gracious hath it pleased
  To shine on my contemptible estate.   75
  Lo, whilst I waited on my tender lambs,
  And to sun's parching heat displayed my cheeks,
  God's mother deignèd to appear to me
  And in a vision full of majesty
  Willed me to leave my base vocation°   80
  And free my country from calamity.
  Her aid she promised and assured success;
  In complete glory she revealed herself;
  And, whereas I was black and swart° before,
  With those clear rays which she infused° on me   85
  That beauty am I blessed with which you may see.
  Ask me what question thou canst possible,
  And I will answer unpremeditated;
  My courage try by combat, if thou dar'st,
  And thou shalt find that I exceed my sex.   90
  Resolve on this,° thou shalt be fortunate
  If thou receive me for thy warlike mate.°

Dauphin. Thou hast astonished me with thy high
    terms;°
  Only this proof I'll of thy valor make,
  In single combat thou shalt buckle° with me,   95
  And if thou vanquishest, thy words are true;
  Otherwise I renounce all confidence.

71 **She . . . dash** she acts bravely at the first encounter   73 **wit** mind
74 **our Lady** the Virgin Mary   80 **vocation** occupation   84 **swart**
dark-complexioned   85 **infused** shed   91 **resolve on this** be assured of this   92 **mate** (1) comrade (2) sweetheart (?)   93 **high
terms** i.e., mastery of the grand rhetorical style   95 **buckle** (1)
grapple (2) embrace as lovers

Pucelle. I am prepared: here is my keen-edged sword,
  Decked with fine flower-de-luces on each side,
  The which at Touraine, in Saint Katherine's
100   churchyard,
  Out of a great deal of old iron I chose forth.

Dauphin. Then come, a° God's name, I fear no
  woman.

Pucelle. And while I live, I'll ne'er fly from a man.

Here they fight, and Joan la Pucelle overcomes.

Dauphin. Stay, stay thy hands! thou art an Amazon
105   And fightest with the sword of Deborah.°

Pucelle. Christ's mother helps me, else I were too
  weak.

Dauphin. Whoe'er helps thee, 'tis thou that must help
  me:
  Impatiently I burn with thy desire;
  My heart and hands thou hast at once subdued.
110 Excellent Pucelle, if thy name be so,°
  Let me thy servant° and not sovereign be;
  'Tis the French Dolphin sueth to° thee thus.

Pucelle. I must not yield to any rites of love,
  For my profession's sacred from above;
115 When I have chasèd all thy foes from hence,
  Then will I think upon a recompense.

Dauphin. Meantime look gracious on thy prostrate
  thrall.°

Reignier. My lord, methinks, is very long in talk.

Alençon. Doubtless he shrives this woman to her
  smock;°
120 Else ne'er could he so long protract his speech.

---

102 **a** in   105 **Deborah** prophetess who delivered Israel from oppression by the Canaanites (Judges 4–5)   110 **if thy name be so**
if you really are a virgin   111 **servant** lover   112 **sueth to** woos
117 **thrall** slave   119 **shrives . . . smock** (1) questions her closely
(2) hears her confession to the most minute detail

Reignier. Shall we disturb him, since he keeps no
    mean?°

Alençon. He may mean more than we poor men do
    know:
    These women are shrewd tempters with their
    tongues.

Reignier. My lord, where are you? What devise you
    on?°
    Shall we give o'er Orleans, or no?   125

Pucelle. Why, no, I say, distrustful recreants!°
    Fight till the last gasp; I'll be your guard.

Dauphin. What she says I'll confirm: we'll fight it out.

Pucelle. Assigned am I to be the English scourge.
    This night the siege assuredly I'll raise;   130
    Expect Saint Martin's summer,° halcyon's days,°
    Since I have enterèd into these wars.
    Glory is like a circle in the water,
    Which never ceaseth to enlarge itself
    Till by broad spreading it disperse to nought.   135
    With Henry's death the English circle ends;
    Dispersèd are the glories it included.
    Now am I like that proud insulting° ship
    Which Caesar and his fortune bare° at once.

Dauphin. Was Mahomet inspirèd with a dove?   140
    Thou with an eagle° art inspirèd then.
    Helen,° the mother of great Constantine,
    Nor yet Saint Philip's daughters,° were like thee.

---

121 **keeps no mean** does not control himself   124 **devise you on**
are you deliberating   126 **recreants** cowards   131 **Saint Martin's
summer** Indian summer (named after the feast of Saint Martin of
Tours, November 11)   131 **halcyon's days** peaceful times (the an-
cients believed that the bird called the halcyon nested on the sea
and that the waters remained calm during its breeding season)
138 **insulting** insolently triumphant   139 **bare** bore   141 **eagle** i.e.,
like Saint John the Evangelist, with the highest source of inspiration   142 **Helen** Saint Helena, inspired by a vision to find the cross
of Jesus   143 **Saint Philip's daughters** (who had the gift of prophecy; see Acts 21:9)

Bright star of Venus, fall'n down on the earth,
145 How may I reverently worship thee enough?

Alençon. Leave off delays, and let us raise the siege.

Reignier. Woman, do what thou canst to save our
    honors;
Drive them from Orleans and be immortalized.

Dauphin. Presently° we'll try. Come, let's away about
    it;
150 No prophet will I trust, if she prove false.   *Exeunt.*

[Scene III. *London. Before the Tower.*]

Enter Gloucester, with his Servingmen [in blue coats°].

Gloucester. I am come to survey° the Tower this
    day:
Since Henry's death, I fear, there is conveyance.°
Where be these warders,° that they wait not here?
Open the gates; 'tis Gloucester° that calls.

First Warder. [*Within*] Who's there that knocks so
5   imperiously?

Gloucester's First [*Serving*]*man.* It is the noble Duke
    of Gloucester.

Second Warder. [*Within*] Whoe'er he be, you may not
    be let in.

Gloucester's First [*Serving*]*man.* Villains, answer you
    so the Lord Protector?

149 **Presently** immediately I.iii.s.d. **blue coats** (blue clothing was
customary for servants) 1 **survey** inspect 2 **conveyance** under-
hand dealing 3 **warders** guards 4 **Gloucester** (trisyllabic here
and often, for metrical purposes, elsewhere in the play)

First Warder. [*Within*] The Lord protect him! so we
    answer him;
  We do no otherwise than we are willed.   *10*

Gloucester. Who willèd you? Or whose will stands
    but mine?
  There's none Protector of the realm but I.
  Break up the gates, I'll be your warrantize;°
  Shall I be flouted thus by dunghill grooms?°
      Gloucester's men rush at the Tower gates, and
          Woodville the Lieutenant speaks within.
Woodville. What noise is this? What traitors have
    we here?   *15*

Gloucester. Lieutenant, is it you whose voice I hear?
  Open the gates; here's Gloucester that would enter.

Woodville. Have patience, noble duke, I may not
    open;
  The Cardinal of Winchester forbids:
  From him I have express commandment°   *20*
  That thou nor none of thine shall be let in.

Gloucester. Faint-hearted Woodville, prizest him 'fore
    me?°
  Arrogant Winchester, that haughty prelate,
  Whom Henry, our late sovereign, ne'er could
    brook?°
  Thou art no friend to God or to the king;   *25*
  Open the gates, or I'll shut thee out shortly.

Servingmen. Open the gates unto the Lord Protector,
  Or we'll burst them open, if that° you come not
    quickly.

*Enter to the Protector at the Tower gates Winchester
    and his men in tawny coats.°*

---

13 **warrantize** pledge of security   14 **dunghill grooms** vile servingmen   20 **commandment** (trisyllabic; spelled *commandement* in the
Folio)   22 **prizest him 'fore me** rank him above me   24 **brook**
endure   28 **if that** if   28s.d. **tawny coats** (servants of churchmen
traditionally wore tawny, or brownish-yellow, coats)

Winchester. How now, ambitious Humphrey, what
    means this?

Gloucester. Peeled° priest, dost thou command me to
30   be shut out?

Winchester. I do, thou most usurping proditor,°
    And not Protector, of the king or realm.

Gloucester. Stand back, thou manifest conspirator,
    Thou that contriv'dst to murder our dead lord,
35   Thou that giv'st whores indulgences° to sin;
    I'll canvas thee in thy broad cardinal's hat,°
    If thou proceed in this thy insolence.

Winchester. Nay, stand thou back, I will not budge
        a foot;
    This be Damascus,° be thou cursèd Cain,
40   To slay thy brother° Abel, if thou wilt.

Gloucester. I will not slay thee, but I'll drive thee
        back;
    Thy scarlet robes as a child's bearing-cloth°
    I'll use to carry thee out of this place.

Winchester. Do what thou dar'st, I beard° thee to
    thy face.

Gloucester. What! am I dared and bearded to my
45   face?
    Draw, men, for all this privilegèd place,°
    Blue coats to tawny coats. Priest, beware your
        beard;
    I mean to tug it, and to cuff you soundly.
    Under my feet I stamp thy cardinal's hat;

---

30 **Peeled** tonsured, bald   31 **proditor** traitor   35 **indulgences** (the
brothels near the theaters on the south bank of the Thames were
within the jurisdiction of the Bishops of Winchester)   36 **canvas
. . . hat** toss you in your wide-brimmed ecclesiastical hat as if it were
a blanket   39 **Damascus** (supposed to have been built in the place
where Cain killed Abel)   40 **brother** (Winchester was half-brother
to Gloucester's father, King Henry IV)   42 **bearing-cloth** christen-
ing robe   44 **beard** defy   46 **for . . . place** (even though drawing
of weapons is forbidden under pain of death in royal residences)

In spite of pope or dignities of church,°   *50*
Here by the cheeks I'll drag thee up and down.

Winchester. Gloucester, thou wilt answer this before
　　the pope.

Gloucester. Winchester goose,° I cry, a rope!° a rope!
　　Now beat them hence; why do you let them stay?
　　Thee I'll chase hence, thou wolf in sheep's array.   *55*
　　Out, tawny coats! out, scarlet° hypocrite!

*Here Gloucester's men beat out the Cardinal's men,
and enter in the hurly-burly° the Mayor of London
and his Officers.*

Mayor. Fie, lords! that you, being supreme
　　magistrates,°
　　Thus contumeliously° should break the peace!

Gloucester. Peace, mayor! thou know'st little of my
　　wrongs:
　　Here's Beaufort, that regards nor God nor king,   *60*
　　Hath here distrained° the Tower to his use.

Winchester. Here's Gloucester, a foe to citizens,
　　One that still motions° war and never peace,
　　O'ercharging your free purses with large fines,°
　　That seeks to overthrow religion   *65*
　　Because he is Protector of the realm,
　　And would have armor here out of the Tower
　　To crown himself king and suppress° the prince.

Gloucester. I will not answer thee with words,
　　but blows.   *Here they skirmish again.*

Mayor. Nought rests for me in this tumultuous strife   *70*
　　But to make open proclamation.

50 **dignities of church** your high ecclesiastical rank   53 **Winchester goose** (1) venereal infection (2) prostitute (see note to line 35)   53 **rope** hangman's cord   56 **scarlet** (a derisive allusion to the red robes of the cardinal)   56 s.d. **hurly-burly** tumult   57 **magistrates** administrators of the kingdom   58 **contumeliously** insolently   61 **distrained** seized   63 **still motions** always proposes   64 **O'ercharging . . . fines** overburdening you with excessive special taxes   68 **suppress** depose

Come, officer, as loud as e'er thou canst,
Cry.

[*Officer.*] All manner of men assembled here in arms
75   this day against God's peace and the king's, we
charge and command you, in his highness' name,
to repair° to your several° dwelling-places; and not
to wear, handle, or use any sword, weapon, or
dagger henceforward, upon pain° of death.

80   *Gloucester.* Cardinal, I'll be no breaker of the law,
But we shall meet, and break our minds at large.°

Winchester. Gloucester, we'll meet to thy cost, be
sure:
Thy heart-blood I will have for this day's work.

Mayor. I'll call for clubs,° if you will not away.
85   This cardinal's more haughty than the devil.

Gloucester. Mayor, farewell; thou dost but what thou
mayst.

Winchester. Abominable Gloucester, guard thy head,
For I intend to have it ere long.   *Exeunt.*

Mayor. See the coast cleared, and then we will depart.
Good God, these nobles should such stomachs
90   bear!°
I myself fight not once in forty year.   *Exeunt.*

---

77 **repair** return   77 **several** own   79 **pain** penalty   81 **break . . .
large** reveal our thoughts fully   84 **call for clubs** i.e., summon the
apprentices of the city to come with clubs and assist the officers in
putting down the riot   90 **these . . . bear** that these noblemen
should have such quarrelsome tempers

[Scene IV. *Orleans.*]

Enter the Master Gunner of Orleans and his Boy.

Master Gunner. Sirrah,° thou know'st how Orleans is
    besieged,
And how the English have the suburbs won.

Boy. Father, I know, and oft have shot at them,
Howe'er, unfortunate, I missed my aim.

Master Gunner. But now thou shalt not. Be thou ruled
    by me: 5
Chief master-gunner am I of this town;
Something I must do to procure me grace.°
The prince's espials° have informèd me
How the English, in the suburbs close intrenched,
Went through a secret grate of iron bars   10
In yonder tower to overpeer° the city
And thence discover how with most advantage
They may vex us with shot or with assault.
To intercept° this inconvenience,
A piece of ordnance° 'gainst it I have placed,   15
And even these three days have I watched
If I could see them. Now do thou watch,
For I can stay no longer.
If thou spy'st any, run and bring me word,
And thou shalt find me at the governor's.   *Exit.*   20

Boy. Father, I warrant you, take you no care;
I'll never trouble you, if I may spy them.   *Exit.*

*Enter Salisbury and Talbot on the turrets, with [Sir
William Glansdale, Sir Thomas Gargrave, and] others.*

I.iv.1 **Sirrah** a term used in addressing children or inferiors 7
grace favor 8 **espials** spies 11 **overpeer** look down upon 14
intercept stop 15 **piece of ordnance** cannon

Salisbury. Talbot, my life, my joy, again returned!
How wert thou handled, being prisoner?
25   Or by what means gots thou° to be released?
Discourse,° I prithee,° on this turret's top.

Talbot. The Earl of Bedford had a prisoner
Called the brave Lord Ponton de Santrailles;
For him was I exchanged and ransomèd.
30   But with a baser° man of arms by far
Once in contempt they would have bartered me;
Which I disdaining scorned and cravèd death
Rather than I would be so pilled-esteemed.°
In fine,° redeemed I was as I desired.
35   But O! the treacherous Falstaff wounds my heart,
Whom with my bare fists I would execute,
If I now had him brought into my power.

Salisbury. Yet tell'st thou not how thou wert enter-
          tained.

Talbot. With scoffs and scorns and contumelious
          taunts,
40   In open marketplace produced they me,
To be a public spectacle to all:
Here, said they, is the terror of the French,
The scarecrow that affrights° our children so.
Then broke I from the officers that led me,
45   And with my nails digged stones out of the ground
To hurl at the beholders of my shame.
My grisly° countenance made others fly;
None durst come near for fear of sudden death.
In iron walls they deemed me not secure;
50   So great fear of my name 'mongst them were spread
That they supposed I could rend bars of steel
And spurn in pieces posts of adamant.°
Wherefore a guard of chosen shot° I had

---

25 **gots thou** did you manage   26 **Discourse** relate   26 **prithee**
pray thee   30 **baser** less well born   33 **pilled-esteemed** poorly
valued   34 **In fine** finally   43 **affrights** frightens   47 **grisly** grim
52 **adamant** indestructible material   53 **chosen shot** picked marks-
men

That walked about me every minute while,°
And if I did but stir out of my bed,   55
Ready they were to shoot me to the heart.

Enter the Boy with a linstock.°

Salisbury. I grieve to hear what torments you endured,
But we will be revenged sufficiently.
Now it is supper-time in Orleans;
Here, through this grate, I count each one   60
And view the Frenchmen how they fortify;
Let us look in; the sight will much delight thee.
Sir Thomas Gargrave, and Sir William Glansdale,
Let me have your express° opinions
Where is best place to make our batt'ry° next.   65

Gargrave. I think at the north gate, for there stands
lords.

Glansdale. And I, here, at the bulwark° of the bridge.

Talbot. For aught I see, this city must be famished,
Or with light skirmishes enfeeblèd.°   *Here they
shoot, and Salisbury [and Gargrave] fall down.*

Salisbury. O Lord, have mercy on us, wretched
sinners!   70

Gargrave. O Lord, have mercy on me, woeful man!

Talbot. What chance is this that suddenly hath
crossed° us?
Speak, Salisbury; at least, if thou canst speak,
How far'st thou, mirror of° all martial men?
One of thy eyes and thy cheek's side struck off!   75
Accursèd tower! accursèd fatal hand°
That hath contrived this woful tragedy!
In thirteen battles Salisbury o'ercame;
Henry the Fifth he first trained to the wars;

---

54 **every minute while** incessantly   56s.d. **linstock** staff to hold the
match for lighting a cannon   64 **express** precise   65 **make our
batt'ry** direct our fire   67 **bulwark** fortification   69 **enfeeblèd**
weakened   72 **crossed** thwarted   74 **mirror of** model for   76 **fatal
hand** hand of fate

80   Whilst any trump° did sound, or drum struck up,
      His sword did ne'er leave striking in the field.
      Yet liv'st thou, Salisbury? Though thy speech doth
          fail,
      One eye thou hast, to look to heaven for grace.
      The sun with one eye vieweth all the world.
85   Heaven, be thou gracious to none alive
      If Salisbury wants° mercy at thy hands!
      Bear hence his body; I will help to bury it.
      Sir Thomas Gargrave, hast thou any life?
      Speak unto Talbot; nay, look up to him.
90   Salisbury, cheer thy spirit with this comfort:
      Thou shalt not die whiles°—
      He beckons with his hand and smiles on me,
      As who° should say, "When I am dead and gone,
      Remember to avenge me on the French."
95   Plantagenet,° I will; and like thee, [Nero,]
      Play on the lute, beholding the towns burn.
      Wretched shall France be only in° my name.

      Here an alarum, and it thunders and lightens.

      What stir° is this? What tumult's in the heavens?
      Whence cometh this alarum, and the noise?

                Enter a Messenger.

      Messenger. My lord, my lord, the French have gath-
100   ered head:°
      The Dolphin, with one Joan la Pucelle joined,
      A holy prophetess new risen up,
      Is come with a great power to raise the siege.

      Here Salisbury lifteth himself up and groans.

      Talbot. Hear, hear how dying Salisbury doth groan!
105   It irks his heart he cannot be revenged.

      80 **trump** trumpet 86 **wants** lacks 91 **whiles** until 93 **As who**
      as if he 95 **Plantagenet** (though Salisbury's name was Thomas
      Montacute, he was related to the royal family, which adopted the
      name Plantagenet in the fifteenth century) 97 **only in** merely at
      the sound of (?) 98 **stir** commotion 100 **gathered head** raised
      forces

Frenchmen, I'll be a Salisbury to you.
Pucelle or pussel,° Dolphin or dogfish,
Your hearts I'll stamp out with my horse's heels,
And make a quagmire of your mingled brains.
Convey me° Salisbury into his tent,   *110*
And then we'll try what these dastard Frenchmen
     dare.

                                        Alarum. Exeunt.

[Scene V. *Orleans.*]

*Here an alarum again, and Talbot pursueth the
Dauphin, and driveth him. Then enter Joan la Pucelle, driving Englishmen before her [and exit after
them]. Then [re-]enter Talbot.*

Talbot. Where is my strength, my valor, and my
     force?
Our English troops retire, I cannot stay them;
A woman clad in armor chaseth them.

                     Enter [La] Pucelle.

Here, here she comes. I'll have a bout with thee;
Devil or devil's dam,° I'll conjure thee:°   *5*
Blood will I draw on thee,° thou art a witch,
And straightway give thy soul to him thou serv'st.

Pucelle. Come, come, 'tis only° I that must disgrace
     thee.   *Here they fight.*

Talbot. Heavens, can you suffer hell so to prevail?
My breast I'll burst with straining of my courage   *10*

107 **pussel** lewd woman, strumpet   110 **convey me** carry I.v.5 **dam**
(1) mistress (2) mother   5 **conjure thee** i.e., back to hell whence
you came   6 **Blood . . . thee** (whoever could draw blood from a
witch was free of her power)   8 **only** with no other assistance

And from my shoulders crack my arms asunder,
But I will chastise this high-minded° strumpet.
                              They fight again.

Pucelle. Talbot, farewell; thy hour is not yet come;
I must go victual° Orleans forthwith.°

A short alarum. Then enter the town with soldiers.

15 O'ertake me if thou canst; I scorn thy strength.
Go, go, cheer up thy hungry-starvèd men;
Help Salisbury to make his testament;
This day is ours, as many more shall be.   *Exit.*

Talbot. My thoughts are whirlèd like a potter's wheel;
20 I know not where I am, nor what I do.
A witch, by fear, not force, like Hannibal,°
Drives back our troops and conquers as she lists;°
So bees with smoke and doves with noisome stench
Are from their hives and houses driven away.
25 They called us for our fierceness English dogs;
Now, like to whelps,° we crying run away.
                              A short alarum.
Hark, countrymen! either renew the fight,
Or tear the lions° out of England's coat;
Renounce your soil,° give sheep in lions' stead:
30 Sheep run not half so treacherous° from the wolf,
Or horse or oxen from the leopard,
As you fly from your oft-subduèd slaves.
                              Alarum. Here another skirmish.
It will not be. Retire into your trenches.
You all consented unto Salisbury's death,
35 For none would strike a stroke in his revenge.
Pucelle is entered into Orleans
In spite of us or aught that we could do.

---

12 **high-minded** arrogant   14 **victual** bring provisions into   14 **forth-with** immediately   21 **Hannibal** (who terrified the Romans by driving among them oxen with lighted torches fixed to their horns) 22 **lists** pleases   26 **whelps** puppies   28 **lions** heraldic royal symbol of England   29 **soil** (possibly a misprint for *style;* the line appears to mean· replace the lions in your royal coat of arms with sheep)   30 **treacherous** fearfully

O, would I were to die with Salisbury!
The shame hereof will make me hide my head.
Exit Talbot. Alarum. Retreat.°

[Scene VI. *Orleans.*]

*Flourish. Enter on the walls [La] Pucelle, Dauphin,
Reignier, Alençon, and Soldiers.*

Pucelle. Advance° our waving colors on the walls;
Rescued is Orleans from the English.
Thus Joan la Pucelle hath performed her word.

Dauphin. Divinest creature, Astraea's daughter,°
How shall I honor thee for this success?   5
Thy promises are like Adonis'° garden
That one day bloomed and fruitful were the next.
France, triumph in thy glorious prophetess!
Recovered is the town of Orleans;
More blessèd hap° did ne'er befall our state.   10

Reignier. Why ring not out the bells aloud throughout
      the town?
Dolphin, command the citizens make bonfires
And feast and banquet in the open streets
To celebrate the joy that God hath given us.

Alençon. All France will be replete with mirth and joy   15
When they shall hear how we have played the
      men.°

Dauphin. 'Tis Joan, not we, by whom the day is won;

39s.d. **Retreat** signal for withdrawal from battle   I.vi.1 **Advance**
raise   4 **Astraea's daughter** daughter of the goddess of justice
(compare *Deborah*, I.ii.105)   6 **Adonis'** of the youth loved by
Venus (for a description of his garden, see Edmund Spenser,
Faerie Queene, III.vi.29–50)   10 **hap** good fortune   16 **played the
men** proved our courage

For which I will divide my crown with her,
And all the priests and friars in my realm
20 Shall in procession sing her endless praise.
A statelier pyramis° to her I'll rear
Than Rhodope's° or Memphis' ever was.
In memory of her when she is dead,
Her ashes, in an urn more precious
25 Than the rich-jeweled coffer of Darius,°
Transported shall be at high festivals
Before the kings and queens of France.
No longer on Saint Denis° will we cry,
But Joan la Pucelle shall be France's saint.
30 Come in, and let us banquet royally,
After this golden day of victory.   *Flourish. Exeunt.*

21 **pyramis** pyramid   22 **Rhodope's** (according to lengend, the famous Greek courtesan Rhodopis built the third pyramid)   25 **coffer of Darius** (the Persian monarch's jewel chest, said to have been used by Alexander the Great to hold a copy of Homer)   28 **Saint Denis** patron saint of France

ACT II

Scene I. [*Orleans.*]

*Enter a [French] Sergeant of a band, with two
Sentinels.*

Sergeant. Sirs, take your places and be vigilant;
  If any noise or soldier you perceive
  Near to the walls, by some apparent sign
  Let us have knowledge at the court of guard.°

Sentinel. Sergeant, you shall. Thus are poor servi-
  tors,°   [*Exit Sergeant.*]   5
  When others sleep upon their quiet beds,
  Constrained to watch in darkness, rain, and cold.

*Enter Talbot, Bedford, and Burgundy, [and forces,]
with scaling-ladders, their drums beating a dead
march.*

Talbot. Lord Regent, and redoubted° Burgundy,
  By whose approach° the regions of Artois,
  Wallon, and Picardy° are friends to us,   10

II.i.4 **court of guard** headquarters of the guard   5 **servitors** soldiers
8 **redoubted** distinguished   9 **approach** presence   9–10 **Artois,
Wallon, and Picardy** (provinces in northeastern France, parts of
which are now in Belgium)

This happy night the Frenchmen are secure,°
Having all day caroused and banqueted;
Embrace we° then this opportunity
As fitting best to quittance° their deceit
15 Contrived by art° and baleful° sorcery.

Bedford. Coward of France! how much he wrongs his
      fame,
Despairing of his own arm's fortitude,
To join with witches and the help of hell.

Burgundy. Traitors have never other company.
20 But what's that Pucelle whom they term so pure?

Talbot. A maid, they say.

Bedford.   A maid? And be so martial?

Burgundy. Pray God she prove not masculine° ere
      long,
If underneath the standard of the French
She carry armor as she hath begun.

Talbot. Well, let them practice° and converse with
25   spirits.
God is our fortress, in whose conquering name
Let us resolve to scale their flinty° bulwarks.

Bedford. Ascend, brave Talbot; we will follow thee.

Talbot. Not all together: better far, I guess,
30 That we do make our entrance several° ways;
That, if it chance the one of us do fail,
The other yet may rise against their force.

Bedford. Agreed; I'll to yond° corner.

Burgundy.   And I to this.

Talbot. And here will Talbot mount, or make his
      grave.

---

11 **secure** careless   13 **Embrace we** let us seize   14 **quittance** re-
pay   15 **art** (black) magic   15 **baleful** harmful   22 **prove not mas-**
culine (1) does not turn out to be a man (?) (2) does not become
pregnant with a male child   24 **practice** conjure   27 **flinty** rugged
30 **several** by separate   33 **yond** yonder

Now, Salisbury, for thee, and for the right   35
Of English Henry, shall this night appear
How much in duty I am bound to both.

Sentinel. Arm! arm! the enemy doth make assault!
[*The English, scaling the walls,*] *cry* "St. George!
                    a Talbot!" [*and enter the town*].

*The French leap o'er the walls in their shirts. Enter
several ways Bastard, Alençon, Reignier, half ready,*°
                and half unready.

Alençon. How now, my lords! what, all unready so?

Bastard. Unready? Ay, and glad we 'scaped so well.   40

Reignier. 'Twas time, I trow,° to wake and leave our
        beds,
    Hearing alarums at our chamber doors.

Alençon. Of all exploits since first I followed arms,
    Ne'er heard I of a warlike enterprise
    More venturous or desperate than this.   45

Bastard. I think this Talbot be a fiend of hell.

Reignier. If not of hell, the heavens, sure, favor him.

Alençon. Here cometh Charles; I marvel how he
        sped.°

        Enter Charles [the Dauphin] and Joan.

Bastard. Tut, holy Joan was his defensive guard.

Dauphin. Is this thy cunning,° thou deceitful dame?   50
    Didst thou at first, to flatter us withal,°
    Make us partakers of a little gain,
    That now our loss might be ten times so much?

Pucelle. Wherefore is Charles impatient with his
        friend?
    At all times will you have my power alike?   55
    Sleeping or waking must I still° prevail,

38s.d. **ready** dressed   41 **trow** think   48 **marvel how he sped** wonder how he fared   50 **cunning** craftiness   51 **to flatter us withal**
in order to deceive us   56 **still** always

Or will you blame and lay the fault on me?
Improvident° soldiers! had your watch been good,
This sudden mischief never could have fall'n.

60 *Dauphin.* Duke of Alençon, this was your default,°
That, being captain of the watch tonight,
Did look no better to that weighty charge.°

Alençon. Had all your quarters been as safely kept
As that whereof I had the government,°
65 We had not been thus shamefully surprised.

Bastard. Mine was secure.

Reignier.   And so was mine, my lord.

Dauphin. And, for myself, most part of all this night,
Within her quarter° and mine own precinct°
I was employed in passing to and fro,
70 About relieving of the sentinels.
Then how or which way should they first break in?

Pucelle. Question, my lords, no further of the case,
How or which way; 'tis sure they found some place
But weakly guarded, where the breach was made.
75 And now there rests no other shift° but this,
To gather our soldiers, scattered and dispersed,
And lay new platforms to endamage them.°

*Alarum. Enter an [English] Soldier, crying, "A Tal-
bot! a Talbot!" They fly, leaving their clothes behind.*

Soldier. I'll be so bold to take what they have left.
The cry of Talbot serves me for a sword,
80 For I have loaden me° with many spoils,
Using no other weapon but his name.   *Exit.*

---

58 **Improvident** unwary   60 **default** fault   62 **weighty charge** important responsibility   64 **government** command   68 **quarter** (1)
assigned area for defense (2) chamber   68 **precinct** area of command   75 **shift** expedient, stratagem   77 **lay . . . them** make new
plans to harm the English   80 **loaden me** burdened myself

[Scene II. *Orleans. Within the town.*]

Enter Talbot, Bedford, Burgundy, [a Captain, and others].

Bedford. The day begins to break, and night is fled,
  Whose pitchy° mantle over-veiled the earth.
  Here sound retreat, and cease our hot pursuit.
                                                Retreat.

Talbot. Bring forth the body of old Salisbury,
  And here advance it° in the marketplace,   5
  The middle center of this cursèd town.
  Now have I paid my vow unto his soul;
  For every drop of blood was drawn from him
  There hath at least five Frenchmen died tonight.
  And that hereafter ages may behold   10
  What ruin happened in revenge of him,
  Within their chiefest temple° I'll erect
  A tomb, wherein his corpse shall be interred;
  Upon the which, that everyone may read,
  Shall be engraved the sack° of Orleans,   15
  The treacherous manner of his mournful death,
  And what a terror he had been to France.
  But, lords, in all our bloody massacre,
  I muse° we met not with the Dolphin's grace,°
  His new-come champion, virtuous Joan of Arc,   20
  Nor any of his false confederates.°

Bedford. 'Tis thought, Lord Talbot, when the fight
    began,
  Roused on the sudden from their drowsy beds,

II.ii.2 **pitchy** dark **5 advance it** raise it up **12 chiefest temple** cathedral **15 sack** plundering **19 muse** wonder why **19 the Dolphin's grace** i.e., his grace, the Dauphin **21 confederates** companions

They did amongst the troops of armèd men
25   Leap o'er the walls for refuge in the field.

Burgundy. Myself, as far as I could well discern
For° smoke and dusky vapors of the night,
Am sure I scared the Dolphin and his trull,°
When arm in arm they both came swiftly running,
30   Like to a pair of loving turtle-doves
That could not live asunder day or night.
After that things are set in order here,
We'll follow them with all the power we have.

Enter a Messenger.

Messenger. All hail, my lords! Which of this princely
train°
35   Call ye the warlike Talbot, for his acts
So much applauded through the realm of France?

Talbot. Here is the° Talbot; who would speak with
him?

Messenger. The virtuous lady, Countess of Auvergne,
With modesty admiring thy renown,
40   By me entreats, great lord, thou wouldst vouchsafe°
To visit her poor castle where she lies,°
That she may boast she hath beheld the man
Whose glory fills the world with loud report.

Burgundy. Is it even so? Nay, then, I see our wars
45   Will turn unto a peaceful comic sport,
When ladies crave to be encountered° with.
You may not, my lord, despise her gentle suit.°

Talbot. Ne'er trust me then; for when a world of men
Could not prevail with all their oratory,
50   Yet hath a woman's kindness overruled;°

---

27 **For** because of   28 **trull** concubine, harlot   34 **princely train**
noble company   37 **the** (used with the surname to designate the
head of a family or clan)   40 **vouchsafe** condescend   41 **lies** re-
sides   46 **encountered** met (for an amatory interview)   47 **gentle
suit** mannerly request   50 **overruled** prevailed

And therefore tell her I return great thanks
And in submission° will attend on her.
Will not your honors bear me company?

Bedford. No, truly, 'tis more than manners will,°
And I have heard it said, unbidden° guests   55
Are often welcomest when they are gone.

Talbot. Well then, alone, since there's no remedy,
I mean to prove this lady's courtesy.°
Come hither, captain. (*Whispers*) You perceive my
mind?°

Captain. I do, my lord, and mean accordingly.   60
                                        Exeunt.

[Scene III. *Auvergne. The Countess' castle.*]

Enter Countess [and her Porter].

Countess. Porter, remember what I gave in charge,°
And when you have done so, bring the keys to me.

Porter. Madam, I will.   *Exit.*

Countess. The plot is laid; if all things fall out right,
I shall as famous be by this exploit   5
As Scythian Tomyris° by Cyrus' death.
Great is the rumor° of this dreadful knight,
And his achievements of no less account;
Fain° would mine eyes be witness with mine ears,
To give their censure° of these rare reports.   10

Enter Messenger and Talbot.

52 **in submission** deferentially   54 **will** require   55 **unbidden** un-
invited   58 **prove . . . courtesy** try out this lady's hospitality   59
perceive my mind understand my plan   II.iii.1 **gave in charge** instructed you to do   6 **Tomyris** queen of a fierce Central Asian people who slew Cyrus the Great in battle   7 **rumor** reputation   9
Fain gladly   10 **censure** judgment

Messenger. Madam,
    According as your ladyship desired,
    By message craved,° so is Lord Talbot come.

Countess. And he is welcome. What! is this the man?

Messenger. Madam, it is.

15 *Countess.*   Is this the scourge of France?
    Is this the Talbot, so much feared abroad
    That with his name the mothers still° their babes?
    I see report is fabulous° and false.
    I thought I should have seen some Hercules,
20 A second Hector, for his grim aspect°
    And large proportion of his strong-knit° limbs.
    Alas, this is a child, a silly° dwarf!
    It cannot be this weak and writhled° shrimp
    Should strike such terror to his enemies.

25 *Talbot.* Madam, I have been bold to trouble you,
    But since your ladyship is not at leisure,
    I'll sort° some other time to visit you.

Countess. What means he now? Go ask him whither
    he goes.

Messenger. Stay, my Lord Talbot, for my lady craves
30 To know the cause of your abrupt departure.

Talbot. Marry,° for that° she's in a wrong belief,
    I go to certify° her Talbot's here.

                    Enter Porter with keys.

Countess. If thou be he, then art thou prisoner.

Talbot. Prisoner! to whom?

Countess.   To me, bloodthirsty lord;
35 And for that cause I trained° thee to my house.
    Long time thy shadow hath been thrall to me,

---

13 **craved** invited   17 **still** silence   18 **fabulous** merely fictional
20 **aspect** countenance   21 **strong-knit** well-muscled   22 **silly** feeble
23 **writhled** wrinkled   27 **sort** choose   31 **Marry** why   31 **for that**
because   32 **certify** inform   35 **trained** lured

For in my gallery thy picture° hangs.
But now the substance shall endure the like,
And I will chain these legs and arms of thine
That hast by tyranny these many years   40
Wasted our country, slain our citizens,
And sent our sons and husbands captivate.°

Talbot. Ha, ha, ha!

Countess. Laughest thou, wretch? Thy mirth shall turn
   to moan.

Talbot. I laugh to see your ladyship so fond°   45
   To think that you have aught but Talbot's shadow
   Whereon to practice your severity.°

Countess. Why, art not thou the man?

Talbot.   I am indeed.

Countess. Then have I substance too.

Talbot. No, no, I am but shadow of myself: 50
   You are deceived, my substance is not here,
   For what you see is but the smallest part
   And least proportion of humanity.
   I tell you, madam, were the whole frame° here,
   It is of such a spacious lofty pitch,°   55
   Your roof were not sufficient to contain 't.

Countess. This is a riddling merchant° for the
   nonce;°
   He will be here, and yet he is not here.
   How can these contrarieties° agree?

Talbot. That will I show you presently.   60
            *Winds° his horn; drums strike up; a peal
                of ordnance;° enter Soldiers.*
   How say you, madam? Are you now persuaded
   That Talbot is but shadow of himself?

---

37 picture (possibly implying that the Countess was trying to practice witchcraft on him)   **42 captive** captive   **45 fond** foolish   **47
severity** cruelty   **54 frame** structure   **55 pitch** stature   **57 riddling
merchant** enigmatic fellow   **57 for the nonce** for the occasion
(merely a line-filler)   **59 contrarieties** contradictions   **60s.d. Winds**
blows   **60s.d. peal of ordnance** salute of guns

These are his substance, sinews, arms, and strength,
With which he yoketh° your rebellious necks,
65   Razeth your cities and subverts° your towns,
And in a moment makes them desolate.

Countess. Victorious Talbot, pardon my abuse;
I find thou art no less than fame hath bruited°
And more than may be gathered by thy shape.
70   Let my presumption not provoke thy wrath,
For I am sorry that with reverence°
I did not entertain thee as thou art.

Talbot. Be not dismayed, fair lady, nor misconster°
The mind of Talbot, as you did mistake
75   The outward composition° of his body.
What you have done hath not offended me,
Nor other satisfaction do I crave,
But only, with your patience, that we may
Taste of your wine and see what cates° you have,
80   For soldiers' stomachs always serve them well.

Countess. With all my heart, and think me honorèd
To feast so great a warrior in my house.   *Exeunt.*

[Scene IV. *London. The Temple Garden.°*]

Enter Richard Plantagenet, Warwick, Somerset, [William de la] Pole [Earl of Suffolk, Vernon, and another Lawyer].

Plantagenet. Great lords and gentlemen, what means
this silence?
Dare no man answer in a case of truth?

64 **yoketh** brings into subjection 65 **subverts** overthrows 68 **bruited** reported 71 **reverence** respect 73 **misconster** misunderstand 75 **composition** form 79 **cates** choice foods II.iv.s.d. **Temple Garden** (the Inner and Middle Temples were residences for students of the common law)

Suffolk. Within the Temple Hall we were too loud;
　The garden here is more convenient.

Plantagenet. Then say at once if I maintained the
　　truth;
　Or else was wrangling° Somerset in th' error?

Suffolk. Faith,° I have been a truant° in the law,
　And never yet could frame° my will to it,
　And therefore frame° the law unto my will.

Somerset. Judge you, my lord of Warwick, then,
　　between us.

Warwick. Between two hawks, which flies the higher
　　pitch;
　Between two dogs, which hath the deeper mouth;°
　Between two blades, which bears the better temper;
　Between two horses, which doth bear him° best;
　Between two girls, which hath the merriest eye—
　I have perhaps some shallow spirit° of judgment;
　But in these nice sharp quillets° of the law,
　Good faith, I am no wiser than a daw.°

Plantagenet. Tut, tut, here is a mannerly forbearance.
　The truth appears so naked on my side
　That any purblind° eye may find it out.

Somerset. And on my side it is so well appareled,°
　So clear, so shining, and so evident,
　That it will glimmer through a blind man's eye.

Plantagenet. Since you are tongue-tied and so loath
　　to speak,
　In dumb significants° proclaim your thoughts:
　Let him that is a true-born gentleman
　And stands upon° the honor of his birth,

5

10

15

20

25

---

6 **wrangling** quarrelsome　7 **Faith** in truth　7 **truant** lazy student
8 **frame** dispose　9 **frame** twist　12 **mouth** bark, bay　14 **bear him**
behave himself　16 **shallow spirit** small amount　17 **nice sharp
quillets** precise and subtle distinctions　18 **daw** simpleton　21
purblind nearly blind　22 **appareled** (1) dressed (2) ordered　26 **In
dumb significants** by mute signs　28 **stands upon** takes pride in

If he suppose that I have pleaded truth,
30 From off this brier pluck a white rose with me.

Somerset. Let him that is no coward nor no flatterer,
But dare maintain the party of the truth,
Pluck a red rose from off this thorn with me.

Warwick. I love no colors;° and without all color
35 Of base insinuating flattery
I pluck this white rose with Plantagenet.

Suffolk. I pluck this red rose with young Somerset
And say withal° I think he held the right.

Vernon. Stay, lords and gentlemen, and pluck no more
40 Till you conclude that he upon whose side
The fewest roses are cropped° from the tree
Shall yield the other in the right opinion.

Somerset. Good Master Vernon, it is well objected;°
If I have fewest, I subscribe in silence.

45 *Plantagenet.* And I.

Vernon. Then for the truth and plainness of the case,
I pluck this pale and maiden° blossom here,
Giving my verdict on the white rose side.

Somerset. Prick not your finger as you pluck it off,
50 Lest bleeding you do paint the white rose red
And fall on my side so against your will.

Vernon. If I, my lord, for my opinion bleed,
Opinion shall be surgeon to my hurt
And keep me on the side where still I am.

55 *Somerset.* Well, well, come on, who else?

Lawyer. Unless my study and my books be false,
The argument you held was wrong in you;
In sign whereof I pluck a white rose too.

Plantagenet. Now, Somerset, where is your argument?

34 **colors** (1) pretenses (2) adornments of speech   38 **withal** thereby
41 **cropped** plucked   43 **objected** proposed   47 **maiden** flawless

Somerset. Here in my scabbard, meditating° that   60
  Shall dye your white rose in a bloody red.

Plantagenet. Meantime your cheeks do counterfeit°
    our roses,
  For pale they look with fear, as witnessing
  The truth on our side.

Somerset.   No, Plantagenet,
  'Tis not for fear, but anger that thy cheeks   65
  Blush for pure shame to counterfeit our roses,
  And yet thy tongue will not confess thy error.

Plantagenet. Hath not thy rose a canker,° Somerset?

Somerset. Hath not thy rose a thorn, Plantagenet?

Plantagenet. Ay, sharp and piercing, to maintain his
    truth   70
  Whiles thy consuming canker eats his falsehood.

Somerset. Well, I'll find friends to wear my bleeding
    roses,
  That shall maintain what I have said is true
  Where false Plantagenet dare not be seen.

Plantagenet. Now, by this maiden blossom in my
    hand,   75
  I scorn thee and thy fashion,° peevish boy.

Suffolk. Turn not thy scorns this way, Plantagenet.

Plantagenet. Proud Pole, I will, and scorn both him
    and thee.

Suffolk. I'll turn my part thereof into thy throat.

Somerset. Away, away, good William de la Pole!   80
  We grace the yeoman° by conversing with him.

Warwick. Now, by God's will, thou wrong'st him,
    Somerset;

---

60 **meditating** planning   62 **counterfeit** imitate   68 **canker** (1) disease (2) caterpillar larva   76 **fashion** (1) manner of behavior (2) faction (?)   81 **grace the yeoman** dignify this commoner

His grandfather° was Lionel Duke of Clarence,
Third son to the third Edward King of England:
85   Spring crestless° yeomen from so deep a root?

Plantagenet. He bears him on the place's privilege,°
    Or durst not, for his craven heart, say thus.

Somerset. By him that made me, I'll maintain my words
    On any plot of ground in Christendom.
90   Was not thy father, Richard Earl of Cambridge,
    For treason executed in our late king's days?
    And, by his treason, stand'st not thou attainted,
    Corrupted, and exempt from ancient gentry?°
    His trespass° yet lives guilty in thy blood,
95   And, till thou be restored, thou art a yeoman.°

Plantagenet. My father was attachèd,° not attainted,
    Condemned to die for treason, but no traitor;
    And that I'll prove° on better men than Somerset,
    Were growing time once ripened to my will.°
100   For your partaker° Pole and you yourself,
    I'll note you in my book of memory
    To scourge you for this apprehension.°
    Look to it well and say you are well warned.

Somerset. Ah, thou shalt find us ready for thee still,
105   And know us by these colors for thy foes,
    For these my friends in spite of thee shall wear.

Plantagenet. And, by my soul, this pale and angry rose,
    As cognizance° of my blood-drinking° hate,

---

83 **grandfather** i.e., great-great-grandfather   85 **crestless** not having the right to a coat of arms   86 **privilege** i.e., of sanctuary (since the Temple was founded as a religious house)   92–93 **attainted . . . gentry** (legal penalties by which the heirs of a person convicted of treason were prevented from inheriting his property and titles)   94 **trespass** crime   95 **And . . . yeoman** (therefore, you shall remain a commoner until your titles are legally restored)   96 **attachèd** arrested   98 **prove** establish through trial by combat   99 **Were . . . will** i.e., if I should ever be restored to the nobility   100 **partaker** partisan   102 **apprehension** notion, display of wit   108 **cognizance** a badge   108 **blood-drinking** bloodthirsty

Will I forever and my faction wear
Until it wither with me to my grave   110
Or flourish to the height of my degree.°

Suffolk. Go forward and be choked with thy ambition!
And so farewell until I meet thee next.   *Exit.*

Somerset. Have with thee,° Pole. Farewell, ambitious Richard.   *Exit.*

Plantagenet. How I am braved° and must perforce°
endure it!   115

Warwick. This blot that they object against your house
Shall be whipped° out in the next parliament
Called for the truce of Winchester and Gloucester,
And if thou be not then created York,°
I will not live to be accounted° Warwick.   120
Meantime, in signal of my love to thee,
Against proud Somerset and William Pole,
Will I upon thy party° wear this rose.
And here I prophesy: this brawl° today,
Grown to this faction in the Temple garden,   125
Shall send, between the red rose and the white,
A thousand souls to death and deadly night.

Plantagenet. Good Master Vernon, I am bound to
you
That you on my behalf would pluck a flower.

Vernon. In your behalf still will I wear the same.   130

Lawyer. And so will I.

Plantagenet. Thanks, gentle [sir].
Come, let us four to dinner: I dare say
This quarrel will drink blood° another day. *Exeunt.*

---

111 **to . . . degree** until I regain my high rank   114 **Have with thee**
I'll go with you   115 **braved** defied   115 **perforce** necessarily
117 **whipped** quickly stricken   119 **York** i.e., Duke of York   120
accounted considered   123 **upon thy party** in support of you   124
brawl quarrel   134 **drink blood** result in bloodshed

[Scene V. *The Tower of London.*]

Enter Mortimer, brought in a chair, and Jailers.

Mortimer. Kind keepers of my weak decaying age,
Let dying Mortimer here rest himself.
Even like a man new halèd from the rack,°
So fare my limbs with long imprisonment,
5   And these gray locks, the pursuivants° of death,
Nestor-like° agèd in an age of care,
Argue° the end of Edmund Mortimer.
These eyes, like lamps whose wasting° oil is spent,
Wax° dim, as drawing to their exigent;°
10   Weak shoulders, overborne with burthening° grief,
And pithless° arms, like to a withered vine
That droops his sapless branches to the ground.
Yet are these feet, whose strengthless stay° is numb,
Unable to support this lump of clay,
15   Swift-wingèd with desire to get a grave,
As witting I no other comfort have.
But tell me, keeper, will my nephew come?

First Jailer. Richard Plantagenet, my lord, will come:
We sent unto the Temple, unto his chamber,
20   And answer was returned that he will come.

Mortimer. Enough; my soul shall then be satisfied.
Poor gentleman! his wrong doth equal mine.
Since Henry Monmouth° first began to reign,
Before whose glory I was great in arms,

II.v.3 **new . . . rack** just released from the torturer's rack   5 **pursuivants** heralds   6 **Nestor-like** (the Greek king Nestor, in Homer's *Iliad,* is a type of old age)   7 **Argue** foretell   8 **wasting** consuming   9 **Wax** grow   9 **exigent** end   10 **burthening** (dissyllabic) burdensome   11 **pithless** strengthless   13 **stay** support   23 **Henry Monmouth** King Henry V

This loathsome sequestration° have I had;   25
And even since then hath Richard been obscured,°
Deprived of honor and inheritance.
But now the arbitrator of despairs,
Just Death, kind umpire° of men's miseries,
With sweet enlargement° doth dismiss me hence.   30
I would his° troubles likewise were expired,
That so he might recover what was lost.

Enter Richard [Plantagenet].

First Jailer. My lord, your loving nephew now is
    come.

Mortimer. Richard Plantagenet, my friend, is he
    come?

Plantagenet. Ay, noble uncle, thus ignobly used,   35
    Your nephew, late despisèd° Richard, comes.

Mortimer. Direct mine arms I may° embrace his neck
    And in his bosom spend my latter gasp.°
    O, tell me when my lips do touch his cheeks,
    That I may kindly give one fainting kiss.   40
    And now declare, sweet stem from York's great
        stock,°
    Why didst thou say, of late thou wert despised?

Plantagenet. First, lean thine agèd back against mine
        arm,
    And, in that ease, I'll tell thee my disease.°
    This day, in argument upon a case,   45
    Some words there grew 'twixt Somerset and me;
    Among which terms he used his lavish° tongue
    And did upbraid° me with my father's death:
    Which obloquy° set bars before my tongue,
    Else with the like I had requited° him.   50

25 **sequestration** imprisonment   26 **obscured** degraded   29 **umpire**
arbitrator   30 **enlargement** release   31 **his** i.e., Plantagenet's   36
late despisèd just insulted   37 **I may** (so that) I may   38 **spend
my latter gasp** draw my last breath   41 **stock** trunk (i.e., lineage)
44 **disease** source of my discomfort   47 **lavish** licentious, unre-
strained   48 **upbraid** insult   49 **obloquy** reproach   50 **requited**
repaid

Therefore, good uncle, for my father's sake,
In honor of a true Plantagenet,
And for alliance' sake, declare the cause°
My father, Earl of Cambridge, lost his head.

Mortimer. That cause, fair nephew, that imprisoned
55   me
And hath detained me all my flow'ring° youth
Within a loathsome dungeon, there to pine,
Was cursèd instrument of his decease.

Plantagenet. Discover° more at large what cause that
      was,
60   For I am ignorant and cannot guess.

Mortimer. I will, if that my fading breath permit
And death approach not ere my tale be done.
Henry the Fourth, grandfather to this king,
Deposed his nephew° Richard, Edward's son,
65   The first-begotten and the lawful heir
Of Edward king, the third of that descent:°
During whose reign the Percies° of the north,
Finding his usurpation most unjust,
Endeavored my advancement to the throne,
70   The reason moved° these warlike lords to this
Was, for that—young° Richard thus removed,
Leaving no heir begotten of his body—
I was the next by birth and parentage:
For by my mother° I derivèd° am
75   From Lionel Duke of Clarence, third son
To King Edward the Third; whereas he
From John of Gaunt doth bring his pedigree,
Being but fourth of that heroic line.
But mark:° as in this haughty° great attempt

---

53 **the cause** for what reason   56 **flow'ring** vigorous, flourishing
59 **Discover** explain   64 **nephew** (cousin)   64–66 **Edward's . . .
descent** i.e., Richard II, son of Edward the Black Prince and grand-
son of King Edward III   67 **Percies** noble family of Northumber-
land   70 **moved** that provoked   71 **young** (Richard was actually
over thirty at the time of his deposition)   74 **mother** (actually,
grandmother)   74 **derivèd** descended   79 **mark** listen attentively
79 **haughty** lofty

They laborèd to plant the rightful heir,   80
I lost my liberty and they their lives.
Long after this, when Henry the Fifth,
Succeeding his father Bolingbroke, did reign,
Thy father, Earl of Cambridge, then derived
From famous Edmund Langley, Duke of York,   85
Marrying my sister that thy mother was,
Again, in pity of my hard distress,
Levied an army, weening to redeem
And have installed me in the diadem;°
But, as the rest, so fell that noble earl   90
And was beheaded. Thus the Mortimers,
In whom the title rested, were suppressed.

Plantagenet. Of which, my lord, your honor is the
     last.

Mortimer. True; and thou seest that I no issue have
And that my fainting words do warrant° death.   95
Thou art my heir; the rest I wish thee gather,°
But yet be wary in thy studious care.°

Plantagenet. Thy grave admonishments prevail with
     me,
But yet, methinks, my father's execution
Was nothing less than bloody tyranny.   100

Mortimer. With silence, nephew, be thou politic:
Strong-fixèd is the house of Lancaster,
And like a mountain, not to be removed.
But now thy uncle is removing hence,
As princes do their courts, when they are cloyed°   105
With long continuance in a settled place.

Plantagenet. O, uncle, would some part of my young
     years

88–89 **Levied . . . diadem** raised an army, with the intention of
rescuing me and having me crowned king   95 **warrant** give assur-
ance of   96 **the rest . . . gather** (1) I want you to conclude for yourself (2) I hope that you may gain all that is rightfully yours   97
But . . . care i.e., but always be careful even as you take pains in
this enterprise   105 **cloyed** satiated

Might but redeem the passage° of your age!

Mortimer. Thou dost then wrong me, as that
slaughterer doth
110 Which giveth many wounds when one will kill.
Mourn not, except thou sorrow for my good;
Only give order° for my funeral.
And so farewell, and fair be all thy hopes,
And prosperous be thy life in peace and war! *Dies.*

Plantagenet. And peace, no war, befall thy parting
115 soul!
In prison hast thou spent a pilgrimage°
And like a hermit overpassed° thy days.
Well, I will lock his counsel in my breast,
And what I do imagine, let that rest.
120 Keepers, convey him hence, and I myself
Will see his burial better than his life.°

[*Exeunt Jailers with the body of Mortimer.*]

Here dies the dusky° torch of Mortimer,
Choked with ambition of the meaner sort.°
And for those wrongs, those bitter injuries
125 Which Somerset hath offered to my house,
I doubt not but with honor to redress.°
And therefore haste I to the parliament,
Either to be restorèd to my blood,
Or make my will th'advantage of my good.°

Exit.

108 **redeem the passage** buy back the passing   112 **give order** make
arrangements   116 **pilgrimage** full life's journey   117 **overpassed**
lived out   121 **Will . . . life** will see that he receives the honor in
his funeral that was denied him during his lifetime   122 **dusky**
gloomy   123 **Choked . . . sort** stifled by the ambition of men of
inferior birth (i.e., the House of Lancaster)   126 **redress** remedy
129 **will . . . good** determination of purpose the means of achieving
my ambition (see Textual Note)

ACT III

Scene I. [*London. The Parliament-house.*]

Flourish. Enter King, Exeter, Gloucester, Winchester, Warwick, Somerset, Suffolk, Richard Plantagenet. Gloucester offers to put up a bill;° Winchester snatches it, tears it.

Winchester. Com'st thou with deep premeditated
    lines,°
  With written pamphlets studiously devised?
  Humphrey of Gloucester, if thou canst accuse
  Or aught intend'st to lay unto my charge,
  Do it without invention,° suddenly,   *5*
  As I with sudden and extemporal° speech
  Purpose to answer what thou canst object.

Gloucester. Presumptuous priest! this place commands
    my patience,
  Or thou shouldst find thou hast dishonored me.
  Think not, although in writing I preferred°   *10*
  The manner of thy vile outrageous crimes,

III.i.s.d. **offers . . . bill** attempts to post a statement of accusations
1 **deep premeditated lines** statements carefully thought out in advance 5 **invention** (seeking out the grounds for argument in the manner of a rhetorician or a lawyer trained in oratory) 6 **extemporal** extemporaneous 10 **preferred** set forth

That therefore I have forged,° or am not able
Verbatim to rehearse the method of my pen.°
No, prelate, such is thy audacious wickedness,
15   Thy lewd, pestiferous, and dissentious pranks,°
As very° infants prattle of thy pride.
Thou art a most pernicious usurer,°
Froward° by nature, enemy to peace,
Lascivious, wanton, more than well beseems°
20   A man of thy profession and degree.
And for thy treachery, what's more manifest?
In that thou laid'st a trap to take my life,
As well at London Bridge as at the Tower.
Beside, I fear me, if thy thoughts were sifted,°
25   The king, thy sovereign, is not quite exempt
From envious malice of thy swelling° heart.

Winchester. Gloucester, I do defy thee. Lords,
      vouchsafe
To give me hearing what I shall reply.
If I were covetous, ambitious, or perverse,
30   As he will have me,° how am I so poor?
Or how haps it° I seek not to advance
Or raise myself, but keep my wonted calling?°
And for dissension, who preferreth peace
More than I do?—except I be provoked.
35   No, my good lords, it is not that offends;
It is not that that hath incensed° the duke:
It is, because no one should sway° but he,
No one but he should be about the king,
And that engenders thunder in his breast
40   And makes him roar these accusations forth.
But he shall know I am as good—

---

12 **forged** fabricated lies   13 **rehearse . . . pen** repeat the contents of what I have written   15 **lewd . . . pranks** wicked, mischievous, and quarrelsome offenses   16 **As very** that even   17 **pernicious usurer** (alluding to Winchester's reputation for gaining riches through extortions and loans made at exorbitant rates of interest) 18 **Froward** inclined to evil   19 **beseems** is fitting to   24 **sifted** closely examined   26 **swelling** proud   30 **have me** make me out to be   31 **haps it** does it happen   32 **calling** religious vocation   36 **incensed** enraged   37 **sway** rule

Gloucester.   As good?
  Thou bastard° of my grandfather!

Winchester. Ay, lordly° sir; for what are you, I pray,
  But one imperious° in another's throne?

Gloucester. Am I not Protector, saucy priest?   45

Winchester. And am not I a prelate of the church?

Gloucester. Yes, as an outlaw in a castle keeps
  And useth it to patronage° his theft.

Winchester. Unreverent Gloucester!

Gloucester.   Thou art reverent
  Touching thy spiritual function,° not thy life.   50

Winchester. Rome shall remedy this.

Warwick.   Roam thither, then.
  My lord, it were your duty to forbear.

Somerset. Ay, see the bishop be not overborne.°
  Methinks my lord° should be religious
  And know the office° that belongs to such.   55

Warwick. Methinks his lordship° should be humbler;
  It fitteth not a prelate so to plead.

Somerset. Yes, when his holy state is touched so
  near.°

Warwick. State holy or unhallowed,° what of that?
  Is not his grace° Protector to the king?   60

Plantagenet. [*Aside*] Plantagenet, I see, must hold
  his tongue,
  Lest it be said, "Speak, sirrah, when you should;

---

42 **bastard** (Winchester was an illegitimate son of John of Gaunt,
Duke of Lancaster)   43 **lordly** haughty   44 **imperious** ruling   48
patronage defend   50 **Touching . . . function** only in respect of
your high ecclesiastical office   53 **overborne** prevailed over   54
lord i.e., Gloucester   55 **office** respect   56 **lordship** Winchester
58 **holy . . . near** ecclesiastical office is so directly involved   59
holy or unhallowed ecclesiastical or secular   60 **grace** i.e.,
Gloucester

Must your bold verdict° enter talk with lords?"
Else would I have a fling at° Winchester.

65 *King.* Uncles of Gloucester and of Winchester,
The special watchmen° of our Engish weal,°
I would prevail, if prayers might prevail,
To join your hearts in love and amity.
O, what a scandal is it to our crown,
70 That two such noble peers as ye should jar!
Believe me, lords, my tender years can tell
Civil dissension is a viperous worm°
That gnaws the bowels of the commonwealth.

A noise within, "Down with the tawny-coats!"

What tumult's this?

Warwick   An uproar, I dare warrant,°
75 Begun through malice of the bishop's men.

A noise again, "Stones! stones!"

Enter Mayor.

Mayor. O my good lords, and virtuous Henry,
Pity the city of London, pity us!
The bishop° and the Duke of Gloucester's men,
Forbidden late° to carry any weapon,
80 Have filled their pockets full of pebble stones
And banding themselves in contrary parts°
Do pelt so fast at one another's pate°
That many have their giddy° brains knocked out.
Our windows are broke down in every street,
85 And we for fear compelled to shut our shops.

*Enter [Servingmen of Gloucester and Winchester]
in skirmish, with bloody pates.*

King. We charge you, on allegiance to ourself,
To hold your slaught'ring hands and keep the
peace.

---

63 **bold verdict** presumptuous opinion   64 **have a fling at** reprove
66 **watchmen** guardians   66 **weal** state   72 **worm** serpent   74 **warrant** swear   78 **bishop** bishop's   79 **late** recently   81 **parts** parties
82 **pate** head   83 **giddy** foolish

Pray, uncle Gloucester, mitigate° this strife.

First Servingman. Nay, if we be forbidden stones,
   we'll fall to it with our teeth.   *90*

Second Servingman. Do what ye dare, we are as
   resolute.   *Skirmish again.*

Gloucester. You of my household, leave this peevish
   broil
   And set this unaccustomed° fight aside.

Third Servingman. My lord, we know your grace to be
   a man   *95*
   Just and upright; and, for your royal birth,
   Inferior to none but to his majesty,
   And ere that we will suffer° such a prince,
   So kind a father of the commonweal,
   To be disgracèd by an inkhorn mate,°   *100*
   We and our wives and children all will fight
   And have our bodies slaughtered by thy foes.

First Servingman. Ay, and the very parings of our
   nails
   Shall pitch a field° when we are dead. *Begin again.*

Gloucester.   Stay, stay, I say!
   And if you love me, as you say you do,   *105*
   Let me persuade you to forbear awhile.

King. O, how this discord doth afflict my soul!
   Can you, my Lord of Winchester, behold
   My sighs and tears and will not once relent?
   Who should be pitiful, if you be not?   *110*
   Or who should study° to prefer a peace,
   If holy churchmen take delight in broils?

Warwick. Yield, my Lord Protector; yield, Winchester,

---

88 **mitigate** appease   94 **unaccustomed** indecorous   98 **suffer** permit   100 **inkhorn mate** scribbling fellow (an unlettered person's
disparaging allusion to the literacy of clergymen)   104 **pitch a
field** i.e., serve as stakes in a pitched battlefield   111 **study** make
it his aim

Except° you mean with obstinate repulse°
115 To slay your sovereign and destroy the realm.
You see what mischief and what murder too
Hath been enacted through your enmity;
Then be at peace, except ye thirst for blood.

Winchester. He shall submit, or I will never yield.

Gloucester. Compassion on the king commands me
120   stoop;
Or I would see his heart out ere the priest
Should ever get that privilege° of me.

Warwick. Behold, my Lord of Winchester, the duke
Hath banished moody discontented fury,
125 As by his smoothèd brows it doth appear:
Why look you still so stern and tragical?°

Gloucester. Here, Winchester, I offer thee my hand.

King. Fie, uncle Beaufort! I have heard you preach
That malice was a great and grievous sin,
130 And will not you maintain the thing you teach,
But prove a chief offender in the same?

Warwick. Sweet king! the bishop hath a kindly gird.°
For shame, my Lord of Winchester, relent!
What, shall a child instruct you what to do?

Winchester. Well, Duke of Gloucester, I will yield
135   to thee
Love for thy love, and hand for hand I give.

Gloucester. [*Aside*] Ay, but, I fear me, with a hollow°
    heart.
[*Aloud*] See here, my friends and loving countrymen;
This token° serveth for a flag of truce
140 Betwixt ourselves and all our followers.
So help me God, as I dissemble not!

---

114 **Except** unless   114 **repulse** refusal   122 **privilege** advantage
yielded   126 **tragical** gloomy   132 **kindly gird** fitting gibe   137
hollow insincere   139 **token** i.e., handclasp

Winchester. [*Aside*] So help me God, as I intend it
    not!

King. O loving uncle, kind Duke of Gloucester,
    How joyful am I made by this contract!°
    Away, my masters! trouble us no more,   145
    But join in friendship, as your lords have done.

First Servingman. Content; I'll to the surgeon's.

Second Servingman.   And so will I.

Third Servingman. And I will see what physic° the
    tavern affords.°   *Exeunt.*

Warwick. Accept this scroll,° most gracious sovereign, 150
    Which in the right of Richard Plantagenet
    We do exhibit to your majesty.

Gloucester. Well urged, my Lord of Warwick: for,
      sweet prince,
    And if° your grace mark° every circumstance,
    You have great reason to do Richard right,   155
    Especially for those occasions°
    At Eltham Place I told your majesty.

King. And those occasions, uncle, were of force.
    Therefore, my loving lords, our pleasure is
    That Richard be restorèd to his blood.°   160

Warwick. Let Richard be restorèd to his blood;
    So shall his father's wrongs be recompensed.

Winchester. As will the rest, so willeth Winchester.

King. If Richard will be true, not that all alone
    But all the whole inheritance I give   165
    That doth belong unto the house of York,
    From whence you spring by lineal descent.

Plantagenet. Thy humble servant vows obedience
    And humble service till the point of death.

---

144 **contract** agreement   148 **physic** remedy   149 **affords** provides
150 **scroll** document   154 **And if** if   154 **mark** take notice of   156
occasions reasons   160 **blood** i.e., title and rights of nobility

170 *King.* Stoop then and set your knee against my foot,
　　　And in reguerdon° of that duty done,
　　　I girt° thee with the valiant sword of York.
　　　Rise, Richard, like a true Plantagenet,
　　　And rise created princely Duke of York.

　　　Plantagenet. And so thrive Richard as thy foes may
175　　fall!
　　　And as my duty springs, so perish they
　　　That grudge one thought° against your majesty!

　　　All. Welcome, high prince, the mighty Duke of York!

　　　Somerset. [*Aside*] Perish, base prince, ignoble Duke
　　　of York!

180 *Gloucester.* Now will it best avail your majesty
　　　To cross the seas and to be crowned in France:
　　　The presence of a king engenders love
　　　Amongst his subjects and his loyal friends,
　　　As it disanimates° his enemies.

　　　King. When Gloucester says the word, King Henry
185　　goes,
　　　For friendly counsel cuts off many foes.

　　　Gloucester. Your ships already are in readiness.

　　　　　Sennet.° Flourish. Exeunt. Manet° Exeter.

　　　Exeter. Ay, we may march in England or in France,
　　　Not seeing what is likely to ensue.
190　This late dissension grown betwixt the peers
　　　Burns under feignèd ashes of forged° love
　　　And will at last break out into a flame;
　　　As festered members° rot but by degree°
　　　Till bones and flesh and sinews fall away,
195　So will this base and envious discord breed.
　　　And now I fear that fatal prophecy

171 **reguerdon** ample reward   172 **girt** gird   177 **grudge one
thought** entertain one grudging thought   184 **disanimates** disheart-
ens   187s.d. **Sennet** trumpet signal for the exit of an important
personage   187s.d. **Manet** remains (Latin)   191 **forged** pretended
193 **members** parts of the body   193 **by degree** little by little,
gradually

Which in the time of Henry named the Fifth
Was in the mouth of every sucking° babe,
That Henry born at Monmouth should win all
And Henry born at Windsor lose all: *200*
Which is so plain that Exeter doth wish
His days may finish ere that hapless time.   *Exit.*

[Scene II. *France. Before Rouen.*]

*Enter [La] Pucelle disguised, with four Soldiers
with sacks upon their backs.*

Pucelle. These are the city gates, the gates of Rouen,
Through which our policy° must make a breach.
Take heed, be wary how you place your words;
Talk like the vulgar° sort of market men°
That come to gather money for their corn.°   *5*
If we have entrance, as I hope we shall,
And that we find the slothful watch but weak,
I'll by a sign give notice to our friends
That Charles the Dolphin may encounter° them.

Soldier. Our sacks shall be a mean° to sack the city, *10*
And we be lords and rulers over Rouen;
Therefore we'll knock.   *Knock.*

Watchman. [*Within*] Qui est là?°

Pucelle. Paysans là, pauvres gens de France:°
Poor market folks that come to sell their corn.   *15*

Watchman. Enter, go in, the market bell is rung.

Pucelle. Now, Rouen, I'll shake thy bulwarks to the
ground.   *Exeunt.*

198 **sucking** nursing III.ii.2 **policy** stratagem   4 **vulgar** common
4 **market men** people going to market 5 **corn** grain 9 **encounter**
assail 10 **mean** means 13 **Qui est là** who is there? 14 **Paysans**
... **France** peasants here, poor folk of France

Enter Charles [the Dauphin], Bastard, Alençon,
[Reignier, and forces].

Dauphin. Saint Denis bless this happy stratagem,
And once again we'll sleep secure in Rouen!

20 *Bastard.* Here entered Pucelle and her practisants.°
Now she is there, how will she specify:
Here is the best and safest passage in?

Reignier. By thrusting out a torch from yonder tower,
Which, once discerned, shows that her meaning is:
25 No way to° that, for weakness, which she entered.

Enter [La] Pucelle on the top, thrusting out a
torch burning.

Pucelle. Behold, this is the happy wedding torch
That joineth Rouen unto her countrymen,
But burning fatal to the Talbonites!°   [*Exit.*]

Bastard. See, noble Charles, the beacon of our friend,
30 The burning torch, in yonder turret stands.

Dauphin. Now shine it° like a comet of revenge,
A prophet to the fall of all our foes!

Reignier. Defer° no time, delays have dangerous
ends;
Enter and cry, "The Dolphin!" presently,
35 And then do execution on the watch.

                                        Alarum. [*Exeunt.*]

An alarum. Talbot in an excursion.°

Talbot. France, thou shalt rue this treason with thy
tears,
If Talbot but survive thy treachery.
Pucelle, that witch, that damnèd sorceress,
Hath wrought this hellish mischief unawares,
40 That hardly we escaped the pride° of France.
                                        Exit.

20 **practisants** companions in the stratagem 25 **to** comparable to
28 **Talbonites** followers of Talbot 31 **shine it** may it shine 33
Defer waste 35s.d. **excursion** sortie 40 **pride** finest warriors

*An alarum: excursions. Bedford, brought in sick in
a chair. Enter Talbot and Burgundy without: within
[La] Pucelle, Charles [the Dauphin], Bastard,
[Alençon,] and Reignier on the walls.*

Pucelle. Good morrow, gallants!° Want ye corn for
    bread?
 I think the Duke of Burgundy will fast
 Before he'll buy again at such a rate.
 'Twas full of darnel;° do you like the taste?

Burgundy. Scoff on, vile fiend and shameless
    courtesan!°   45
 I trust ere long to choke thee with thine own
 And make thee curse the harvest of that corn.

Dauphin. Your grace may starve perhaps before that
    time.

Bedford. O, let no words, but deeds, revenge this
    treason!

Pucelle. What will you do, good gray-beard? Break
    a lance,   50
 And run a-tilt° at death within a chair?

Talbot. Foul fiend of France, and hag of all despite,°
 Encompassed° with thy lustful paramours!°
 Becomes it thee to taunt his valiant age
 And twit° with cowardice a man half dead?   55
 Damsel,° I'll have a bout with you again,
 Or else let Talbot perish with this shame.

Pucelle. Are ye so hot,° sir? Yet, Pucelle, hold thy
    peace;
 If Talbot do but thunder, rain will follow.

      [The English] whisper together in council.

 God speed the parliament! who shall be the
    Speaker?°   60

41 **gallants** gentlemen   44 **darnel** weeds   45 **courtesan** prostitute
50–51 **Break . . . a-tilt** joust, combat   52 **of all despite** full of malice   53 **Encompassed** surrounded   53 **paramours** lovers   55 **twit**
chide   56 **Damsel** girl   58 **hot** angry   60 **Speaker** presiding officer

Talbot. Dare ye come forth and meet us in the field?

Pucelle. Belike° your lordship takes us then for fools,
  To try if that our own be ours or no.

Talbot. I speak not to that railing Hecate,°
65 But unto thee, Alençon, and the rest.
  Will ye, like soldiers, come and fight it out?

Alençon. Signior,° no.

Talbot. Signior, hang! base muleters° of France!
  Like peasant foot-boys° do they keep the walls
70 And dare not take up arms like gentlemen.

Pucelle. Away, captains! let's get us from the walls;
  For Talbot means no goodness by his looks.
  Good-bye, my lord! we came but to tell you
  That we are here.   *Exeunt from the walls.*

75 *Talbot.* And there will we be too, ere it be long,
  Or else reproach be Talbot's greatest fame.
  Vow, Burgundy, by honor of thy house,
  Pricked on° by public wrongs sustained in France,
  Either to get the town again or die.
80 And I, as sure as English Henry lives
  And as his father here was conqueror,
  As sure as in this late-betrayèd town
  Great Cordelion's° heart was burièd,
  So sure I swear to get° the town or die.

85 *Burgundy.* My vows are equal partners with thy vows.

Talbot. But, ere we go, regard° this dying prince,
  The valiant Duke of Bedford. Come, my lord,
  We will bestow you in some better place,
  Fitter for sickness and for crazy° age.

90 *Bedford.* Lord Talbot, do not so dishonor me;
  Here will I sit before the walls of Rouen

62 **Belike** perhaps   64 **railing Hecate** abusive witch (after Hecate, goddess of sorcery)   67 **Signior** sir   68 **muleters** mule-drivers   69 **foot-boys** boy-servants   78 **Pricked on** provoked   83 **Cordelion's** King Richard the Lion-Hearted's   84 **get** retake   86 **regard** behold   89 **crazy** infirm, decrepit

And will be partner of your weal or woe.°

Burgundy. Courageous Bedford, let us now persuade
  you.

Bedford. Not to be gone from hence, for once I read
  That stout Pendragon° in his litter° sick   95
  Came to the field and vanquishèd his foes.
  Methinks I should revive the soldiers' hearts,
  Because I ever found them as myself.

Talbot. Undaunted spirit in a dying breast!
  Then be it so: heavens keep old Bedford safe!   100
  And now no more ado, brave Burgundy,
  But gather we our forces out of hand
  And set upon our boasting enemy.

  [*Exeunt all but Bedford and his Attendants.*]

*An alarum: excursions.° Enter Sir John Falstaff
            and a Captain.*

Captain. Whither away, Sir John Falstaff, in such
  haste?

Falstaff. Whither away? To save myself by flight;   105
  We are like to have the overthrow° again.

Captain. What! Will you fly, and leave Lord Talbot?

Falstaff.   Ay,
  All the Talbots in the world, to save my life.

                                        Exit.

Captain. Cowardly knight, ill fortune follow thee!

                                        Exit.

Retreat. Excursions. [*La*] *Pucelle, Alençon, and
    Charles* [*the Dauphin enter and*] *fly.*

Bedford. Now, quiet soul, depart when heaven please, 110

_____

92 **weal or woe** good or bad fortune   95 **Pendragon** Uther Pendragon, father of King Arthur   95 **litter** stretcher-bed   103s.d. **excursions** entries and exits of skirmishing troops   106 **have the overthrow** be defeated

For I have seen our enemies' overthrow.
What is the trust or strength of foolish man?
They that of late were daring with their scoffs
Are glad and fain° by flight to save themselves.

Bedford dies and is carried in by two in his chair.

An alarum. Enter Talbot, Burgundy, and the rest
[of their men].

115 *Talbot.* Lost, and recovered in a day again!
This is a double honor, Burgundy;
Yet heavens have glory for this victory!

Burgundy. Warlike and martial Talbot, Burgundy
Enshrines thee in his heart and there erects
120 Thy noble deeds as valor's monuments.

Talbot. Thanks, gentle duke. But where is Pucelle
now?
I think her old familiar° is asleep.
Now where's the Bastard's braves,° and Charles
his gleeks?°
What, all amort?° Rouen hangs her head for grief
125 That such a valiant company are fled.
Now will we take some order° in the town,
Placing therein some expert° officers,
And then depart to Paris to the king,
For there young Henry with his nobles lie.°

130 *Burgundy.* What wills Lord Talbot pleaseth Burgundy.

Talbot. But yet, before we go, let's not forget
The noble Duke of Bedford, late deceased,
But see his exequies° fulfilled in Rouen.
A braver soldier never couchèd° lance,
135 A gentler° heart did never sway° in court.
But kings and mightiest potentates must die,
For that's the end of human misery.   *Exeunt.*

---

114 **fain** eager   122 **familiar** servant demon   123 **braves** boasts
123 **gleeks** jests, scoffs   124 **amort** dejected   126 **take some order**
restore order   127 **expert** experienced   129 **lie** reside   133 **exe-
quies** funeral ceremonies   134 **couchèd** leveled for the assault   135
gentler nobler   135 **sway** prevail

Scene III. [*The plains near Rouen.*]

Enter Charles [*the Dauphin*], *Bastard, Alençon,* [*La*]
Pucelle, [*and forces*].

Pucelle. Dismay not, princes, at this accident,
  Nor grieve that Rouen is so recoverèd.
  Care is no cure, but rather corrosive,°
  For things that are not to be remedied.
  Let frantic° Talbot triumph for a while   5
  And like a peacock sweep along his tail;
  We'll pull° his plumes and take away his train,°
  If Dolphin and the rest will be but ruled.°

Dauphin. We have been guided by thee hitherto
  And of thy cunning had no diffidence;°   10
  One sudden foil° shall never breed distrust.

Bastard. Search out thy wit° for secret policies,
  And we will make thee famous through the world.

Alençon. We'll set thy statue in some holy place,
  And have thee reverenced like a blessèd saint.   15
  Employ thee° then, sweet virgin, for our good.

Pucelle. Then thus it must be; this doth Joan devise:°
  By fair persuasions mixed with sugared° words
  We will entice the Duke of Burgundy
  To leave the Talbot and to follow us.   20

Dauphin. Ay, marry, sweeting,° if we could do that,
  France were no place for Henry's warriors,

III.iii.3 **corrosive** a caustic drug   5 **frantic** raging   7 **pull** pluck
7 **train** (1) followers (2) equipment for battle   8 **ruled** guided (by
Joan)   10 **diffidence** lack of confidence   11 **foil** defeat   12 **Search
out thy wit** examine your mind   16 **Employ thee** apply your efforts   17 **devise** determine   18 **sugared** sweet-sounding   21 **sweeting** sweetheart

Nor should that nation boast it so with° us,
But be extirpèd° from our provinces.

Alençon. Forever should they be expulsed° from
25   France
And not have title of° an earldom here.

Pucelle. Your honors shall perceive how I will work
To bring this matter to the wishèd end.

                        Drum sounds afar off.

Hark! by the sound of drum you may perceive
30   Their powers are marching unto Paris-ward.°

                Here sound an English march.

There goes the Talbot, with his colors spread,°
And all the troops of English after him.

French march. [*Enter the Duke of Burgundy and
forces.*]
Now in the rearward comes the duke and his;
Fortune in favor° makes him lag behind.
35   Summon a parley; we will talk with him.

                Trumpets sound a parley.

Dauphin. A parley with the Duke of Burgundy!

Burgundy. Who craves a parley with the Burgundy?

Pucelle. The princely Charles of France, thy
countryman.

Burgundy. What say'st thou, Charles? For I am
marching hence.

Dauphin. Speak, Pucelle, and enchant him with thy
40   words.

Pucelle. Brave Burgundy, undoubted hope of France!
Stay, let thy humble handmaid speak to thee.

Burgundy. Speak on, but be not over-tedious.

23 **boast it so with** lord it over   24 **extirpèd** rooted out   25 **expulsed**
driven out   26 **title of** claim to   30 **unto Paris-ward** toward Paris
31 **colors spread** banners unfurled   34 **in favor** to our advantage

Pucelle. Look on thy country, look on fertile France,
And see the cities and the towns defaced   45
By wasting ruin of the cruel foe,
As looks the mother on her lowly babe
When death doth close his tender-dying° eyes.
See, see the pining° malady of France;
Behold the wounds, the most unnatural wounds,   50
Which thou thyself hast given her woeful breast.
O, turn thy edgèd° sword another way;
Strike those that hurt, and hurt not those that help.
One drop of blood drawn from thy country's bosom
Should grieve thee more than streams of foreign
    gore.   55
Return thee therefore with a flood of tears,
And wash away thy country's stainèd° spots.

Burgundy. Either she hath bewitched me with her
    words,
Or nature makes me suddenly relent.

Pucelle. Besides, all French and France exclaims on°
    thee,   60
Doubting thy birth and lawful progeny.°
Who join'st thou with, but with a lordly° nation
That will not trust thee but for profit's sake?
When Talbot hath set footing° once in France
And fashioned thee° that instrument of ill,   65
Who then but English Henry will be lord,
And thou be thrust out like a fugitive?
Call we to mind, and mark but this for proof:
Was not the Duke of Orleans thy foe?
And was he not in England prisoner?   70
But when they heard he was thine enemy,
They set him free without his ransom paid,
In spite of Burgundy and all his friends.
See then, thou fight'st against thy countrymen

---

48 **tender-dying** prematurely dying   49 **pining** consuming   52
edgèd sharp   57 **stainèd** disgraceful   60 **exclaims on** cries out
against   61 **lawful progeny** legitimate parentage   62 **lordly** imperious, disdainful   64 **set footing** entered   65 **fashioned thee** made
you into

75   And join'st with them will be thy slaughter-men.°
     Come, come, return; return, thou wandering lord;
     Charles and the rest will take thee in their arms.

Burgundy. I am vanquishèd; these haughty° words of
     hers
     Have battered me like roaring cannon-shot,
80   And made me almost yield upon my knees.
     Forgive me, country, and sweet countrymen,
     And, lords, accept this hearty kind° embrace.
     My forces and my power of men° are yours.
     So farewell, Talbot; I'll no longer trust thee.

Pucelle. [*Aside*] Done like a Frenchman: turn and
85   turn again!°

Dauphin. Welcome, brave duke! thy friendship makes
     us fresh.°

Bastard. And doth beget new courage in our breasts.

Alençon. Pucelle hath bravely played her part in this,
     And doth deserve a coronet° of gold.

Dauphin. Now let us on, my lords, and join our
90   powers,
     And seek how we may prejudice° the foe.   *Exeunt.*

---

75 **slaughter-men** executioners   78 **haughty** loftily brave   82 **kind**
(1) friendly (2) of a kinsman   83 **my power of men** (1) my full com-
plement of troops (?) (2) command over my troops   85 **turn and
turn again** change sides frequently   86 **makes us fresh** renews our
spirits   89 **coronet** a small crown worn on state occasions by members of the nobility   91 **prejudice** damage

Scene IV. [*Paris. The Palace.*]

Enter the King, Gloucester, Winchester, York, Suf-
folk, Somerset, Warwick, Exeter, [Vernon, Basset,
and others]. To them, with his Soldiers, Talbot.

Talbot. My gracious prince, and honorable peers,
　Hearing of your arrival in this realm,
　I have awhile given truce unto my wars
　To do my duty to my sovereign.
　In sign whereof, this arm, that hath reclaimed°　　5
　To your obedience fifty fortresses,
　Twelve cities, and seven wallèd towns of strength,
　Beside five hundred prisoners of esteem,°
　Lets fall his sword before your highness' feet,
　And with submissive loyalty of heart　　10
　Ascribes the glory of his conquest got
　First to my God and next unto your grace.

King. Is this the Lord Talbot, uncle Gloucester,
　That hath so long been resident in France?

Gloucester. Yes, if it please your majesty, my liege.°　　15

King. Welcome, brave captain and victorious lord!
　When I was young (as yet I am not old)
　I do remember° how my father said
　A stouter champion never handled sword.
　Long since we were resolvèd of your truth,°　　20
　Your faithful service, and your toil in war;
　Yet never have you tasted our reward
　Or been reguerdoned° with so much as thanks,

III.iv.5 **reclaimed** subdued　8 **esteem** good reputation in battle and
high birth (thus likely to command a profitable ransom)　15 **liege**
sovereign lord　18 **remember** (but Henry VI was only nine months
old when his father died)　20 **resolvèd of your truth** convinced of
your loyalty　23 **reguerdoned** repaid

Because till now we never saw your face.
25   Therefore, stand up, and for these good deserts
We here create you Earl of Shrewsbury,
And in our coronation take your place.

Sennet. Flourish. Exeunt. Manet° Vernon and Basset.

Vernon. Now, sir, to you, that were so hot° at sea,
Disgracing of° these colors that I wear
30   In honor of my noble Lord of York—
Dar'st thou maintain the former words thou
spak'st?

Basset. Yes, sir, as well as you dare patronage°
The envious barking of your saucy tongue
Against my lord the Duke of Somerset.

35 *Vernon.* Sirrah, thy lord I honor as he is.

Basset. Why, what is he? As good a man as York.

Vernon. Hark ye, not so: in witness,° take ye that.

Strikes him.

Basset. Villain, thou knowest the law of arms is such
That whoso draws a sword,° 'tis present° death,
40   Or else this blow should broach° thy dearest blood.
But I'll unto his majesty and crave°
I may have liberty to venge° this wrong.
When thou shalt see I'll meet thee to thy cost.

Vernon. Well, miscreant,° I'll be there as soon as
you,
45   And, after, meet you sooner than you would.

Exeunt.

27s.d. **Manet** remains (the Latin singular with a plural subject is common in Elizabethan stage directions)   28 **hot** passionate   29 **Disgracing of** disparaging   32 **patronage** (1) maintain (2) defend   37 **in witness** as proof   39 **draws a sword** i.e., in a royal residence   39 **present** immediate   40 **broach** draw as with a tap   41 **crave** beg   42 **venge** avenge   44 **miscreant** coward

ACT IV

Scene I. [*Paris. A hall of state.*]

Enter King, Gloucester, Winchester, York, Suffolk, Somerset, Warwick, Talbot, Exeter, Governor [of Paris and others].

Gloucester. Lord bishop, set the crown upon his head.

Winchester. God save King Henry, of that name the
    sixth!

Gloucester. Now, governor of Paris, take your oath,
    That you elect no other king but him;
    Esteem none friends but such as are his friends,   *5*
    And none your foes but such as shall pretend°
    Malicious practices° against his state:
    This shall ye do, so help you righteous God!

Enter Falstaff.

Falstaff. My gracious sovereign, as I rode from Calais
    To haste unto your coronation,   *10*
    A letter was delivered to my hands,
    Writ to your grace from th' Duke of Burgundy.

Talbot. Shame to the Duke of Burgundy and thee!
    I vowed, base knight, when I did meet thee next,
15 To tear the garter° from thy craven's° leg,

                         [Plucking it off.]

    Which I have done, because unworthily
    Thou wast installèd in that high degree.°
    Pardon me, princely Henry, and the rest:
    This dastard, at the battle of Poictiers,°
20 When but in all I was six thousand strong
    And that the French were almost ten to one,
    Before we met or that a stroke was given,
    Like to a trusty squire° did run away.
    In which assault we lost twelve hundred men;
25 Myself and divers gentlemen beside
    Were there surprised and taken prisoners.
    Then judge, great lords, if I have done amiss,
    Or whether that such cowards ought to wear
    This ornament of knighthood, yea or no.

30 *Gloucester.* To say the truth, this fact° was infamous
    And ill beseeming any common man,
    Much more a knight, a captain, and a leader.

Talbot. When first this order was ordained, my lords,
    Knights of the Garter were of noble birth,
35 Valiant and virtuous, full of haughty° courage,
    Such as were grown to credit° by the wars;
    Not fearing death, nor shrinking for distress,°
    But always resolute in most extremes.°
    He then that is not furnished in this sort°
40 Doth but usurp the sacred name of knight,
    Profaning this most honorable order,
    And should (if I were worthy to be judge)

---

15 **garter** badge of the Order of the Garter, England's highest degree of knighthood   15 **craven's** coward's   17 **degree** dignity   19 **Poictiers** i.e., Patay (1429)   23 **trusty squire** (used contemptuously: a person of inferior character)   30 **fact** deed   35 **haughty** high   36 **credit** honorable reputation   37 **distress** adversity   38 **in most extremes** in the most difficult situations   39 **furnished in this sort** possessed of such qualities

Be quite degraded, like a hedge-born swain°
That doth presume to boast of gentle blood.

King. Stain to thy countrymen, thou hear'st
    thy doom!°   45
Be packing,° therefore, thou that wast a knight:
Henceforth we banish thee on pain of death.

                    [*Exit Falstaff.*]

And now, Lord Protector, view the letter
Sent from our uncle Duke of Burgundy.

Gloucester. What means his grace, that he hath
    changed his style?°   50
No more but plain and bluntly, "To the king!"
Hath he forgot he is his sovereign?
Or doth this churlish superscription
Pretend° some alteration in good will?
What's here? "I have, upon especial cause,   55
Moved with compassion of my country's wrack,°
Together with the pitiful complaints
Of such as your oppression feeds upon,
Forsaken your pernicious faction
And joined with Charles, the rightful King of
    France."   60
O monstrous treachery! can this be so,
That in alliance, amity, and oaths,
There should be found such false dissembling
    guile?

King. What! doth my uncle Burgundy revolt?

Gloucester. He doth, my lord, and is become your foe.   65

King. Is that the worst this letter doth contain?

Gloucester. It is the worst, and all, my lord, he writes.

King. Why, then, Lord Talbot there shall talk with
    him

---

43 **hedge-born swain** low peasant   45 **doom** judgment, condemna-
tion   46 **Be packing** begone   50 **style** form of address   54 **Pretend**
signify   56 **wrack** misfortune

And give him chastisement for this abuse.
70   How say you, my lord; are you not content?

Talbot. Content, my liege? Yes, but that I am prevented,°
I should have begged I might have been employed.

King. Then gather strength, and march unto him
straight;
Let him perceive how ill we brook° his treason
75   And what offense it is to flout his friends.

Talbot. I go, my lord, in heart desiring still
You may behold confusion of your foes.   [*Exit.*]

Enter Vernon and Basset.

Vernon. Grant me the combat,° gracious sovereign.

Basset. And me, my lord, grant me the combat too.

80   *York.* This is my servant; hear him, noble prince.

Somerset. And this is mine; sweet Henry, favor him.

King. Be patient, lords, and give them leave to
speak.
Say, gentlemen, what makes you thus exclaim,
And wherefore crave you combat? Or with whom?

Vernon. With him, my lord, for he hath done me
85   wrong.

Basset. And I with him, for he hath done me wrong.

King. What is that wrong whereof you both complain?
First let me know, and then I'll answer you.

Basset. Crossing the sea from England into France,
90   This fellow here, with envious carping° tongue,
Upbraided° me about the rose I wear,
Saying, the sanguine° color of the leaves

71 **prevented** anticipated   74 **brook** bear with   78 **combat** trial by
arms   90 **carping**   fault-finding   91 **Upbraided**   reproached   92
sanguine blood-red

Did represent my master's blushing cheeks,
When stubbornly he did repugn° the truth
About a certain question in the law   *95*
Argued betwixt the Duke of York and him;
With other vile and ignominious terms;
In confutation of which rude reproach
And in defense of my lord's worthiness,
I crave the benefit of law of arms.°   *100*

Vernon. And that is my petition, noble lord:
For though he seem with forgèd quaint conceit°
To set a gloss upon° his bold intent,
Yet know, my lord, I was provoked by him,
And he first took exceptions at° this badge,   *105*
Pronouncing that the paleness of this flower
Bewrayed° the faintness of my master's heart.

York. Will not this malice, Somerset, be left?

Somerset. Your private grudge, my Lord of York, will
     out,
Though ne'er so cunningly you smother it.   *110*

King. Good Lord, what madness rules in brain-
     sick men,
When for so slight and frivolous a cause
Such factious emulations° shall arise!
Good cousins both, of York and Somerset,
Quiet yourselves, I pray, and be at peace.   *115*

York. Let this dissension first be tried by fight,
And then your highness shall command a peace.

Somerset. The quarrel toucheth° none but us alone;
Betwixt ourselves let us decide it then.

York. There is my pledge;° accept it, Somerset.   *120*

Vernon. Nay, let it rest where it began at first.

94 **repugn** resist   100 **benefit . . . arms** privilege of trial by combat
102 **forgèd quaint conceit** crafty manner of expression   103 **set a
gloss upon** veil in specious language   105 **took exceptions at** disap-
proved of   107 **Bewrayed** revealed   113 **emulations** contentions
118 **toucheth** concerns   120 **pledge** challenge (made by casting
down one's glove)

Basset. Confirm it so, mine honorable lord.

Gloucester. Confirm it so? Confounded be your strife!
And perish ye with your audacious prate!°
125 Presumptuous vassals, are you not ashamed
With this immodest° clamorous outrage
To trouble and disturb the king and us?
And you, my lords, methinks you do not well
To bear with their perverse objections,
130 Much less to take occasion from their mouths
To raise a mutiny betwixt yourselves.
Let me persuade you take a better course.

Exeter. It grieves his highness. Good my lords, be
friends.

King. Come hither, you that would be com-
batants:
135 Henceforth I charge you, as you love our favor,
Quite to forget this quarrel and the cause.
And you, my lords, remember where we are:
In France, amongst a fickle wavering nation;
If they perceive dissension in our looks
140 And that within ourselves we disagree,
How will their grudging stomachs° be provoked
To wilful disobedience, and rebel!
Beside, what infamy will there arise,
When foreign princes shall be certified°
145 That for a toy,° a thing of no regard,
King Henry's peers and chief nobility
Destroyed themselves and lost the realm of France!
O, think upon the conquest of my father,
My tender years, and let us not forgo
150 That for a trifle that was bought with blood!
Let me be umpire in this doubtful strife.
I see no reason, if I wear this rose,

[*Putting on a red rose.*]

That anyone should therefore be suspicious

124 **prate** chatter   126 **immodest** arrogant   141 **grudging stomachs**
resentful dispositions   144 **certified** informed   145 **toy** trifle

I more incline to Somerset than York;
Both are my kinsmen, and I love them both.   *155*
As well they may upbraid me with my crown
Because, forsooth,° the King of Scots is crowned.
But your discretions° better can persuade
Than I am able to instruct or teach,
And therefore, as we hither came in peace,   *160*
So let us still continue peace and love.
Cousin of York, we institute your grace
To be our Regent in these parts of France;
And, good my Lord of Somerset, unite
Your troops of horsemen with his bands of foot,   *165*
And, like true subjects, sons of your progenitors,
Go cheerfully together and digest
Your angry choler° on your enemies.
Ourself, my Lord Protector, and the rest
After some respite will return to Calais;   *170*
From thence to England, where I hope ere long
To be presented, by your victories,
With Charles, Alençon, and that traitorous rout.°

> *Flourish. Exeunt. Manet York, Warwick,
> Exeter, Vernon.*

Warwick. My Lord of York, I promise you, the king
Prettily, methought, did play the orator.   *175*

York. And so he did, but yet I like it not,
In that he wears the badge of Somerset.

Warwick. Tush, that was but his fancy, blame him
not;
I dare presume, sweet prince, he thought no harm.

York. And if—I wish—he did. But let it rest;   *180*
Other affairs must now be managèd.

> *Exeunt. Manet Exeter.*

---

157 **forsooth** in truth (used derisively)   158 **discretions** lordships,
judgments   168 **choler** bile (according to earlier physiology, the
cause of anger or hot temper)   173 **rout** crowd

Exeter. Well didst thou, Richard, to suppress thy
    voice;
    For, had the passions of thy heart burst out,
    I fear we should have seen deciphered° there
185   More rancorous spite, more furious raging broils,
    Than yet can be imagined or supposed.
    But howsoe'er, no simple man that sees
    This jarring discord of nobility,
    This shouldering° of each other in the court,
190   This factious bandying° of their favorites,
    But that it doth presage some ill event.°
    'Tis much° when scepters are in children's hands,
    But more when envy breeds unkind division;°
    There comes the ruin, there begins confusion. *Exit.*

[Scene II.] *Before Bordeaux.*

Enter Talbot, with trump and drum.

Talbot. Go to the gates of Bordeaux, trumpeter;
    Summon their general unto the wall.

                      [Trumpet] sounds.

Enter General aloft [with others].

    English John Talbot, captains, calls you forth,
    Servant in arms to Harry King of England,
5   And thus he would: open your city gates,
    Be humble to us, call my sovereign yours
    And do him homage as obedient subjects,
    And I'll withdraw me and my bloody power.
    But, if you frown upon this proffered peace,
10   You tempt the fury of my three attendants,

---

184 **deciphered** revealed   189 **shouldering** jostling   190 **bandying**
contention   191 **presage some ill event** predict some evil outcome
192 **much** difficult   193 **unkind division** unnatural disunion

Lean Famine, quartering° Steel, and climbing Fire,
Who in a moment even° with the earth
Shall lay your stately and air-braving° towers,
If you forsake the offer of their love.

General. Thou ominous and fearful owl of death,°   15
Our nation's terror and their bloody scourge!
The period° of thy tyranny approacheth.
On us thou canst not enter but by death,
For, I protest, we are well fortified
And strong enough to issue out and fight.   20
If thou retire, the Dolphin, well appointed,°
Stands with the snares of war to tangle thee.
On either hand° thee there are squadrons pitched
To wall thee from the liberty of flight,
And no way canst thou turn thee for redress,°   25
But death doth front° thee with apparent spoil,°
And pale destruction meets thee in the face.
Ten thousand French have ta'en the sacrament°
To rive° their dangerous artillery
Upon no Christian soul but English Talbot.   30
Lo, there thou stand'st, a breathing valiant man,
Of an invincible unconquered spirit!
This is the latest° glory of thy praise
That I, thy enemy, due° thee withal,
For ere the glass that now begins to run   35
Finish the process of his sandy hour,
These eyes, that see thee now well colorèd,°
Shall see thee withered, bloody, pale, and dead.

Drum afar off.

Hark! hark! The Dolphin's drum, a warning bell,
Sings heavy° music to thy timorous soul,   40

IV.ii.11 **quartering** that cuts men into quarters   12 **even** level   13
air-braving skyscraping   15 **owl of death** (alluding to the owl as a
supposed harbinger of death or misfortune)   17 **period** end   21
appointed equipped   23 **hand** side of   25 **redress** relief   26 **front**
confront   26 **apparent spoil** obvious destruction   28 **ta'en the
sacrament** confirmed their oaths by receiving holy communion
29 **rive** burst   33 **latest** final   34 **due** endue   37 **well colorèd** of
healthy complexion   40 **heavy** doleful

And mine shall ring thy dire departure out.

Exit [with his followers].

Talbot. He fables not,° I hear the enemy;
Out, some light° horsemen, and peruse their wings.°
O, negligent and heedless discipline!
45 How are we parked and bounded in a pale,°
A little herd of England's timorous deer,
Mazed with° a yelping kennel of French curs!
If we be English deer, be then in blood,°
Not rascal-like° to fall down with a pinch,°
50 But rather moody-mad;° and, desperate stags,
Turn on the bloody° hounds with heads of steel
And make the cowards stand aloof at bay.
Sell every man his life as dear as mine,
And they shall find dear° deer of us, my friends.
55 God and Saint George, Talbot and England's right,
Prosper our colors in this dangerous fight! *[Exeunt.]*

[Scene III. *Plains in Gascony.*]

*Enter a Messenger that meets York. Enter York with
trumpet and many Soldiers.*

York. Are not the speedy scouts returned again
That dogged° the mighty army of the Dolphin?

Messenger. They are returned, my lord, and give it
out°
That he is marched to Bordeaux with his power
5 To fight with Talbot. As he marched along,
By your espials° were discovered

42 **fables not** does not speak falsely   43 **light** lightly armed   43
peruse their wings scout their flanks   45 **parked . . . pale** surrounded and hemmed in by a fence   47 **Mazed with** terrified by
48 **in blood** (1) in full vigor (2) in temper   49 **rascal-like** like inferior deer   49 **pinch** nip   50 **moody-mad** furious in mood   51
bloody bloodthirsty   54 **dear** costly   IV.iii.2 **dogged** tracked, closely
pursued   3 **give it out** report   6 **espials** spies

Two mightier troops than that the Dolphin led,
Which joined with him and made their march for
  Bordeaux.

York. A plague upon that villain Somerset,
That thus delays my promisèd supply   10
Of horsemen that were levied for this siege!
Renownèd Talbot doth expect° my aid,
And I am louted° by a traitor villain
And cannot help the noble chevalier.°
God comfort him in this necessity!   15
If he miscarry,° farewell wars in France.

Enter another Messenger: [Sir William Lucy.]

Lucy. Thou princely leader of our English strength,
Never so needful on the earth of France,
Spur to the rescue of the noble Talbot,
Who now is girdled with a waist of iron   20
And hemmed about with grim destruction.
To Bordeaux, warlike duke! to Bordeaux, York!
Else, farewell Talbot, France, and England's honor.

York. O God, that Somerset, who in proud heart
Doth stop my cornets,° were in Talbot's place!   25
So should we save a valiant gentleman
By forfeiting a traitor and a coward.
Mad ire and wrathful fury makes me weep,
That thus we die, while remiss traitors sleep.

Lucy. O, send some succor to the distressed lord!   30

York. He dies, we lose; I break my warlike word;
We mourn, France smiles; we lose, they daily get;
All long° of this vile traitor Somerset.

Lucy. Then God take mercy on brave Talbot's soul,
And on his son young John, who two hours since   35
I met in travel toward his warlike father!
This seven years did not Talbot see his son,
And now they meet where both their lives are done.

---

12 **expect** await   13 **louted** mocked   14 **chevalier** knight   16 **miscarry** be destroyed   25 **stop my cornets** withhold my squadrons of cavalry   33 **long** on account

York. Alas, what joy shall noble Talbot have
40   To bid his young son welcome to his grave?
  Away! vexation almost stops my breath,
  That sundered° friends greet in the hour of death.
  Lucy, farewell, no more my fortune can°
  But curse the cause° I cannot aid the man.
45   Maine, Blois, Poictiers, and Tours are won away,
  Long all of Somerset and his delay.
                    Exit [with his Soldiers].

Lucy. Thus, while the vulture of sedition
  Feeds in the bosom of such great commanders,
  Sleeping neglection° doth betray to loss
50   The conquest of our scarce-cold° conqueror,
  That ever living man of memory,
  Henry the Fifth. Whiles they each other cross,
  Lives, honors, lands, and all hurry to loss.

[Scene IV. *Other plains in Gascony.*]

*Enter Somerset with his army, [a Captain of Talbot's
with him].*

Somerset. It is too late, I cannot send them now;
  This expedition was by York and Talbot
  Too rashly plotted. All our general° force
  Might with a sally° of the very° town
5   Be buckled with. The over-daring Talbot
  Hath sullied all his gloss° of former honor
  By this unheedful, desperate, wild adventure;
  York set him on to fight and die in shame,
  That, Talbot dead, great York might bear the name.

42 **sundered** separated 43 **fortune can** circumstances enable me to
do 44 **cause** reason why 49 **neglection** negligence 50 **scarce-cold**
barely dead IV.iv.3 **general** whole 4 **sally** sudden outrush 4 **very**
itself 6 **gloss** luster

Captain. Here is Sir William Lucy, who with me   10
  Set from our o'er-matched° forces forth for aid.

Somerset. How now, Sir William! whither were you
    sent?

Lucy. Whither, my lord? from bought and sold Lord
    Talbot;
  Who, ringed about with bold adversity,°
  Cries out for noble York and Somerset   15
  To beat assailing death from his weak regions;°
  And whiles the honorable captain there
  Drops bloody sweat from his war-wearied limbs,
  And in advantage ling'ring° looks for rescue,
  You, his false hopes, the trust of England's honor,   20
  Keep off aloof with worthless emulation.°
  Let not your private discord keep away
  The levied succors° that should lend him aid
  While he, renownèd noble gentleman,
  Yield up his life unto a world of odds: 25
  Orleans the Bastard, Charles, Burgundy,
  Alençon, Reignier compass him about,
  And Talbot perisheth by your default.

Somerset. York set him on, York should have sent
    him aid.

Lucy. And York as fast upon your grace exclaims,   30
  Swearing that you withhold his levied host,
  Collected for this expedition.

Somerset. York lies; he might have sent and had the
    horse!
  I owe him little duty, and less love,
  And take° foul scorn to fawn on him by sending.   35

Lucy. The fraud of England, not the force of France,
  Hath now entrapped the noble-minded Talbot;

---

11 **o'er-matched** outnumbered   14 **bold adversity** confident op-
ponents   16 **regions** places   19 **in advantage ling'ring** (1) desper-
ately clinging to every advantage (?) (2) while holding out on
advantageous ground (?)   21 **emulation** rivalry   23 **succors** rein-
forcements   35 **take** submit to

Never to England shall he bear his life,
But dies betrayed to fortune by your strife.

Somerset. Come, go; I will dispatch the horsemen
40   straight;
Within six hours they will be at his aid.

Lucy. Too late comes rescue, he is ta'en or slain,
For fly he could not, if he would have fled,
And fly would Talbot never though he might.

45 *Somerset.* If he be dead, brave Talbot, then adieu!

Lucy. His fame lives in the world, his shame in you.
                                        Exeunt.

[Scene V. *The English camp near Bordeaux.*]

Enter Talbot and his son.

Talbot. O young John Talbot! I did send for thee
To tutor thee in stratagems of war,
That Talbot's name might be in thee revived
When sapless° age and weak unable° limbs
5   Should bring thy father to his drooping chair.°
But, O malignant and ill-boding stars!
Now thou art come unto a feast of death,
A terrible and unavoided° danger:
Therefore, dear boy, mount on my swiftest horse,
10   And I'll direct thee how thou shalt escape
By sudden flight. Come, dally not, be gone.

John. Is my name Talbot? And am I your son?
And shall I fly? O, if you love my mother,
Dishonor not her honorable name,
15   To make a bastard and a slave of me.

IV.v.4 **sapless** withered   4 **unable** powerless   5 **drooping chair** decline from vigor   8 **unavoided** unavoidable

The world will say, he is not Talbot's blood,
That basely fled when noble Talbot stood.

Talbot. Fly, to revenge my death, if I be slain.

John. He that flies so will ne'er return again.

Talbot. If we both stay, we both are sure to die.   20

John. Then let me stay, and, father, do you fly:
Your loss is great, so your regard should be;
My worth unknown, no loss is known in me.
Upon my death the French can little boast;
In yours they will, in you all hopes are lost.   25
Flight cannot stain the honor you have won,
But mine it will, that no exploit have done;
You fled for vantage,° everyone will swear,
But, if I bow,° they'll say it was for fear.
There is no hope that ever I will stay   30
If the first hour I shrink and run away.
Here on my knee I beg mortality,°
Rather than life preserved with infamy.

Talbot. Shall all thy mother's hopes lie in one tomb?

John. Ay, rather than I'll shame my mother's womb.   35

Talbot. Upon my blessing, I command thee go.

John. To fight I will, but not to fly the foe.

Talbot. Part of thy father may be saved in thee.

John. No part of him but will be shame in me.

Talbot. Thou never hadst renown, nor canst not lose
it.   40

John. Yes, your renownèd name: shall flight abuse it?

Talbot. Thy father's charge° shall clear thee from that
stain.

John. You cannot witness for me, being slain.
If death be so apparent, then both fly.

28 **for vantage** to gain a tactical advantage   29 **bow** flee   32 **mortality** death   42 **charge** attack

45 *Talbot.* And leave my followers here to fight and die?
       My age was never tainted with such shame.

    John. And shall my youth be guilty of such blame?
       No more can I be severed from your side
       Than can yourself yourself in twain° divide.
50   Stay, go, do what you will, the like do I;
       For live I will not, if my father die.

    Talbot. Then here I take my leave of thee, fair son,
       Born to eclipse° thy life this afternoon.
       Come, side by side together live and die;
55   And soul with soul from France to heaven fly.
                                   Exit [with Son].

                [Scene VI. *A field of battle.*]

    *Alarum: excursions, wherein Talbot's Son is hemmed
              about, and Talbot rescues him.*

    Talbot. Saint George and victory! fight, soldiers, fight!
       The Regent hath with Talbot broke his word
       And left us to the rage of France his sword.
       Where is John Talbot? Pause, and take thy breath;
5   I gave thee life and rescued thee from death.

    John. O, twice my father, twice am I thy son!
       The life thou gav'st me first was lost and done,
       Till with thy warlike sword, despite of° fate,
       To my determined° time thou gav'st new date.

    Talbot. When from the Dolphin's crest thy sword
10   struck fire,
       It warmed thy father's heart with proud desire
       Of bold-faced victory. Then leaden° age,
       Quickened° with youthful spleen° and warlike rage,

49 **twain** two   53 **eclipse** end   IV.vi.8 **despite of** in spite of   9
determined predestined, fated   12 **leaden** spiritless   13 **Quickened**
animated   13 **spleen** high spirits, courage

Beat down Alençon, Orleans, Burgundy,
And from the pride of Gallia° rescued thee.   15
The ireful bastard Orleans, that drew blood
From thee, my boy, and had the maidenhood
Of thy first fight, I soon encounterèd,
And interchanging blows I quickly shed
Some of his bastard blood; and in disgrace   20
Bespoke him thus: "Contaminated, base,
And misbegotten blood I spill of thine,
Mean and right poor, for that pure blood of mine
Which thou didst force from Talbot, my brave
    boy."
Here,° purposing the Bastard to destroy,   25
Came in strong rescue. Speak, thy father's care,
Art thou not weary, John? How dost thou fare?
Wilt thou yet leave the battle, boy, and fly,
Now thou art sealed° the son of chivalry?
Fly, to revenge my death when I am dead;   30
The help of one stands me in little stead.
O, too much folly is it, well I wot,°
To hazard° all our lives in one small boat!
If I today die not with Frenchmen's rage,
Tomorrow I shall die with mickle° age.   35
By me they nothing gain and if I stay;
'Tis but the short'ning of my life one day.
In thee thy mother dies, our household's name,
My death's revenge, thy youth, and England's fame:
All these and more we hazard by thy stay;   40
All these are saved if thou wilt fly away.

John. The sword of Orleans hath not made me smart;
    These words of yours draw life-blood from my
        heart.
    On that advantage, bought with such a shame,
    To save a paltry life and slay bright fame,   45
    Before young Talbot from old Talbot fly,
    The coward horse that bears me fall and die!
    And like° me to the peasant boys of France,

15 **Gallia** France   25 **Here** i.e., here I   29 **sealed** authenticated
(by his deeds)   32 **wot** know   33 **hazard** gamble   35 **mickle** much,
advanced   48 **like** compare

To be shame's scorn and subject of mischance!°
50 Surely, by all the glory you have won,
And if I fly, I am not Talbot's son.
Then talk no more of flight, it is no boot;°
If son to Talbot, die at Talbot's foot.

Talbot. Then follow thou thy desperate sire of Crete,°
55 Thou Icarus; thy life to me is sweet;
If thou wilt fight, fight by thy father's side;
And, commendable proved, let's die in pride.°

                              Exit [with Son].

[Scene VII. *Another part of the field.*]

Alarum: excursions. Enter old Talbot, led [by a Servant].

Talbot. Where is my other life? Mine own is gone.
O, where's young Talbot? Where is valiant John?
Triumphant death, smeared with captivity,°
Young Talbot's valor makes me smile at thee.
5 When he perceived me shrink° and on my knee,
His bloody sword he brandished over me,
And like a hungry lion did commence
Rough deeds of rage and stern impatience,
But when my angry guardant° stood alone,
10 Tend'ring° my ruin and assailed of° none,
Dizzy-eyed° fury and great rage of heart
Suddenly made him from my side to start
Into the clust'ring battle° of the French,
And in that sea of blood my boy did drench

49 **subject of mischance** an example of unhappy fate   52 **boot** use
54 **sire of Crete** Daedalus (who made wings of feathers and wax on
which he and his son Icarus attempted to escape from King Minos
of Crete)   57 **pride** glory   IV.vii.3 **captivity** the blood of your
captives (?)   5 **shrink** give way   9 **guardant** protector   10 **Tend'ring** tenderly caring for me in   10 **of** by   11 **Dizzy-eyed** giddy
13 **clust'ring battle** close-grouped battle formation

His over-mounting° spirit and there died,   *15*
My Icarus, my blossom, in his pride.

Enter [Soldiers,] with John Talbot, borne.

Servant. O my dear lord, lo, where your son is
    borne!

Talbot. Thou antic° death, which laugh'st us here to
    scorn,
Anon,° from thy insulting tyranny,
Coupled in bonds of perpetuity,°   *20*
Two Talbots, wingèd through the lither° sky,
In thy despite shall 'scape mortality.
O thou, whose wounds become hard-favored°
    death,
Speak to thy father ere thou yield thy breath!
Brave Death by speaking, whether he will or no;   *25*
Imagine him a Frenchman and thy foe.
Poor boy! he smiles, methinks, as who should say,
"Had Death been French, then Death had died
    today."
Come, come and lay him in his father's arms;
My spirit can no longer bear these harms.   *30*
Soldiers, adieu! I have what I would have,
Now my old arms are young John Talbot's grave.
                                                    Dies.

*Enter Charles [the Dauphin], Alençon, Burgundy,
    Bastard, and [La] Pucelle, [with forces].*

Dauphin. Had York and Somerset brought rescue in,
We should have found a bloody day of this.

Bastard. How the young whelp of Talbot's, raging
    wood,°   *35*
Did flesh his puny-sword° in Frenchmen's blood!

Pucelle. Once I encountered him, and thus I said:

---

15 **over-mounting** too highly aspiring   18 **antic** (1) grinning (2)
buffoon   19 **Anon** immediately   20 **of perpetuity** eternal   21 **lither**
yielding, pliant   23 **hard-favored** ugly-looking   35 **wood** mad   36
flesh his puny-sword initiate his untried sword in battle

"Thou maiden youth, be vanquished by a maid."
But, with a proud majestical high scorn,
40 He answered thus: "Young Talbot was not born
To be the pillage° of a giglot° wench."
So, rushing in the bowels°of the French,
He left me proudly, as unworthy fight.°

Burgundy. Doubtless he would have made a noble
        knight.
45 See, where he lies inhearsèd° in the arms
Of the most bloody nurser° of his harms!

Bastard. Hew them to pieces, hack their bones
        asunder,
Whose life was England's glory, Gallia's wonder.

Dauphin. O no, forbear! for that which we have fled
50 During the life, let us not wrong it dead.

        Enter Lucy, [attended by a French Herald].

Lucy. Herald, conduct me to the Dolphin's tent,
To know who hath obtained the glory of the day.

Dauphin. On what submissive message art thou sent?

Lucy. Submission, Dolphin! 'Tis a mere French word;
55 We English warriors wot not what it means.
I come to know what prisoners thou hast ta'en
And to survey the bodies of the dead.

Dauphin. For prisoners ask'st thou? Hell our prison
        is.°
But tell me whom thou seek'st.

60 *Lucy.* But where's the great Alcides° of the field,
Valiant Lord Talbot, Earl of Shrewsbury,
Created, for his rare success in arms,
Great Earl of Washford, Waterford, and Valence,
Lord Talbot of Goodrig and Urchinfield,
65 Lord Strange of Blackmere, Lord Verdun of Alton,

41 **pillage** plunder 41 **giglot** wanton 42 **bowels** midst 43 **un-worthy fight** not worthy of fighting with 45 **inhearsèd** enclosed as in a hearse 46 **nurser** fosterer 58 **Hell our prison is** i.e., we kill all our enemies 60 **Alcides** Hercules

Lord Cromwell of Wingfield, Lord Furnival of
    Sheffield,
The thrice-victorious Lord of Falconbridge,
Knight of the noble order of Saint George,
Worthy Saint Michael, and the Golden Fleece,°
Great Marshal to Henry the Sixth   70
Of all his wars within the realm of France?

Pucelle. Here's a silly stately style° indeed!
The Turk,° that two and fifty kingdoms hath,
Writes not so tedious a style as this.
Him that thou magnifi'st with all these titles   75
Stinking and fly-blown lies here at our feet.

Lucy. Is Talbot slain, the Frenchmen's only scourge,
Your kingdom's terror and black Nemesis?
O, were mine eyeballs into bullets turned,
That I in rage might shoot them at your faces!   80
O, that I could but call these dead to life,
It were enough to fright the realm of France!
Were but his picture left amongst you here,
It would amaze° the proudest of you all.
Give me their bodies, that I may bear them hence   85
And give them burial as beseems their worth.

Pucelle. I think this upstart is old Talbot's ghost,
He speaks with such a proud commanding spirit.
For God's sake, let him have him; to keep them
    here,
They would but stink and putrefy the air.   90

Dauphin. Go, take their bodies hence.

Lucy. I'll bear them hence, but from their ashes shall
    be reared
A phoenix° that shall make all France afeard.°

68–70 Saint George . . . Saint Michael . . . the Golden Fleece
chivalric orders of England, France, and the Holy Roman Empire
respectively   **72 stately style** imposing title   **73 the Turk** the Sultan
84 amaze stupefy, terrify   **93 phoenix** in mythology, an Arabian
bird that is resurrected from the ashes of its own funeral pyre   **93
afeard** afraid

Dauphin. So we be rid of them, do with him what
    thou wilt.
95   And now to Paris, in this conquering vein:°
All will be ours, now bloody Talbot's slain.

                         Exeunt.

95 **vein** mood

ACT V

[Scene I. *London. The palace.*]

Sennet. Enter King, Gloucester, and Exeter.

King. Have you perused the letters from the pope,
   The emperor, and the Earl of Armagnac?

Gloucester. I have, my lord, and their intent is this:
   They humbly sue unto your excellence
   To have a godly peace concluded of   5
   Between the realms of England and of France.

King. How doth your grace affect° their motion?

Gloucester. Well, my good lord, and as the only
     means
   To stop effusion of our Christian blood
   And stablish° quietness on every side.   10

King. Ay, marry, uncle, for I always thought
   It was both impious and unnatural
   That such immanity° and bloody strife
   Should reign among professors of° one faith.

Gloucester. Beside, my lord, the sooner to effect   15
   And surer bind this knot of amity,
   The Earl of Armagnac, near knit° to Charles,
   A man of great authority in France,

V.i.7 **affect** like 10 **stablish** establish 13 **immanity** monstrous
cruelty 14 **professors of** believers in 17 **near knit** closely bound
by blood relationship

Proffers his only daughter to your grace
20 In marriage, with a large and sumptuous dowry.

King. Marriage, uncle! alas, my years are young,
And fitter is my study and my books
Than wanton dalliance with a paramour.°
Yet call th' ambassadors, and, as you please,
25 So let them have their answers every one:
I shall be well content with any choice
Tends to God's glory and my country's weal.

*Enter Winchester [in Cardinal's habit], and three Am-
bassadors, [one of them a Legate°].*

Exeter. What! is my Lord of Winchester installed,
And called unto a cardinal's degree?
30 Then I perceive that will be verified
Henry the Fifth did sometime° prophesy:
"If once he come to be a cardinal,
He'll make his cap° co-equal with the crown."

King. My lords ambassadors, your several suits°
35 Have been considered and debated on.
Your purpose is both good and reasonable,
And therefore are we certainly resolved
To draw conditions of a friendly peace,
Which by my Lord of Winchester we mean
40 Shall be transported presently to France.

Gloucester. And for the proffer of my lord your mas-
ter,°
I have informed his highness so at large
As,° liking of the lady's virtuous gifts,
Her beauty and the value of her dower,°
45 He doth intend she shall be England's queen.

King. In argument and proof of which contract,
Bear her this jewel, pledge of my affection.

23 **wanton ... paramour** lascivious sport with a mistress   27s.d.
Legate representative of the Pope   31 **sometime** once   33 **cap** red
cardinal's skullcap   34 **several suits** individual requests   41 **master**
i.e., the Count of Armagnac   43 **As** that   44 **dower** marriage set-
tlement

And so, my Lord Protector, see them guarded
And safely brought to Dover, wherein shipped,°
Commit them to the fortune of the sea.   50
        Exeunt [all but Winchester and the Legate].

Winchester. Stay, my Lord Legate; you shall first
    receive
The sum of money which I promisèd
Should be delivered to his Holiness
For clothing me in these grave ornaments.°

Legate. I will attend upon your lordship's leisure.   55

Winchester. [Aside] Now Winchester will not submit,
    I trow,
Or be inferior to the proudest peer.
Humphrey of Gloucester, thou shalt well perceive
That, neither in birth or for authority,
The bishop will be overborne by thee.   60
I'll either make thee stoop and bend thy knee,
Or sack this country with a mutiny.°   *Exeunt.*

[Scene II. *France. Plains in Anjou*].

*Enter Charles [the Dauphin], Burgundy, Alençon,
Bastard, Reignier, and Joan [la Pucelle, with forces].*

Dauphin. These news, my lords, may cheer our droop-
    ing spirits:
'Tis said the stout Parisians do revolt
And turn again unto the warlike French.

Alençon. Then march to Paris, royal Charles of
    France.
And keep not back your powers in dalliance.°   5

49 **shipped** embarked   54 **grave ornaments** symbols of high rank
62 **mutiny** rebellion   V.ii.5 **dalliance** idleness

Pucelle. Peace be amongst them, if they turn to us;
   Else, ruin combat with their palaces!

                    Enter Scout.

Scout. Success unto our valiant general,
   And happiness to his accomplices!

Dauphin. What tidings send our scouts? I prithee,
10   speak.

Scout. The English army, that divided was
   Into two parties, is now conjoined° in one,
   And means to give you battle presently.

Dauphin. Somewhat too sudden, sirs, the warning is,
15   But we will presently provide for them.

Burgundy. I trust the ghost of Talbot is not there;
   Now he is gone, my lord, you need not fear.

Pucelle. Of all base passions, fear is most accursed.
   Command the conquest, Charles, it shall be thine;
20   Let Henry fret and all the world repine.°

Dauphin. Then on, my lords, and France be fortunate!
                    Exeunt.

         [Scene III. *Before Angiers.*]

   Alarum. Excursions. Enter Joan la Pucelle.

Pucelle. The Regent° conquers, and the Frenchmen
      fly.
   Now help, ye charming° spells and periapts,°
   And ye choice° spirits that admonish° me
   And give me signs of future accidents.° *Thunder.*

---

12 **conjoined** united   20 **repine** complain   V.iii.1 **Regent** i.e., York
2 **charming** exercising magic power   2 **periapts** amulets   3 **choice**
excellent   3 **admonish** inform   4 **accidents** events

You speedy helpers, that are substitutes　　　　　5
Under the lordly monarch of the north,°
Appear and aid me in this enterprise.

Enter Fiends.

This speedy and quick appearance argues proof
Of your accustomed diligence to me.
Now, ye familiar spirits, that are culled°　　　　　10
Out of the powerful regions under earth,
Help me this once, that France may get° the field.
　　　　　　　They walk, and speak not.
O, hold me not with silence over-long!
Where I was wont to feed you with my blood,
I'll lop a member° off and give it you　　　　　15
In earnest° of a further benefit,
So you do condescend to help me now.
　　　　　　　They hang their heads.
No hope to have redress? My body shall
Pay recompense, if you will grant my suit.
　　　　　　　They shake their heads.
Cannot my body nor blood-sacrifice　　　　　20
Entreat you to your wonted furtherance?°
Then take my soul; my body, soul, and all,
Before that England give the French the foil.°
　　　　　　　They depart.
See, they forsake me! Now the time is come
That France must vail° her lofty plumèd crest　　　25
And let her head fall into England's lap.
My ancient° incantations are too weak,
And hell too strong for me to buckle with.
Now, France, thy glory droopeth to the dust.　*Exit.*

*Excursions. Burgundy and York fight hand to hand.
French fly, [pursued. York returns with La Pucelle
captive].*

---

6 **monarch of the north** the devil (evil spirits were traditionally
thought to dwell in the regions of the north)　10 **culled** gathered
12 **get** win　15 **member** part of the body　16 **earnest** pledge　21
furtherance assistance　23 **the foil** defeat, repulse　25 **vail** lower
or take off in token of submission　27 **ancient** former

30 *York.* Damsel of France, I think I have you fast;
      Unchain your spirits now with spelling° charms
      And try if they can gain your liberty.
      A goodly prize, fit for the devil's grace!
      See, how the ugly witch doth bend her brows,
35   As if, with Circe,° she would change my shape!

    Pucelle. Changed to a worser shape thou canst not be.

    York. O, Charles the Dolphin is a proper man;
      No shape but his can please your dainty° eye.

    Pucelle. A plaguing° mischief light on Charles and
        thee!
40   And may ye both be suddenly surprised
      By bloody hands, in sleeping on your beds!

    York. Fell banning° hag, enchantress, hold thy
        tongue!

    Pucelle. I prithee, give me leave to curse awhile.

    York. Curse, miscreant, when thou comest to the
        stake.   *Exeunt.*

    Alarum. Enter Suffolk, with Margaret in his hand.

45 *Suffolk.* Be what thou wilt, thou art my prisoner.
                                        Gazes on her.
      O fairest beauty, do not fear nor fly!
      For I will touch thee but with reverent° hands;
      I kiss these fingers for eternal peace
      And lay them gently on thy tender side.
50   Who art thou? Say, that I may honor thee.

    Margaret. Margaret my name, and daughter to a
        king,
      The King of Naples, whosoe'er thou art.

    Suffolk. An earl I am, and Suffolk am I called.
      Be not offended, nature's miracle,

---

31 **spelling** spell-casting   35 **with Circe** like Circe (the sorceress in
the *Odyssey* who transformed men into beasts)   38 **dainty** fastidi-
ous   39 **plaguing** tormenting   42 **Fell banning** evil cursing   47
reverent respectful

Thou art allotted° to be ta'en by me: *55*
So doth the swan her downy cygnets save,
Keeping them prisoner underneath her wings.
Yet if this servile usage° once offend,
Go and be free again as Suffolk's friend.
                    She is going.
O, stay! [*Aside*] I have no power to let her pass;   *60*
My hand would free her, but my heart says no.
As plays the sun upon the glassy° streams,
Twinkling another counterfeited° beam,
So seems this gorgeous beauty to mine eyes.
Fain would I woo her, yet I dare not speak;   *65*
I'll call for pen and ink, and write my mind.
Fie, De la Pole! disable° not thyself.
Hast not a tongue? Is she not here?
Wilt thou be daunted at a woman's sight?
Ay, beauty's princely majesty is such,   *70*
Confounds the tongue and makes the senses
    rough.°

Margaret. Say, Earl of Suffolk, if thy name be so,
What ransom must I pay before I pass?
For I perceive I am thy prisoner.

Suffolk. [*Aside*] How canst thou tell she will deny thy
    suit,   *75*
Before thou make a trial of her love?

Margaret. Why speak'st thou not? What ransom must
I pay?

Suffolk. [*Aside*] She's beautiful and therefore to be
    wooed;
She is a woman, therefore to be won.

Margaret. Wilt thou accept of ransom, yea or no?   *80*

Suffolk. [*Aside*] Fond man, remember that thou hast
    a wife;
Then how can Margaret be thy paramour?

---

55 **allotted** fated 58 **servile usage** unworthy treatment 62 **glassy**
smooth 63 **counterfeited** reflected 67 **disable** disparage 71 **rough**
dull

Margaret. I were best to leave him, for he will not
hear.

Suffolk. [*Aside*] There all is marred; there lies a
cooling card.°

85 *Margaret.* He talks at random; sure, the man is mad.

Suffolk. [*Still aside, but more loudly*] And yet a
dispensation° may be had.

Margaret. And yet I would that you would answer
me.

Suffolk. [*Aside*] I'll win this Lady Margaret. For
whom?
Why, for my king. [*Somewhat more loudly*] Tush,
that's a wooden° thing!

90 *Margaret.* He talks of wood: it° is some carpenter.

Suffolk. [*Aside*] Yet so my fancy may be satisfied
And peace establishèd between these realms.
But there remains a scruple° in that too:
For though her father be the King of Naples,
95 Duke of Anjou and Maine, yet is he poor,
And our nobility will scorn the match.

Margaret. Hear ye, captain, are you not at leisure?

Suffolk. [*Aside*] It shall be so, disdain they ne'er so
much:
Henry is youthful and will quickly yield.
100 [*Aloud*] Madam, I have a secret to reveal.

Margaret. [*Aside*] What though I be enthralled?° he
seems a knight,
And will not any way dishonor me.

Suffolk. Lady, vouchsafe to listen what I say.

Margaret. [*Aside*] Perhaps I shall be rescued by the
French,

---

84 **cooling card** something to cool my ardor   86 **dispensation** i.e.,
annulment of a previous marriage   89 **wooden** dull   90 **it** he   93
scruple difficulty   101 **enthralled** captured

And then I need not crave his courtesy.   *105*

Suffolk. Sweet madam, give me hearing in a cause.

Margaret. [*Aside*] Tush, women have been captivate
  ere now.

Suffolk. Lady, wherefore talk you so?

Margaret. I cry you mercy,° 'tis but *quid* for *quo.*°

Suffolk. Say, gentle princess, would you not suppose   *110*
  Your bondage happy, to be made a queen?

Margaret. To be a queen in bondage is more vile
  Than is a slave in base servility,
  For princes should be free.

Suffolk.   And so shall you,
  If happy England's royal king be free.   *115*

Margaret. Why, what concerns his freedom unto me?

Suffolk. I'll undertake to make thee Henry's queen,
  To put a golden scepter in thy hand
  And set a precious crown upon thy head,
  If thou wilt condescend to be my—

Margaret.   What?   *120*

Suffolk. His love.

Margaret. I am unworthy to be Henry's wife.

Suffolk. No, gentle madam, I unworthy am
  To woo so fair a dame to be his wife,
  And have no portion in° the choice myself.   *125*
  How say you, madam, are ye so content?

Margaret. And if my father please, I am content.

Suffolk. Then call our captains and our colors forth.
  And, madam, at your father's castle walls
  We'll crave a parley, to confer with him.   *130*

---

109 **cry you mercy** beg your pardon   109 **quid for quo** even ex-
change, tit for tat   125 **no portion in** (1) no share in (2) nothing to
gain by

Sound [a parley.] Enter Reignier on the walls.

See, Reignier, see, thy daughter prisoner!

Reignier. To whom?

Suffolk.   To me.

Reignier.   Suffolk, what remedy?
I am a soldier and unapt° to weep
Or to exclaim on fortune's fickleness.

135 *Suffolk.* Yes, there is remedy enough, my lord:
Consent, and for thy honor give consent,
Thy daughter shall be wedded to my king,
Whom° I with pain° have wooed and won thereto,
And this her easy-held imprisonment
140 Hath gained thy daughter princely liberty.

Reignier. Speaks Suffolk as he thinks?

Suffolk.   Fair Margaret knows
That Suffolk doth not flatter, face,° or feign.

Reignier. Upon thy princely warrant, I descend
To give thee answer of thy just demand.

                    [Exit.]

145 *Suffolk.* And here I will expect° thy coming.

Trumpets sound. Enter Reignier.

Reignier. Welcome, brave earl, into our territories;
Command in Anjou what your honor pleases.

Suffolk. Thanks, Reignier, happy for° so sweet a child,
Fit to be made companion with a king.
150 What answer makes your grace unto my suit?

Reignier. Since thou dost deign to woo her little worth°
To be the princely bride of such a lord,
Upon condition I may quietly

---

133 **unapt** not ready   138 **Whom** i.e., Margaret   138 **pain** much
effort   142 **face** deceive   145 **expect** await   148 **for** in having   151
her little worth a lady of such modest rank and fortune

Enjoy mine own, the country Maine and Anjou,
Free from oppression or the stroke of war,   *155*
My daughter shall be Henry's, if he please.

Suffolk. That is her ransom; I deliver her,
And those two counties I will undertake
Your grace shall well and quietly enjoy.

Reignier. And I again, in Henry's royal name,   *160*
As deputy° unto that gracious king,
Give thee her hand, for sign of plighted faith.°

Suffolk. Reignier of France, I give thee kingly thanks
Because this is in traffic° of a king.
[*Aside*] And yet, methinks, I could be well content *165*
To be mine own attorney° in this case.
[*Aloud*] I'll over then to England with this news,
And make this marriage to be solemnized.
So farewell, Reignier; set this diamond safe
In golden palaces, as it becomes.   *170*

Reignier. I do embrace thee, as I would embrace
The Christian prince, King Henry, were he here.

Margaret. Farewell, my lord; good wishes, praise, and
    prayers
Shall Suffolk ever have of Margaret.   *She is going.*

Suffolk. Farewell, sweet madam; but hark you,
    Margaret: *175*
No princely commendations to my king?

Margaret. Such commendations as becomes a maid,
A virgin, and his servant, say to him.

Suffolk. Words sweetly placed and modestly di-
    rected.°
But, madam, I must trouble you again: *180*
No loving token to his majesty?

Margaret. Yes, my good lord, a pure unspotted heart,
Never yet taint with love,° I send the king.

161 **deputy** i.e., Suffolk   162 **plighted faith** promise to marry   164 **in traffic** in negotiation   166 **attorney** pleader   179 **directed** uttered   183 **taint with love** tinged with immodest desire

Suffolk. And this withal.   *Kisses her.*

185 *Margaret.* That for thyself; I will not so presume
    To send such peevish tokens° to a king.

                        [*Exeunt Reignier and Margaret.*]

Suffolk. O, wert thou for myself! But, Suffolk, stay;
    Thou mayst not wander in that labyrinth;
    There Minotaurs° and ugly treasons lurk.
190 Solicit° Henry with her wondrous praise;
    Bethink thee on her virtues that surmount,
    And natural graces that extinguish° art;
    Repeat their semblance° often on the seas,
    That, when thou com'st to kneel at Henry's feet,
195 Thou mayst bereave° him of his wits with wonder.
                                        Exit.

[Scene IV. *Camp of the Duke of York in Anjou.*]

Enter York, Warwick, [and others].

York. Bring forth that sorceress condemned to burn.

    [*Enter La Pucelle, guarded, and a Shepherd.*]

Shepherd. Ah, Joan, this kills thy father's heart out-
        right!
    Have I sought° every country far and near,
    And now° it is my chance to find thee out,
5   Must I behold thy timeless° cruel death?
    Ah, Joan, sweet daughter Joan, I'll die with thee!

186 **peevish tokens** foolish signs of affection   189 **Minotaurs** (alluding to the mythological monster of Crete, half-bull and half-
man, who was slain by Theseus)   190 **Solicit** allure   192 **extin-
guish** obscure by greater brilliancy   193 **Repeat their semblance**
remind yourself of their appearance   195 **bereave** dispossess
V.iv.3 **sought** searched   4 **now** now that   5 **timeless** untimely

Pucelle. Decrepit miser!° base ignoble wretch!
  I am descended of a gentler blood.
  Thou art no father nor no friend of mine.

Shepherd. Out, out!° My lords, and° please you, 'tis
    not so.   10
  I did beget her, all the parish knows;
  Her mother liveth yet, can testify
  She was the first fruit of my bachelorship.°

Warwick. Graceless! wilt thou deny thy parentage?

York. This argues what her kind of life hath been, *15*
  Wicked and vile, and so her death concludes.

Shepherd. Fie, Joan, that thou wilt be so obstacle!°
  God knows thou art a collop° of my flesh,
  And for thy sake have I shed many a tear.
  Deny me not, I prithee, gentle Joan.   20

Pucelle. Peasant, avaunt!° You have suborned° this
    man
  Of purpose to obscure° my noble birth.

Shepherd. 'Tis true, I gave a noble° to the priest
  The morn that I was wedded to her mother.
  Kneel down and take my blessing, good my girl. 25
  Wilt thou not stoop? Now cursèd be the time
  Of thy nativity! I would the milk
  Thy mother gave thee when thou suck'dst her
    breast
  Had been a little ratsbane° for thy sake!
  Or else, when thou didst keep my lambs a-field, 30
  I wish some ravenous wolf had eaten thee!
  Dost thou deny thy father, cursèd drab?°
  O, burn her, burn her! hanging is too good.   *Exit.*

---

7 **miser** old wretch 10 **Out, out** alas 10 **and** if it 13 **first . . .
bachelorship** i.e., begotten out of wedlock (but the shepherd apparently is confused about the meaning of *bachelorship*) 17 **obstacle** obstinate (a malapropism) 18 **collop** piece 21 **avaunt** begone
21 **suborned** bribed 22 **obscure** conceal 23 **noble** gold coin worth about ten shillings 29 **ratsbane** rat poison 32 **drab** prostitute

York. Take her away, for she hath lived too long,
35 To fill the world with vicious qualities.

Pucelle. First, let me tell you whom you have con-
    demned:
    Not me begotten of a shepherd swain
    But issued from the progeny of kings;
    Virtuous and holy, chosen from above,
40 By inspiration of celestial grace,
    To work exceeding miracles on earth.
    I never had to do with wicked spirits,
    But you, that are polluted with your lusts,
    Stained with the guiltless blood of innocents,
45 Corrupt and tainted with a thousand vices,
    Because you want the grace that others have,
    You judge it straight a thing impossible
    To compass° wonders but by help of devils.
    No, misconceivèd!° Joan of Arc hath been
50 A virgin from her tender infancy,
    Chaste and immaculate in very thought,
    Whose maiden blood, thus rigorously effused,°
    Will cry for vengeance at the gates of heaven.

York. Ay, ay; away with her to execution!

55 *Warwick.* And hark ye, sirs: because she is a maid,
    Spare for no° faggots, let there be enow;°
    Place barrels of pitch upon the fatal stake,
    That so her torture may be shortenèd.

Pucelle. Will nothing turn your unrelenting hearts?
60 Then, Joan, discover thine infirmity,°
    That warranteth by law to be thy privilege.
    I am with child, ye bloody homicides;
    Murder not then the fruit within my womb,
    Although ye hale° me to a violent death.

York. Now heaven forfend!° the holy maid with
65   child!

48 **compass** accomplish   49 **misconceivèd** deceived person   52
rigorously effused cruelly shed   56 **Spare for no** do not spare
56 **enow** enough   60 **discover thine infirmity** reveal your bodily un-
fitness   64 **hale** drag   65 **forfend** forbid

Warwick. The greatest miracle that e'er ye wrought.
  Is all your strict preciseness° come to this?

York. She and the Dolphin have been juggling;°
  I did imagine° what would be her refuge.°

Warwick. Well, go to;° we'll have no bastards live,   70
  Especially since Charles must father it.

Pucelle. You are deceived, my child is none of his,
  It was Alençon that enjoyed my love.

York. Alençon! that notorious Machiavel!°
  It dies, and if it had a thousand lives.   75

Pucelle. O, give me leave, I have deluded you:
  'Twas neither Charles nor yet the duke I named,
  But Reignier, king of Naples, that prevailed.°

Warwick. A married man! that's most intolerable.

York. Why, here's a girl!° I think she knows not well,   80
  There were so many, whom she may accuse.

Warwick. It's sign she hath been liberal and free.°

York. And yet, forsooth,° she is a virgin pure.
  Strumpet, thy words condemn thy brat and thee.
  Use no entreaty, for it is in vain.   85

Pucelle. Then lead me hence; with whom I leave my
    curse:
  May never glorious sun reflex° his beams
  Upon the country where you make abode,
  But darkness and the gloomy shade of death
  Environ you, till mischief and despair   90
  Drive you to break your necks or hang yourselves!
                  Exit, [guarded].

---

67 **preciseness** pretense of scrupulousness   68 **juggling** playing
tricks   69 **imagine** wonder   69 **refuge** excuse   70 **go to** come,
come   74 **Machiavel** intriguer (after Niccolò Machiavelli, author
of *The Prince*)   78 **prevailed** i.e., gained her love   80 **girl** wench
82 **liberal and free** (used ironically, since a lady was supposed to
have these qualities, without Joan's implied wantonness)   83 **forsooth** in truth   87 **reflex** reflect

York. Break thou in pieces and consume to ashes,
   Thou foul accursèd minister° of hell.

Enter Cardinal [Beaufort, Bishop of Winchester].

Winchester. Lord Regent, I do greet your excellence
95   With letters of commission from the king.
   For know, my lords, the states of Christendom,
   Moved with remorse of° these outrageous broils,
   Have earnestly implored a general peace
   Betwixt our nation and the aspiring French,
100   And here at hand the Dolphin and his train°
   Approacheth, to confer about some matter.

York. Is all our travail° turned to this effect?
   After the slaughter of so many peers,
   So many captains, gentlemen, and soldiers,
105   That in this quarrel have been overthrown
   And sold their bodies for their country's benefit,
   Shall we at last conclude effeminate peace?
   Have we not lost most part of all the towns,
   By treason, falsehood, and by treachery,
110   Our great progenitors had conquerèd?
   O, Warwick, Warwick! I foresee with grief
   The utter loss of all the realm of France.

Warwick. Be patient, York; if we conclude a peace,
   It shall be with such strict and severe covenants°
115   As little shall the Frenchmen gain thereby.

*Enter Charles [the Dauphin], Alençon, Bastard,
   Reignier, [and others].*

Dauphin. Since, lords of England, it is thus agreed
   That peaceful truce shall be proclaimed in France,
   We come to be informèd by yourselves
   What the conditions of that league must be.

120 *York.* Speak, Winchester, for boiling choler chokes
   The hollow passage of my poisoned° voice
   By sight of these our baleful enemies.

93 **minister** agent   97 **remorse of** sorrow at   100 **train** retinue   102
travail labor, trouble   114 **covenants** conditions   121 **poisoned** sickened as though with poison

Winchester. Charles, and the rest, it is enacted thus:
　That, in regard King Henry gives consent,
　Of° mere compassion and of lenity,   *125*
　To ease your country of distressful war
　And suffer you to breathe in fruitful peace,
　You shall become true liegemen° to his crown.
　And, Charles, upon condition thou wilt swear
　To pay him tribute, and submit thyself,   *130*
　Thou shalt be placed as viceroy under him,
　And still enjoy thy regal dignity.

Alençon. Must he be then as shadow of himself?
　Adorn his temples with a coronet,
　And yet, in substance and authority,   *135*
　Retain but privilege of a private man?
　This proffer is absurd and reasonless.

Dauphin. 'Tis known already that I am possessed
　With more than half the Gallian territories,
　And therein reverenced for° their lawful king: *140*
　Shall I, for lucre° of the rest unvanquished,
　Detract so much from that prerogative°
　As to be called but viceroy of the whole?
　No, lord ambassador, I'll rather keep
　That which I have than, coveting for more,   *145*
　Be cast° from possibility of all.

York. Insulting Charles! hast thou by secret means
　Used intercession to obtain a league,°
　And, now the matter grows to compromise,
　Stand'st thou aloof upon comparison?°   *150*
　Either accept the title thou usurp'st,
　Of° benefit proceeding from our king
　And not of any challenge of desert,°
　Or we will plague thee with incessant wars.

Reignier. My lord, you do not well in obstinacy   *155*

125 **Of** out of   128 **liegemen** vassals   140 **reverenced for** honored
as   141 **lucre** gain   142 **prerogative** preeminence (as king)   146
cast driven   148 **league** alliance   150 **upon comparison** weighing
the odds   152 **Of** through   153 **challenge of desert** claim that it
is yours by right

To cavil° in the course of this contract:
If once it be neglected, ten to one
We shall not find like opportunity.

Alençon. To say the truth, it is your policy
160   To save your subjects from such massacre
And ruthless slaughters as are daily seen
By our proceeding in hostility;
And therefore take this compact of° a truce—
[*Aside*] Although you break it when your pleasure
    serves.

Warwick. How say'st thou, Charles? Shall our condi-
165   tion stand?

Dauphin. It shall;
Only reserved, you claim no interest
In any of our towns of garrison.

York. Then swear allegiance to his majesty,
170   As thou art knight, never to disobey
Nor be rebellious to the crown of England,
Thou, nor thy nobles, to the crown of England.

[*The Dauphin and French nobles give signs of fealty.*]

So, now dismiss your army when ye please;
Hang up your ensigns,° let your drums be still,
175   For here we entertain° a solemn peace.

                           Exeunt.

---

156 **cavil** find fault without good reason   163 **compact of** mutual
agreement for   174 **ensigns** banners   175 **entertain** accept

[Scene V. *London. The royal palace.*]

*Enter Suffolk in conference with the King, Gloucester,
and Exeter.*

King. Your wondrous rare description, noble earl,
   Of beauteous Margaret hath astonished me.
   Her virtues, gracèd with external gifts,
   Do breed love's settled passions in my heart,
   And like as rigor° of tempestuous gusts   5
   Provokes° the mightiest hulk° against the tide,
   So am I driven by breath° of her renown
   Either to suffer shipwreck or arrive
   Where I may have fruition of her love.

Suffolk. Tush, my good lord, this superficial° tale   10
   Is but a preface of her worthy praise.
   The chief perfections of that lovely dame,
   Had I sufficient skill to utter them,
   Would make a volume of enticing lines,
   Able to ravish any dull conceit;°   15
   And, which is more, she is not so divine,
   So full replete with choice of all delights,
   But with as humble lowliness of mind
   She is content to be at your command;
   Command, I mean, of virtuous chaste intents,°   20
   To love and honor Henry as her lord.

King. And otherwise will Henry ne'er presume.
   Therefore, my Lord Protector, give consent
   That Margaret may be England's royal queen.

V.v.5 **rigor** violence   6 **Provokes** drives on   6 **hulk** ship   7 **breath**
utterance   10 **superficial** touching only the surface   15 **ravish . . .
conceit** i.e., enchant even the dullest imagination   20 **intents** intentions

25 *Gloucester.* So should I give consent to flatter° sin.
    You know, my lord, your highness is betrothed
    Unto another lady° of esteem.
    How shall we then dispense with that contract,
    And not deface your honor with reproach?

30 *Suffolk.* As doth a ruler with unlawful oaths,
    Or one that, at a triumph° having vowed
    To try his strength, forsaketh yet the lists°
    By reason of his adversary's odds.°
    A poor earl's daughter is unequal odds,
35 And therefore may be broke° without offense.

    Gloucester. Why, what, I pray, is Margaret more than
        that?
    Her father is no better than an earl,
    Although in glorious titles he excel.

    Suffolk. Yes, my lord, her father is a king,
40 The King of Naples and Jerusalem,
    And of such great authority in France
    As his alliance will confirm our peace
    And keep the Frenchmen in allegiance.

    Gloucester. And so the Earl of Armagnac may do
45 Because he is near kinsman unto Charles.

    Exeter. Beside, his wealth doth warrant a liberal
        dower,
    Where Reignier sooner will receive than give.

    Suffolk. A dower, my lords! disgrace not so your king,
    That he should be so abject, base, and poor,
50 To choose for wealth and not for perfect love.
    Henry is able to enrich his queen
    And not to seek a queen to make him rich.
    So worthless peasants bargain for their wives,
    As market men for oxen, sheep, or horse.
55 Marriage is a matter of more worth

---

25 **flatter** condone   27 **another lady** i.e., the daughter of the Earl
of Armagnac   31 **triumph** tournament   32 **lists** tournament ground
33 **odds** inferiority   35 **broke** i.e., the pledge of marriage may be
broken

Than to be dealt in by attorneyship;°
Not whom we will, but whom his grace affects,
Must be companion of his nuptial bed.
And therefore, lords, since° he affects her most,
Most of all these reasons bindeth us,   60
In our opinions she should be preferred.
For what is wedlock forcèd but a hell,
An age of discord and continual strife?
Whereas the contrary bringeth bliss,
And is a pattern of celestial peace.   65
Whom should we match with Henry, being a king,
But Margaret, that is daughter to a king?
Her peerless feature,° joinèd with her birth,
Approves° her fit for none but for a king.
Her valiant courage and undaunted spirit,   70
More than in women commonly is seen,
Will answer our hope in issue of a king;
For Henry, son unto a conqueror,
Is likely to beget more conquerors,
If with a lady of so high resolve   75
As is fair Margaret he be linked in love.
Then yield, my lords, and here conclude with me
That Margaret shall be queen, and none but she.

King. Whether it be through force of your report,
My noble Lord of Suffolk, or for that   80
My tender youth was never yet attaint°
With any passion of inflaming love,
I cannot tell; but this I am assured,
I feel such sharp dissension in my breast,
Such fierce alarums both of hope and fear,   85
As I am sick with working of my thoughts.
Take, therefore, shipping; post, my lord, to France;
Agree to any covenants, and procure
That Lady Margaret do vouchsafe to come
To cross the seas to England and be crowned   90
King Henry's faithful and anointed queen.

---

56 **attorneyship** proxy   59 **since** the fact that   68 **feature** comeliness   69 **Approves** proves   81 **attaint** stained

For your expenses and sufficient charge,°
Among the people gather up a tenth.°
Be gone, I say, for, till you do return,

95 I rest° perplexèd with a thousand cares.
And you, good uncle, banish all offense;
If you do censure° me by what you were,
Not what you are, I know it will excuse
This sudden execution° of my will.

100 And so, conduct me where, from company,
I may revolve and ruminate° my grief.   *Exit.*

Gloucester. Ay, grief, I fear me, both at first and last.

Exit Gloucester [with Exeter].

Suffolk. Thus Suffolk hath prevailed, and thus he
goes,
As did the youthful Paris once to Greece,

105 With hope to find the like event° in love,
But prosper better than the Trojan did.
Margaret shall now be queen, and rule the king;
But I will rule both her, the king, and realm. *Exit.*

F I N I S

92 **sufficient charge** adequate money to meet costs   93 **tenth** (a
levy of a tenth of the value of personal property, collected to meet
unusual expenses such as a royal marriage)   95 **rest** remain   97
censure judge   99 **execution** carrying into effect   101 **revolve and
ruminate** consider and meditate upon   105 **event** result

Textual Note

The First Part of Henry the Sixth is preserved only in the Folio of 1623, the basis of the present edition. Though acted infrequently after Shakespeare's lifetime, apparently the drama was originally well received. In the epilogue to Shakespeare's *Henry V,* the Chorus asks the spectators to applaud this more recent work by reminding them of the company's earlier dramatizations of the reign of Henry VI:

> Which oft our stage hath shown; and for their sake,
> In your fair minds let this acceptance take.

It is even likely that in its earliest production *1 Henry VI* was the theatrical hit of the year. On March 3, 1592, the producer Philip Henslowe recorded in his diary that the first performance of a new (or refurbished) play called "harey the vj." had grossed £3.16s.8d., a sum indicating an exceptionally profitable opening. Over the next ten months this work was acted at least fourteen, perhaps fifteen, additional times. It may be that the patriotic theme appealed strongly to a London audience still exulting over the debacle of the Spanish Armada; for the heroic death of Lord Talbot in the fourth act, as Thomas Nashe wrote during the same year in *Pierce Penniless,* had been found deeply moving by "ten thousand spectators at least (at several times), who, in the tragedian that represents his person, imagine they behold him fresh bleeding."

The entry in Henslowe's diary and Nashe's allusion in his pamphlet to "Talbot (the terror of the French)" suggest that the play in question may have been *1 Henry VI*. Still, some doubt must remain whether this particular version was the same as that printed in the Folio, and whether Shakespeare had participated in its composition. With few exceptions, however, modern Shakespearean critics have assumed that *1 Henry VI* as we know it does come, along with the second and third parts of the trilogy, from Shakespeare's apprentice years as a playwright. In the absence of any positive evidence to the contrary, it thus seems reasonable to declare for late 1591 or early 1592 as the likeliest date of original composition for the play printed in the Folio and to presume that it is substantially, perhaps entirely, from the hand of Shakespeare.

The Folio is the only authority and affords a remarkably clear text, apart from a few baffling words and some apparently mangled lines of verse. In the present edition, therefore, the temptation to emend the original has been resisted as much as possible. Only two words to fill apparent lacunae have been supplied from consultation with the later Folios. These are *Nero* (I.iv.95) and *sir* (II.iv.-132). Both of these are bracketed in the text and their sources given in the notes below. Without editorial comment, punctuation and spelling have been modernized (though "Dolphin" is retained in the dialogue), names prefixed to speeches and appearing in stage directions expanded and regularized, act and scene divisions translated where the Folio gives them in Latin, and obvious typographical errors corrected.

In the few instances where lines of verse are improperly divided in the Folio, they have been rearranged; all such corrections are noted in the table below. Occasionally when the printers of the Folio may seem to have divided a single line into two verses, it is quite clear that the line was too long for the space available, and was simply broken at a clause, rather than at the end of the column. Because the stage directions in the original are on the whole clear and amply descriptive, they have been reproduced with a minimum of emendations and additions;

wherever changes have been made, they are enclosed in square brackets. In dividing acts and scenes the Folio is deficient: no scene divisions are given for Acts I and II; Act III is correctly divided into four scenes; Act IV is not only too long—since nothing but the final scene is left for Act V—but within it the scenes are also inaccurately divided. The act and scene divisions of the present edition are therefore those of the Globe text; wherever they differ from those of the Folio, they are enclosed in square brackets. The table that follows includes emendations and corrections of the Folio text. The altered reading appears first, in italics; the original follows, in roman. Where a Folio reading is retained, but seems extremely dubious, the word is given in roman, and commentary or suggested emendation is placed within square brackets.

I.i.94 *Reignier* Reynold   96 *crownèd* crown'd   132 *vanward* Vau ward

I.ii.30 *bred* breed   99 fine [so F, but later editors, following mention in Holinshed's *Chronicles* of a pattern of "five" fleurs-de-lis on the sword, emend to *five;* conceivably the *n* in F is a mistakenly inverted *u* (i.e., for *v*)]   103s.d. *la* de   113 *rites* rights   132 *enterèd* entred

I.iii.29 *Humphrey* Vmpheir

I.iv.10 Went [so F, but Tyrwhitt's conjecture *Wont* is accepted by some modern editors]   16–18 [two lines in F, but perhaps should be printed as three, divided after *watched, them,* and *longer*]   29 *ransomèd* ransom'd   69s.d. *fall* falls   95 *Nero* [not in F; conjectured by Malone from the Second Folio reading "and *Nero* like will" for "and like thee"]   101 *la* de

I.v.s.d. *la* de

I.vi.3 *la* de   6 garden [so F, but *were* in line 7 suggests that the intended reading may have been *gardens*]   29 *la* de

II.i.7 s.d. drums . . . march [so F, but sounding drums seems a most peculiar way of beginning a surprise attack]   29 *all together* altogether   77 [F reads *Exeunt* here, but the following stage direction renders the word superfluous]   77s.d. *an* a

II.ii.6 *center* Centure   20 *Arc* Acre   59 *Whispers* [printed at end of line in F]

II.iii.11–12 [printed as one line in F]

II.iv.s.d. *Vernon, and another Lawyer* and others   117 whipped [so F, but Second Folio and all subsequent editions read *wiped*]   132 *sir* [not in F; supplied by Second Folio]

II.v.121 s.d. *Exeunt . . . Mortimer* Exit   129 will [so F, though modern editors, following Theobald, conjecture *ill* (i.e., turn my injuries to my benefit)]

III.i.52–53 [most modern editions reassign line 52 to Somerset and line 53 to Warwick]   164 all [so F, but the word is superfluous for both sense and meter]   200 *lose* loose

III.ii.50–51 [printed as three (metrically defective) lines in F, divided after *gray-beard, death,* and *chair*]   59s.d. *The English* They   103s.d. *Exeunt . . . Attendants* Exit   123 *gleeks* glikes

IV.i.s.d. *Exeter . . . Paris* and Gouernor Exeter   173s.d. *Flourish* [apparently misplaced in F in s.d. that follows line 181]

IV.ii. *Before Bordeaux* [supplied by s.d. in F]   3 *calls* call   34 *due* dew   50 *moody-mad* moodie mad

IV.iii.20 *waist* waste

IV.iv.16 regions [so F, but most modern editors emend to *legions*]

IV.vi.18 *encounterèd* encountred

IV.vii.96 s.d. *Exeunt* Exit

V.i. *Scene I* Scena secunda

V.ii. *Scene II* Scena Tertia

V.iii.s.d. *la* de   44 *comest* comst   57 *her* his   179 *modestly* modestie   184s.d. *Kisses* Kisse   188, 195 *mayst* mayest   190 *wondrous* wonderous   192 *And* Mad

V.iv.s.d. *and others* Shepheard, Pucell [who obviously enter after line 1]   49 *Arc* Aire   58 *shortenèd* shortned   60 *discover* discouet   93 s.d. [placed in F after line 91]

V.v. *Scene V* Actus Quintus

The Sources of
Henry VI, Part One

For the plot of *1 Henry VI* Shakespeare drew upon at least four English chronicle histories. His chief sources are Edward Hall's *The Union of the Two Noble and Illustre Families of Lancaster and York* (1548) and the second edition of Raphael Holinshed's *Chronicles of England, Scotland, and Ireland* (1587). For a few details not found in Hall or Holinshed he also consulted the *Chronicles* of Robert Fabyan (1516) and Richard Grafton (1569), the latter substantially a reprint of Hall. Some of the best scenes in the play, however, such as the quarrel of the roses in the Temple Garden, appear to have been invented by the playwright himself.

Although Geoffrey Bullough in his *Narrative and Dramatic Sources of Shakespeare* inclines to Hall as the principal source, in many scenes *1 Henry VI* appears to follow more closely Holinshed's account, which is largely derived from Hall without the latter's invented orations, amplification of detail, and attempts at an eloquence commensurate with the grandeur of his theme. But since Shakespeare improvised so freely upon his source materials, in most episodes of the play it is not possible to determine whether his immediate inspiration is Hall or Holinshed.

In view of this uncertainty, I have decided mainly to quote from Holinshed, to whom Shakespeare turned frequently in composing several other plays based upon British and Scottish history, but to give the account of Talbot's death in Hall's words, so that the reader may gain some idea of the elevated style of the source upon which Shakespeare obviously relied for this particular episode. In order that the reader may also acquire some sense of Shakespeare's juggling of historical chronology to suit his dramatic purposes, the selections are printed below in the sequence in which they occur in Holinshed, with both the actual historical dates and the scenes to which they contribute indicated in square brackets prefixed to the quotations.

RAPHAEL HOLINSHED

from *Chronicles of England, Scotland, and Ireland* (1587)

[1422: I.i] After that death had bereft the world of
that noble prince King Henry the Fifth, his only son
Prince Henry, being of the age of nine months, or there-
abouts, with the sound of trumpets was openly proclaimed
King of England and France the thirtieth day of August,
by the name of Henry the Sixth; in the year of the world
five thousand three hundred eighty and nine, after the
birth of our Savior 1422, about the twelfth year of the
Emperor Frederick the Third, the fortieth and two, and
last, of Charles the Sixth, and the third year of Murdoch's
regiment (after his father Robert) governor of Scotland.
The custody of this young prince was appointed to
Thomas, Duke of Exeter, and to Henry Beaufort, Bishop
of Winchester. The Duke of Bedford was deputed Regent
of France, and the Duke of Gloucester was ordained Protector of England; who, taking upon him that office, called
to him wise and grave councillors, by whose advice he
provided and took order as well for the good government
of the realm and subjects of the same at home, as also
for the maintenance of the wars abroad, and further conquest to be made in France, appointing valiant and expert
captains, which should be ready when need required. Besides this, he gathered great sums of money to maintain

men of war, and left nothing forgotten that might advance the good estate of the realm.

While these things were a-doing in England, the Duke of Bedford, Regent of France, studied most earnestly, not only to keep and well order the countries by King Henry late conquered, but also determined not to leave off war and travail, till Charles the Dauphin (which was now afoot, because King Charles his father in the month of October in this present year was departed to God) should either be subdued, or brought to obeisance. And surely the death of this King Charles caused alterations in France. For a great many of the nobility which before, either for fear of the English puissance, or for the love of this King Charles (whose authority they followed) held on the English part, did now revolt to the Dauphin, with all endeavor to drive the English nation out of the French territories. Whereto they were the more earnestly bent, and thought it a thing of greater facility, because of King Henry's young years; whom (because he was a child) they esteemed not, but with one consent revolted from their sworn fealty: as the recorder of the Englishmen's battles with foreign nations very aptly doth note, saying:

> Hic Franci puerum regem neglectui habentes
> Desciscunt, violatque fidem gens perfida sacro
> Consilio ante datam.

[Here the French revolt, holding in scorn the boy king, and this perfidious race violates allegiance hitherto granted in holy council.]

The Duke of Bedford being greatly moved with these sudden changes, fortified his towns both with garrisons of men, munition, and victuals, assembled also a great army of Englishmen and Normans, and so effectuously exhorted them to continue faithful to their liege and lawful lord, young King Henry, that many of the French captains willingly sware to King Henry fealty and obedience, by whose example the communalty did the same. Thus the people quieted, and the country established in order, nothing was minded but war, and nothing spoken of but conquest.

The Dauphin, which lay the same time in the city of Poitiers, after his father's decease, caused himself to be proclaimed King of France, by the name of Charles the Seventh: and in good hope to recover his patrimony, with an haughty courage preparing war, assembled a great army; and first the war began by light skirmishes, but after it grew into main battles. . . .

[1425: I.iii] Somewhat before this season fell a great division in the realm of England, which of a sparkle was like to have grown to a great flame. For whether the Bishop of Winchester called Henry Beaufort, son to John, Duke of Lancaster, by his third wife, envied the authority of Humphrey, Duke of Gloucester, Protector of the realm; or whether the duke disdained at the riches and pompous estate of the bishop: sure it is that the whole realm was troubled with them and their partakers, so that the citizens of London were fain to keep daily and nightly watches, and to shut up their shops for fear of that which was doubted to have issued of their assembling of people about them. The Archbishop of Canterbury and the Duke of Coimbra, called the Prince of Portugal, rode eight times in one day between the two parties, and so the matter was stayed for a time. But the Bishop of Winchester, to clear himself of blame so far as he might, and to charge his nephew the Lord Protector with all the fault, wrote a letter to the Regent of France, the tenor whereof ensueth.

The Bishop of Winchester's Letter Excusatory.

Right high and mighty prince, and my right noble and, after one, lievest lord, I recommend me unto you with all my heart. And as you desire the welfare of the king, our sovereign lord, and of his realms of England and France, your own health, and ours also: so haste you hither. For by my truth, if you tarry, we shall put this land in adventure with a field; such a brother you have here, God make him a good man. For your wisdom knoweth that the profit of France standeth in the welfare of England, etc. Written in great haste on All Hallowen Even. By your true servant to my life's end, Henry Winchester.

The Duke of Bedford being sore grieved with these news, constituted the Earl of Warwick, which was lately come into France with six thousand men, his lieutenant in the French dominions and in the Duchy of Normandy; and so with a small company, he with the duchess his wife returned again over the seas into England, and the tenth day of January he was with all solemnity received into London, to whom the citizens gave a pair of basins of silver and gilt, and a thousand marks in money. Then from London he rode to Westminster and was lodged in the king's palace. [1426: III.i] The five and twentieth day of March after his coming to London, a parliament began at the town of Leicester, where the Duke of Bedford openly rebuked the lords in general, because that they in the time of war, through their privy malice and inward grudge, had almost moved the people to war and commotion, in which time all men ought or should be of one mind, heart, and consent: requiring them to defend, serve, and dread their sovereign lord King Henry, in performing his conquest in France, which was in manner brought to conclusion. In this parliament the Duke of Gloucester laid certain articles to the Bishop of Winchester his charge, the which with the answers hereafter do ensue, as followeth. . . .

. . . And when this was done [the rivals required to become reconciled by the arbitrators of their dispute], it was decreed by the same arbitrators that every each of my Lord of Gloucester, and Winchester, should take either other by the hand, in the presence of the king and all the parliament, in sign and token of good love and accord, the which was done, and the parliament adjourned till after Easter.

At this reconciliation, such as love peace rejoiced (sith it is a foul and pernicious thing for private men, much more for noblemen, to be at variance, sith upon them depend many in affections diverse, whereby factions might grow to the shedding of blood), though others, to whom contention and heartgrudge is delight, wished to see the uttermost mischief that might thereof ensue, which is the utter overthrow and desolation of populous tribes, even as with a little sparkle whole houses are many times consumed to ashes, as the old proverb saith, and that very well and aptly:

Sola scintilla perit haec domus aut domus illa.

[Gone is this house or that with a single spark.]

But when the great fire of this dissension between these two noble personages was thus by the arbitrators (to their knowledge and judgment) utterly quenched out, and laid under board, all other controversies between other lords, taking part with one party or the other, were appeased and brought to concord, so that for joy the king caused a solemn feast to be kept on Whitsunday; on which day he created Richard Plantagenet, son and heir to the Earl of Cambridge (whom his father at Southampton had put to death, as before ye have heard) Duke of York, not foreseeing that this preferment should be his destruction, nor that his seed should of his generation be the extreme end and final conclusion. . . .

[1427: V.i] After that the Duke of Bedford had set all things in good order in England, he took leave of the king, and together with his wife returned into France, first landing at Calais, where the Bishop of Winchester (that also passed the seas with him) received the habit, hat, and dignity of a cardinal, with all ceremonies to it appertaining: which promotion, the late k[ing] right deeply piercing into the unrestrainable ambitious mind of the man, that even from his youth was ever to check at the highest, and also right well ascertained with what intolerable pride his head should soon be swollen under such a hat, did therefore all his life long keep this prelate back from that presumptuous estate. But now the king being young and the Regent his friend, he obtained his purpose, to his great profit, and the impoverishing of the spirituality of this realm. For by a bull legatine, which he purchased from Rome, he gathered so much treasure that no man in manner had money but he: so that he was called the rich Cardinal of Winchester. . . .

[1428: I.iv] After this, in the month of September the earl came before the city of Orleans and planted his siege on the one side of the River of Loire; but before his coming, the Bastard of Orleans, the bishop of the city, and a great number of Scots, hearing of the earl's intent, made divers fortifications about the town and destroyed the suburbs, in which were twelve parish churches and four orders of friars. They cut also down all the vines, trees, and bushes within five leagues of the city, so that the Englishmen should have neither refuge nor succor.

After the siege had continued full three weeks, the Bastard of Orleans issued out of the gate of the bridge and fought with the Englishmen; but they received him with so fierce and terrible strokes, that he was with all his company compelled to retire and flee back into the city. But the Englishmen followed so fast, in killing and taking of their enemies, that they entered with them.

The bulwark of the bridge, with a great tower standing at the end of the same, was taken incontinently by the Englishmen, who behaved themselves right valiantly under the conduct of their courageous captain, as at this assault, so in divers skirmishes against the French, partly to keep possession of that which Henry the Fifth had by his magnanimity and puissance achieved, as also to enlarge the same. But all helped not. For who can hold that which will away? In so much that some cities by fraudulent practices, other some by martial prowess, were recovered by the French, to the great discouragement of the English and the appalling of their spirits; whose hope was now dashed partly by their great losses and discomfitures (as after you shall hear), but chiefly by the death of the late deceased Henry, their victorious king, as Chr[istopher] Ockland very truly and agreeably to the story noteth:

> *Delphinus comitesque eius fera proelia tentant,*
> *Fraude domi capiunt alias, virtute receptae*
> *Sunt urbes aliae quaedam, sublapsa refertur*

Anglum spes retro, languescere pectora dicas,
Quippe erat Henricus quintus, dux strenuus olim,
Mortuus: hinc damni gravior causa atque doloris.

[The Dauphin and his counts essay fierce battles: through treachery they capture some cities at home, through valor some other cities are recovered. The hope of the English is reported to have declined; you would say it languished in their breasts. To be sure, Henry the Fifth, once an energetic leader, was dead: hence more grievous the cause of the loss and the sorrow.]

In this conflict, many Frenchmen were taken, but more were slain, and the keeping of the tower and bulwark was committed to William Glasdale, Esquire. By the taking of this bridge the passage was stopped, that neither men nor victuals could go or come by that way. After this, the earl caused certain bulwarks to be made round about the town, casting trenches between the one and the other, laying ordnance in every place where he saw that any battery might be devised. When they within saw that they were environed with fortresses and ordnance, they laid gun against gun, and fortified towers against bulwarks, and within cast new rampiers, and fortified themselves as strongly as might be devised.

The Bastard of Orleans and the Hire were appointed to see the walls and watches kept, and the bishop saw that the inhabitants within the city were put in good order, and that victuals were not vainly spent. In the tower that was taken at the bridge end (as before you have heard) there was an high chamber, having a grate full of bars of iron, by the which a man might look all the length of the bridge into the city; at which grate many of the chief captains stood many times, viewing the city and devising in what place it was best to give the assault. They within the city well perceived this tooting hole and laid a piece of ordnance directly against the window.

It so chanced that the nine and fiftieth day after the siege was laid the Earl of Salisbury, Sir Thomas Gargrave,

and William Glasdale, with divers other went into the said
tower, and so into the high chamber, and looked out at
the grate, and within a short space the son of the master-
gunner, perceiving men looking out at the window, took his
match (as his father had taught him who was gone down
to dinner) and fired the gun; the shot whereof brake, and
shivered the iron bars of the grate, so that one of the same
bars strake the earl so violently on the head, that it struck
away one of his eyes and the side of his cheek. Sir Thomas
Gargrave was likewise stricken and died within two days.

The earl was conveyed to Meung on Loire, where after
eight days he likewise departed this world, whose body
was conveyed into England with all funeral appointment,
and buried at Bisham by his progenitors, leaving behind
him an only daughter named Alice, married to Richard
Neville, son to Ralph, Earl of Westmorland, of whom
more shall be said hereafter. The damage that the realm
of England received by the loss of this noble man manifestly appeared, in that immediately after his death the
prosperous good luck which had followed the English
nation began to decline, and the glory of their victories
gotten in the parties beyond the sea fell in decay.

[1429: I.ii] In time of this siege at Orleans (French
stories say), the first week of March, 1428 [i.e., 1429],
unto Charles the Dauphin at Chinon, as he was in very
great care and study how to wrestle against the English
nation, by one Peter Baudricourt, captain of Vaucouleur
(made after Marshal of France by the Dauphin's crea-
tion) was carried a young wench of an eighteen years
old, called Joan Are [Arc], by name of her father (a sorry
shepherd) James of Are, and Isabel her mother, brought
up poorly in their trade of keeping cattle, born at Domremy (therefore reported by Bale: Joan Domremy) upon
Meuse in Lorraine within the diocese of Toul. Of favor
was she counted likesome, of person strongly made and
manly, of courage great, hardy, and stout withal, an un-
derstander of councils though she were not at them, great
semblance of chastity both of body and behavior, the
name of Jesus in her mouth about all her businesses,

humble, obedient, and fasting divers days in the week. A person (as their books make her) raised up by power divine only for succor to the French estate then deeply in distress, in whom, for planting a credit the rather, first the company that toward the Dauphin did conduct her, through places all dangerous as holden by the English, where she never was afore, all the way and by nighter-tale safely did she lead; then at the Dauphin's sending by her assignment, from Saint Katherine's Church of Fierbois in Touraine (where she never had been and knew not) in a secret place there among old iron, appointed she her sword to be sought out and brought her, that with five flower-de-lices was graven on both sides, wherewith she fought and did many slaughters by her own hands. On warfare rode she in armor cap-a-pie and mustered as a man, before her an ensign all white, wherein was Jesus Christ painted with a flower-de-lice in his hand.

Unto the Dauphin in his gallery when first she was brought, and he shadowing himself behind, setting other gay lords before him to try her cunning, from all the company with a salutation (that indeed mars all the matter) she picked him out alone; who thereupon had her to the end of the gallery, where she held him an hour in secret and private talk that of his privy chamber was thought very long, and therefore would have broken it off; but he made them a sign to let her say on. In which (among other) as likely it was, she set out unto him the singular feats (forsooth) given her to understand by revelation divine, that in virtue of that sword she should achieve, which were: how with honor and victory she would raise the siege at Orleans, set him in state of the crown of France, and drive the English out of the country, thereby he to enjoy the kingdom alone. Hereupon he heartened at full, indeed appointed her a sufficient army with absolute power to lead them, and they obediently to do as she bade them. Then fell she to work, and first defeated the siege at Orleans, by and by encouraged him to crown himself King of France at Rheims, that a little before from the English she had won. Thus after pursued she many bold enterprises to our great displeasure a two year together, for the time she kept in state until she were taken and for heresy and witchery burned, as in particularities hereafter followeth. But in her prime time she, armed at all points like a jolly captain, rode from Poitiers to Blois, and there found men of war, victuals, and munition ready to be conveyed to Orleans.

Here was it known that the Englishmen kept not so diligent watch as they had been accustomed to do, and therefore this maid (with other French captains) coming forward in the dead time of the night, and in a great rain and thunder entered into the city with all their victuals, artillery, and other necessary provisions. The next day the Englishmen boldly assaulted the town, but the Frenchmen defended the walls so as no great feat worthy of memory chanced that day betwixt them, though the Frenchmen were amazed at the valiant attempt of the Englishmen, whereupon the Bastard of Orleans gave knowledge to the Duke of Alençon in what danger the town stood without his present help, who, coming within two leagues of the city, gave knowledge to them within that they should be ready the next day to receive him.

This accordingly was accomplished: for the Englishmen willingly suffered him and his army also to enter, supposing that it should be for their advantage to have so great a multitude to enter the city, whereby their victuals (whereof they within had great scarcity) might the sooner be consumed. On the next day in the morning the Frenchmen all together issued out of the town, won by assault the bastille of Saint Lô, and set it on fire. And after they likewise assaulted the tower at the bridge foot, which was manfully defended. But the Frenchmen (more in number) at length took it, ere the Lord Talbot could come to the succors, in the which William Glasdale the captain was slain, with the Lord Moulins and Lord Poinings also.

The Frenchmen, puffed up with this good luck, fetched a compass about and in good order of battle marched toward the bastille, which was in the keeping of the Lord Talbot; the which upon the enemy's approach, like a captain without all fear or dread of that great multitude, issued forth against them and gave them so sharp an encounter that they, not able to withstand his puissance, fled (like sheep before the wolf) again into the city, with great loss of men and small artillery. Of Englishmen were lost in the two battles to the number of six hundred persons, or thereabout, though the French writers multiply this number of hundreds to thousands, as their manner is.

The Earl of Suffolk, the Lord Talbot, the Lord Scales, and other captains assembled together in council, and after causes showed to and fro, it was amongst them determined to leave their fortresses and bastilles, and to assemble in the plain field, and there to abide all the day, to see if the Frenchmen would issue forth to fight with them. This conclusion taken was accordingly executed, but when the Frenchmen durst not once come forth to show their heads, the Englishmen set fire of their lodgings and departed in good order of battle from Orleans. . . .

[1429: IV.i] All which [French lords] being once joined in one army, shortly after fought with the Lord Talbot (who had with him not past six thousand men) near unto a village in Beauce called Patay; at which battle the charge was given by the French so upon a sudden that the Englishmen had not leisure to put themselves in array after they had put up their stakes before their archers, so that there was no remedy but to fight at adventure. This battle continued by the space of three long hours; for the Englishmen, though they were overpressed with multitude of their enemies, yet they never fled back one foot till their captain the Lord Talbot was sore wounded at the back, and so taken.

Then their hearts began to faint, and they fled, in which flight were slain above twelve hundred, and forty taken, of whom the Lord Talbot, the Lord Scales, the Lord Hungerford, and Sir Thomas Rampston were chief. Divers archers, after they had shot all their arrows, having only their swords, defended themselves, and with help of some of their horsemen came safe to Meung. This overthrow, and specially the taking of the Lord Talbot, did not so much rejoice the Frenchmen, but it did as much abash the Englishmen, so that immediately thereupon the towns of

Janville, Meung, Fort, and divers other returned from the
English part and became French. From this battle departed without any stroke stricken Sir John Fastolfe, the
same year for his valiantness elected into the Order of
the Garter. But for doubt of misdealing at this brunt, the
Duke of Bedford took from him the image of Saint
George and his garter, though afterward by means of
friends and apparent causes of good excuse, the same
were to him again delivered against the mind of the Lord
Talbot. . . .

[1430–31: V.iii, iv] In the chase and pursuit [at Com-
piègne] was the Pucelle taken, with divers other, besides
those that were slain, which were no small number.
Divers were hurt also on both parts. Among the Englishmen, Sir John Montgomery had his arm broken and Sir
John Steward was shot into the thigh with a quarrel.

As before ye have heard somewhat of this damsel's
strange beginning and proceedings, so sith the ending of
all such miraclemongers doth (for the most part) plainly
decipher the virtue and power that they work, by her
shall ye be advertised what at last became of her; cast
your opinions as ye have cause. Of her lovers (the Frenchmen) reporteth one how in Compiègne thus besieged,
Guillaume de Flavie the captain, having sold her afore-
hand to the Lord of Luxembourg, under color of hasting
her with a band out of the town towards their king, for
him with speed to come and levy the siege there, so gotten
her forth he shut the gates after her, when anon by the
Burgundians set upon and overmatched in the conflict she
was taken; marry, yet (all things accounted) to no small
marvel how it could come so to pass, had she been of any
devotion or of true belief, and no false miscreant, but all
holy as she made it. For early that morning she gat her
to Saint James's Church, confessed her, and received her
Maker (as the book terms it), and after setting herself
to a pillar, many of the townsmen that with a five or six
score of their children stood about there to see her,
unto them quoth she: "Good children and my dear
friends, I tell you plainly one hath sold me. I am betrayed

and shortly shall be delivered to death. I beseech you, pray to God for me, for I shall never have more power to do service either to the king or to the realm of France again."

Saith another book, she was entrapped by a Picard captain of Soissons, who sold that city to the Duke of Burgundy, and he then put it over into the hands of the Lord of Luxembourg, so by that means the Burgundians approached and besieged Compiègne, for succor whereof as damsel Joan with her captains from Lagny was thither come, and daily to the English gave many a hot skirmish, so happened it on a day in an outsally that she made, by a Picard of the Lord of Luxembourg's band in the fiercest of her fight she was taken, and by him by and by to his lord presented, who sold her over again to the English, who for witchcraft and sorcery burnt her at Rouen. Tillet telleth it thus, that she was caught at Compiègne by one of the Earl of Lagny's soldiers, from him had to Beaurevoir Castle, where kept a three months, she was after for ten thousand pounds in money and three hundred pounds rent (all Tournois) sold into the English hands.

In which for her pranks so uncouth and suspicious, the lord regent by Peter Cauchon, Bishop of Beauvais (in whose diocese she was taken), caused her life and belief after order of law to be inquired upon and examined. Wherein found though a virgin, yet first shamefully her sex abominably in acts and apparel to have counterfeit mankind, and then all damnably faithless to be a pernicious instrument to hostility and bloodshed in devilish witchcraft and sorcery, sentence accordingly was pronounced against her. Howbeit upon humble confession of her iniquities, with a counterfeit contrition pretending a careful sorrow for the same, execution spared and all mollified into this: that from thenceforth she should cast off her unnatural wearing of man's habiliments and keep her to garments of her own kind, abjure her pernicious practices of sorcery and witchery, and have life and leisure in perpetual prison to bewail her misdeeds. Which to perform (according to the manner of abjuration) a solemn oath very gladly she took.

But herein (God help us) she, fully afore possessed of the fiend, not able to hold her in any towardness of grace, falling straightway into her former abominations (and yet seeking to eke out life as long as she might) stake not (though the shift were shameful) to confess herself a strumpet and (unmarried as she was) to be with child. For trial, the lord regent's lenity gave her nine months stay, at the end whereof she, found herein as false as wicked in the rest, an eight days after, upon a further definitive sentence declared against her to be relapsed and a renouncer of her oath and repentance, was she thereupon delivered over to secular power, and so executed by consumption of fire in the old market place at Rouen, in the selfsame stead where now Saint Michael's Church stands, her ashes afterward without the town walls shaken into the wind. . . .

These matters may very rightfully denounce unto all the world her execrable abominations, and well justify the judgment she had, and the execution she was put to for the same. A thing yet (God wot) very smally shadowed and less holpen by the very travail of the Dauphin, whose dignity abroad foully spotted in this point, that, contrary to the holy degree of a right Christian prince (as he called himself), for maintenance of his quarrels in war would not reverence to profane his sacred estate, as dealing in devilish practices with misbelievers and witches. . . .

[1435: III.iii; IV.i] But now to return to the communication at Arras, which after the departure of the English commissioners held betwixt the Frenchmen and Burgundians, till at length a peace was concluded, accorded, and sworn betwixt King Charles and Duke Philip of Burgundy, upon certain conditions, as in the French histories more plainly appeareth.

And after, the Duke of Burgundy, to set a veil before the King of England's eyes, sent Toison d'Or, his chief herald, to King Henry with letters, excusing the matter by way of information that he was constrained to enter in this league with K[ing] Charles by the daily outcries, complaints, and lamentations of his people, alleging against him that he was the only cause of the long continuance of the wars, to the utter impoverishing of his own people and the whole nation of France. Therefore sith he could not otherwise do, but partly to content his own people, and chiefly to satisfy the request of the whole general council, was in manner compelled for his part to grow unto a peace and amity with King Charles.

He likewise wished that King Henry, upon reasonable and honorable conditions of agreement offered, should in no wise refuse the same; whereby the long continued war at length might cease and take end, to the pleasure of almighty God, which is the author of peace and unity; and hereto he promised him his aid and furtherance, with many gay words, which I pass over. The superscription of this letter was thus: "To the high and mighty prince Henry, by the grace of God King of England, his well-beloved cousin"—neither naming him King of France, nor his sovereign lord, according as (ever before that time) he was accustomed to do. This letter was much marveled at of the council after they had thoroughly considered all the contents thereof, and they could not but be much disquieted, so far forth that divers of them offended so much with the untruth of the duke that they could not temper their passions, but openly called him traitor. . . .

[1435: III.ii] After the death of that noble prince the Duke of Bedford, the bright sun in France toward Englishmen began to be cloudy and daily to darken; the Frenchmen began not only to withdraw their obedience by oath to the King of England but also took sword in hand and openly rebelled. Howbeit all these mishaps could not anything abash the valiant courages of the English people; for they, having no mistrust in God and good fortune, set up a new sail, began the war afresh, and appointed for regent in France Richard, Duke of York, son to Richard, Earl of Cambridge.

[1435: IV.iii] Although the Duke of York was worthy

(both for birth and courage) of this honor and preferment, yet so disdained of Edmund, Duke of Somerset,
being cousin to the king, that by all means possible he
sought his hindrance, as one glad of his loss and sorry
of his well doing; by reason whereof, ere the Duke of
York could get his dispatch, Paris and divers other of
the chiefest places in France were gotten by the French
king. The Duke of York, perceiving his evil will, openly
dissembled that which he inwardly minded, either of
them working things to the other's displeasure, till
through malice and division between them, at length by
mortal war they both were consumed, with almost their
whole lines and offspring.

[1441: III.ii] While the French king was in Guienne,
the Lord Talbot took the town of Couchet, and after
marched toward Gallardon, which was besieged by the
Bastard of Orleans, otherwise called the Earl of Dunois;
which earl hearing of the Lord Talbot's approach raised
his siege and saved himself. The Frenchmen a little before this season had taken the town of Évreux by treason
of a fisher. Sir Francis the Aragonois hearing of that
chance appareled six strong fellows like men of the
country, with sacks and baskets as carriers of corn and
victuals, and sent them to the Castle of Corneille, in
the which divers Englishmen were kept as prisoners, and
he with an ambush of Englishmen lay in a valley nigh
to the fortress.

The six counterfeit husbandmen entered the castle un-
suspected, and straight came to the chamber of the captain and, laying hands on him, gave knowledge to them
that lay in ambush to come to their aid. The which
suddenly made forth and entered the castle, slew and
took all the Frenchmen, and set the Englishmen at
liberty; which thing done, they set fire in the castle and
departed to Rouen with their booty and prisoners. This
exploit they had not achieved peradventure by force (as
haply they mistrusted), and therefore by subtlety and
deceit sought to accomplish it, which means to use in
war is tolerable, so the same war be lawful, though both

fraud and bloodshed otherwise be forbidden even by the instinct of nature to be put in practice and use, and that doth the poet insinuate in a proper sententious verse, saying:

Fraus absit, vacuas caedis habete manus.

[Away with treachery, keep your hands free of slaughter.]

[1441: III.i] But now to speak somewhat of the doings in England in the meantime. Whilst the men of war were thus occupied in martial feats, and daily skirmishes within the realm of France, ye shall understand that after the Cardinal of Winchester and the Duke of Gloucester were (as it seemed) reconciled either to other, yet the cardinal and the Archbishop of York ceased not to do many things without the consent of the king or of the duke, being (during the minority of the king) governor and Protector of the realm, whereas the duke (as good cause he had) greatly offended, thereupon in writing declared to the king wherein the cardinal and the archbishop had offended both his majesty and the laws of the realm. This complaint of the Duke of Gloucester was contained in four and twenty articles which chiefly rested in that the cardinal had from time to time, through his ambitious desire to surmount all others in high degrees of honor and dignity, sought to enrich himself, to the great and notorious hindrance of the king, as in defrauding him not only of his treasure, but also in doing and practicing things greatly prejudicial to his affairs in France, and namely by setting at liberty the King of Scots upon so easy conditions as the king's majesty greatly lost thereby. . . .

[1443: V.i] In this year died in Guienne the Countess of Comminges, to whom the French king and also the Earl of Armagnac pretended to be heir, insomuch that the earl entered into all the lands of the said lady. And because he knew the French king would not take the matter well, to have a Roland for an Oliver, he sent solemn

ambassadors to the King of England, offering him his
daughter in marriage with promise to be bound (beside
great sums of money, which he would give with her) to
deliver into the King of England's hands all such castles
and towns as he or his ancestors detained from him
within any part of the Duchy of Aquitaine, either by
conquest of his progenitors or by gift and deliverance of
any French king; and further to aid the same king with
money for the recovery of other cities within the same
duchy from the French king, or from any other person
that against King Henry unjustly kept and wrongfully
withholden them.

This offer seemed so profitable and also honorable to
King Henry and the realm that the ambassadors were
well heard, honorably received, and with rewards sent
home into their country. After whom were sent for the
conclusion of the marriage into Guienne Sir Edward Hull,
Sir Robert Ross, and John Grafton, Dean of St. Severin's,
the which (as all the chronographers agree) both concluded the marriage and by proxy affied the young lady.
The French king, not a little offended herewith, sent his
eldest son Louis, the Dauphin of Vienne, into Rouergue
with a puissant army which took the earl and his young-
est son, with both his daughters, and by force obtained
the countries of Armagnac, L'Auvergne, Rouergue, and
Moulessonois [Limousin?], beside the cities Severac and
Cadeac, chasing the bastard of Armagnac out of his
countries, and so by reason hereof the concluded marriage was deferred, and that so long that it never took
effect, as hereafter it may appear. . . .

[1444–45: V.iii, v] In treating of this truce [between
England and France], the Earl of Suffolk, adventuring
somewhat upon his commission without the assent of his
associates, imagined that the next way to come to a
perfect peace was to contrive a marriage between the
French king's kinswoman, the Lady Margaret, daughter
to Reignier, Duke of Anjou, and his sovereign lord King
Henry. This Reignier, Duke of Anjou, named himself
King of Sicily, Naples, and Jerusalem, having only the

name and style of those realms without any penny, profit, or foot of possession. This marriage was made strange to the earl at the first, and one thing seemed to be a great hindrance to it, which was, because the King of England occupied a great part of the Duchy of Anjou and the whole County of Maine, appertaining (as was alleged) to King Reignier.

The Earl of Suffolk (I cannot say), either corrupted with bribes or too much affectioned to this unprofitable marriage, condescended that the Duchy of Anjou and the County of Maine should be delivered to the king, the bride's father, demanding for her marriage neither penny nor farthing; as who should say, that this new affinity passed all riches and excelled both gold and precious stones. And to the intent that of this truce might ensue a small concord, a day of interview was appointed between the two kings in a place convenient between Chartres and Rouen. When these things were concluded, the Earl of Suffolk with his company returned into England, where he forgat not to declare what an honorable truce he had taken, out of the which there was a great hope that a final peace might grow the sooner for that honorable marriage which he had concluded, omitting nothing that might extol and set forth the personage of the lady or the nobility of her kindred.

But although this marriage pleased the king and divers of his council, yet Humphrey, Duke of Gloucester, Protector of the realm, was much against it, alleging that it should be both contrary to the laws of God and dishonorable to the prince if he should break that promise and contract of marriage, made by ambassadors sufficiently thereto instructed, with the daughter of the Earl of Armagnac, upon conditions both to him and his realm as much profitable and honorable. But the duke's words could not be heard, for the earl's doings were only liked and allowed. So that for performance of the conclusions the French king sent the Earl of Vendôme, great master of his house, and the Archbishop of Rheims, first peer of France, and divers other into England, where they were honorably received; and after that the instruments were once sealed and delivered on both parts, the said ambassadors returned again into their countries with great gifts and rewards.

When these things were done the king, both for honor of his realm and to assure to himself more friends, created John Holland, Earl of Huntington, Duke of Exeter as his father was; Humphrey, Earl of Stafford, was made Duke of Buckingham; and Henry, Earl of Warwick, was elected to the title of Duke of Warwick, to whom the king also gave the castle of Bristol, with the isle of Jersey and Guernsey. Also the Earl of Suffolk was made Marquess of Suffolk, which marquess with his wife and many honorable personages of men and women richly adorned both with apparel and jewels, having with them many costly chariots and gorgeous horselitters, sailed into France for the conveyance of the nominated queen into the realm of England. For King Reignier, her father, for all his long style had too short a purse to send his daughter honorably to the king her spouse.

EDWARD HALL

from *The Union of the Two Noble and Illustre Families of Lancaster and York* (1548)

[1453: IV.ii] When the Earl of Shrewsbury was thus according to his intent of all things furnished and adorned, first he fortified Bordeaux with Englishmen and victual; after that he rode into the country abroad, where he obtained cities and gat towns without stroke or dint of sword, for the poor and needy people being fatigate and weary with the oppression of their new landlords, rendered their towns before they were of them required, and beside this the towns and cities far distant from Bordeaux sent messengers to the Earl, promising to him both service and obeisance. And among other the town and castle of Châtillon in Perigord was to him delivered by the Frenchmen upon composition that they might with their lives safely depart; which town the earl strongly fortified both with men and ordnance. . . .

[IV.v–vii] [Upon learning of Talbot's approach a French force besieging Châtillon] . . . with all diligence left the siege and retired in good order into the place which they had trenched, ditched, and fortified with ordnance. They within the town, seeing the siege removed, sent out word to the Englishmen that the Frenchmen fled. The courageous earl, hearing these news and fearing lest through long tarrying the birds might be flown away, not tarrying till his footmen were come, set forward toward his enemies, which were in mind surely to have fled, as they confessed afterward, if the fear of the French king's rebuke, which was not far off, had not caused them to tarry, and yet in this army were present the marshal and great master of France, the Earl of Ponthieu, the Seneschal of Poitou, the Lord Beziers, and many valiant barons and knights. When the Englishmen were come to the place where the Frenchmen were encamped, in the which (as Aeneas Silvius testifieth) were three hundred pieces of brass, beside divers other small pieces and subtle engines to the Englishmen unknown and nothing suspected, they lighted all on foot, the Earl of Shrewsbury only except, which because of his age rode on a little hackney, and fought fiercely with the Frenchmen, and got the entry of their camp, and by fine force entered into the same. This conflict continued in doubtful judgment of victory two long hours, during which fight the lords of Montauban and Hunaudières with a great company of Frenchmen entered the battle and began a new field, and suddenly the gunners, perceiving the Englishmen to approach near, discharged their ordnance and slew three hundred persons near to the earl, who, perceiving the imminent jeopardy and subtle labyrinth in which he and his people were enclosed and illaqueate, despising his own safeguard and desiring the life of his entirely and well-beloved son the Lord Lisle, willed, advertised, and counseled him to depart out of the field and to save himself. But when the son had answered that it was neither honest nor natural for him to leave his father in the extreme jeopardy of his life, and that he would taste of that draught which his father and parent should assay and begin, the noble earl and comfortable captain said to him: "Oh, son, son, I thy father, which only hath been the terror and scourge of the French people so many years, which hath subverted so many towns, and profligate and discomfited so many of them in open battle and martial conflict, neither can here

die for the honor of my country without great laud
and perpetual fame, nor fly or depart without perpetual
shame and continual infamy. But because this is thy
first journey and enterprise, neither thy flying shall re-
dound to thy shame, nor thy death to thy glory; for
as hardy a man wisely flieth as a temerarious person
foolishly abideth; therefore the fleeing of me shall be
the dishonor, not only of me and my progeny, but
also a discomfiture to all my company; thy departure
shall save thy life and make thee able another time,
if I be slain, to revenge my death and to do honor to
thy prince and profit to his realm." But nature so
wrought in the son that neither desire of life nor thought
of security could withdraw or pluck him from his natural
father; who, considering the constancy of his child and
the great danger that they stood in, comforted his
soldiers, cheered his captains, and valiantly set upon his
enemies and slew of them more in number than he had
in his company. But his enemies, having a greater
company of men and more abundance of ordnance than
before had been seen in a battle, first shot him through
the thigh with a handgun, and slew his horse, and
cowardly killed him, lying on the ground, whom they
never durst look in the face while he stood on his feet;
and with him there died manfully his son the Lord
Lisle, his bastard son, Henry Talbot, and Sir Edward
Hull, elect to the noble Order of the Garter, and thirty
valiant personages of the English nation, and the Lord
Moulins was there taken prisoner with sixty other. The
residue of the English people fled to Bordeaux and
other places, whereof in the flight were slain above a
thousand persons. At this battle of Châtillon, fought the
thirteenth day of July in this year, ended his life John,
lord Talbot, and of his progeny the first Earl of Shrewsbury, after that he with much fame, more glory, and
most victory had for his prince and country, by the
space of twenty-four years and more, valiantly made
war and served the king in the parts beyond the sea;
whose corpse was left on the ground, and after was
found by his friends and conveyed to Whitchurch in

Shropshire, where it is intumulate. This man was to the French people a very scourge and a daily terror, in so much that as his person was fearful and terrible to his adversaries present, so his name and fame was spiteful and dreadful to the common people absent, in so much that women in France to fear their young children would cry, "The Talbot cometh! the Talbot cometh!"

Commentaries

HERMANN ULRICI

from *Shakspeare's Dramatic Art*

The *First Part* forms the real conclusion to *Henry V*, for it is here that we have the termination of the war which was there represented. It ends to the advantage of France, and in the first place because the right, in its ethico-historical significance, has changed sides. For although the French people and the nobility do not prove themselves better, simply more prudent and wiser by experience, still, on the other hand, their arrogance and thoroughly senseless vanity had apparently diminished, and their esteem for their adversaries was already the beginning of victory. On the other hand—and this is the main point—England had lost her moral superiority. In the very first introductory scene, we distinctly see how it has degenerated, owing to the selfish intrigues and quarrels of the nobility, in which the people also have now become involved. Single features of the war —for instance, Fastolfe's cowardly, ignominious flight— prove that the people and the army are no longer animated by the old spirit. The play opens with the coffin

From *Shakspeare's Dramatic Art. History and Character of Shakspeare's Plays* by Dr. Hermann Ulrici. Translated by L. Dora Schmitz. London: George Bell and Sons, 1876.

of Henry V lying in state, thus representing the grave
of the English victories and conquests. These had necessarily to be lost, sooner or later, for it was a grand
mistake, but nevertheless a mistake, to suppose that the
England of the day could maintain a *lasting* supremacy
over France. As long as the political and national energy
of an independent country is not wholly broken, it cannot
sink so far as to become a mere province of another.
This error only maintained the semblance of truth for
a short time, because of the moral weakness of the
French people, and because of the heroic energy of
Henry V. If France had again rallied, the conquest could
not have been maintained even by a monarch more
powerful than Henry VI, because, when more closely
examined, it contained an unjust presumption, as unjust
as every attempt to enslave the liberty of a man as long
as he is morally capable of freedom. The same justice
which had formerly weighed in England's favor, ultimately turns the scales against her.

As this unhappy termination of the war corresponds
with the spirit and character of the whole trilogy, intimated by the above discussion, so we have it reflected
in a peculiar coloring in the character, the doings and the
fate of the Maid of Orleans. She is, as it were, the
soul of the rekindled war on the French side, as Talbot
represents it on that of England. With her appearance
the fortune of war turns from England to France, because she succeeds in arousing the French nation to
enthusiastic patriotism by faith in a higher and divine
aid. The poet does not deny the existence of this higher
aid, which is represented in Joan, but, as a true Eng-
lishman, he looks upon it as the aid of ungodly, de-
moniacal powers. The enthusiastic rise of the French
nation with the appearance of Joan la Pucelle he con-
siders as a stirring of the nightside of nature, as an
interference of the evil principle. He therefore becomes
untrue to himself, and sins against the principle of the
historical drama, which demands strict impartiality for
the inner motives and great turning points in the course
of history. We have a proof of how this error—which

was as much an error against the laws of poetry—
takes its revenge, for the character of Joan is not only
untrue, but also unpoetical. From the very fact of
Shakspeare not being aware of this, and from his having here entirely followed the English view and the
English authorities in regard to the history of the time,
we might infer (even though it were not otherwise established) that the First Part of *Henry VI* is one of
Shakspeare's youthful works, written at a time when he
did not as yet possess a clear idea of what an historical drama should be, in order to be free from the faults
of blind patriotism and national prejudice. On the other
hand we have an excuse for the poet in the circumstance that Shakspeare's conception of the character of
Joan of Arc was quite in keeping with the opinions of
the English nation, nay, that it corresponded pretty
closely with the *general* opinion of the whole age to
which the history belongs. For an *historical* drama,
which represents its substance as actually *present,* ought
at the same time to depict the spirit and character of
the age in which it moves. And moreover it was one of
the features in the character of the age, that it was in-
capable of comprehending that which was great, pure,
and noble, nay, that what was good and beautiful could
not even keep itself quite pure. For Joan of Arc does
not appear quite pure even according to French authorities, nor according to our modern and more accurate
historical investigations. That she was inspired by a great
and beautiful thought before her appearance in public,
is intimated even by Shakspeare through the rumor
which he allows to precede her appearance, and his fault
is only in having merely intimated it, and in not having
given us a vivid representation of it. But Shakspeare
must certainly have had some object in introducing this
intimation; at all events it is in excellent keeping with
the spirit and ideal character of the whole trilogy, especially of the First Part. For if we follow this intimation,
we shall have to assume that Joan—in order to realize
her great and beautiful thought in *such a time,* i.e., when
she entered actively into the current of events—did give

herself up to the evil principle; whether she did this voluntarily, or was overpowered by it, is a point which the poet could justly leave undecided, as it was a matter of indifference to his purpose. In history, and hence in Shakspeare, she therefore fell the victim to the tragic fate which, like a fearful specter, wanders through the whole trilogy.

Joan's death, when conceived in this light, appears at the same time the organic contrast to that of the Earl of Salisbury [sic], of Lord Talbot and his son. Lord Talbot is obviously the noblest character in the whole play, a rough and vigorous knight; battle and war, self-devoted patriotism, knightly honor and bravery, these have constituted his entire life; all higher ideas seem beyond him; he knows how to win a battle, but not how to carry on a war; he is an excellent military captain, but no general, no chief, because, although valiant and even discreet and prudent (as is proved by his interview with the Countess of Auvergne), he does not possess either presence of mind, creative power, or a clear insight into matters. This, together with the roughness and harshness of his virtue, which has in it something of the rage of the lion, is his weak point, and proves the cause of his death. His power was not equal to the complicated circumstances and the depravity of the age; under the iron rod of chastisement, he became equally unbending and iron; he is the representative of the rage and ferocity of the war, to which he falls a victim because he is wholly absorbed in it and therefore unable to become the master in directing it. In such days, however, the honorable death of a noble character proves a blessing; victory and pleasure are found in death when life succumbs to the superior power of evil, to the weight and misery of a decline which affects both the nation and the state.

This is the special modification of the theme which is carried out throughout the play, the special task which the First Part has to solve, and to the solution of which the other parts have to contribute their share. Henry VI, who in himself is pious and innocent and by nature unimpassionate, is led by Suffolk's seductive arts to break his royal word and his already plighted troth, and to conclude his unfortunate marriage with Margaret of Anjou. Even he cannot keep himself pure, and, inasmuch as in youthful levity he follows his sensual desires, he himself lays the foundation of his subsequent unhappy life. Gloster's honest, high-minded, and truly patriotic nature is likewise carried away by party spirit and passion. The quarrel between him and the bishop of Winchester, which has also affected their retainers, the jealousy between Somerset and Richard of York, the powerlessness of old Bedford and Exeter—all this helps to bring about the death of Talbot, the impending and soon no longer inevitable destruction of all the better minds. The citizens and people do not as yet take any direct part in the dissensions of the nobility, the Mayor of London appears more in the light of a mediator, and a promoter of peace. Still some incidents, such as the brawls among the servingmen, the cowardliness of Fastolfe and his troops show that the people are already affected by the general state of corruption. In the following parts this, accordingly, is brought more prominently forward.

E. M. W. TILLYARD

from *Shakespeare's History Plays*

"The First Part of Henry VI"

I am fully in accord with a growing trend of belief that
Shakespeare wrote this play. It is not in the least surprising if the style is hesitant and varied. If a young man
attempts a big thing, a thing beyond his years, he will
imitate others when his own invention flags. Some of the
verse in this play, as in the rest of the tetralogy, is in the
common, little differentiated dramatic idiom of the age:
it is the sort of thing that just was being written. That
Shakespeare should have had recourse to it was perfectly
natural. Why should he, more than another poet, be expected to find himself instantaneously? No one disputes
the authorship of Pope's *Pastorals* because they do not
show the author's achieved and unmistakable genius
throughout, or collects the truly Popean lines and conjectures that he added just these to a lost original. Such
treatment is kept for Shakespeare. One cannot of course
be sure that a manuscript which waited over thirty years
for publication remained in every word or sentence as the
poet penned it. But the editors of the First Folio thought
the play to be Shakespeare's; and this is evidence that
only something very solid on the other side should be

From *Shakespeare's History Plays* by E. M. W. Tillyard. London:
Chatto and Windus, 1944. Reprinted by permission of the publishers
and Mr. Stephen Tillyard. Additional excerpts from this book appear in
the Signet Classic edition of *3 Henry VI*.

allowed to gainsay. The evidence, apart from the First Folio, that is overwhelmingly on the side of Shakespeare's being the author is the masterly structure. None of his contemporary dramatists was capable of this. The steady political earnestness is further proof.

I cannot believe either that this part was written after the other two parts of *Henry VI*. The evidence for a later date is the entry in Henslowe's Diary for 3 March 1591-92 of *Henry VI* as "ne" or new. Alexander has argued that the entry probably refers to another play altogether. Quite apart from the greater immaturity of its style, in itself a strong argument for earlier date, the first part is a portion of a larger organism. The very difference of its structure from that of the second part is an essential and deliberate contrast within a total scheme, while characters, embryonic in the first part, develop in the second in full congruity with their embryonic character.

Nor can I agree with Alexander that the scenes at the end of the play of Suffolk fetching Margaret of Anjou are an afterthought designed to link the play closely with the next. They have the same function as the last scenes in the next two plays, which suggest the opening scenes of their successors. They *all* argue the organic nature of the whole tetralogy.

Apart from the queer reluctance to allow Shakespeare to have written ill or like other dramatists when he was immature, the chief reason why people have been hostile to Shakespeare's authorship is the way he treats Joan of Arc. That the gentle Shakespeare could have been so ungentlemanly as to make his Joan other than a saint was intolerable. This is precisely like arguing that Shakespeare could not have written *King John* because he does not mention Magna Carta. That England adopted the French opinion of Joan of Arc and saw the beginnings of our liberties in Magna Carta may have been excellent things; but these acts are comparatively recent, belonging to the "1066 and All That" phase of history, about which the Elizabethans knew nothing. To an Elizabethan, France did not mean saints, but instability, wars of religion, political intrigue, with the Massacre of St. Bartholomew the outstanding event. Not that moderns can enjoy the way Shakespeare treats the French, Joan of Arc included. But he is just as bad (and with less excuse because older) in *Henry V*; and any argument, based on Joan of Arc, against the Shakespearean authorship of *1 Henry VI* is just as pertinent to the later play. It is some comfort to reflect that in his contribution to *Sir Thomas More* Shakespeare treated the alien like an ordinary human being. George Betts has said that expelling the London aliens will be good for trade, and More replies:

> Grant them remov'd and grant that this your noise
> Had chid down all the majesty of England.
> Imagine that you see the wretched strangers,
> Their babies at their backs and their poor luggage,
> Plodding to th' ports and coasts for transportation—

But these were aliens who could be seen and heard, and taken as individuals. Frenchmen in the mass were judged by other standards.

The *First Part of Henry VI* is the work of an ambitious and reflective young man who has the power to plan but not worthily to execute something great. His style of writing lags behind the powerful imagination that arranged the inchoate mass of historical material into a highly significant order. The characters are well thought out and consistent but they are the correct pieces in a game moved by an external hand rather than self-moving. Yet they come to life now and then and, in promise, are quite up to what we have any right to expect from Shakespeare in his youth.

If this play had been called the *Tragedy of Talbot* it would stand a much better chance of being heeded by a public which very naturally finds it hard to remember which part of *Henry VI* is which, and where Joan of Arc or Jack Cade, or Margaret crowning York with a paper crown, occur. And if we want something by which to distinguish the play, let us by all means give it that title. It is one that contains much truth, but not all. The whole truth in this matter is that though the action revolves around Talbot, though he stands preeminently for loyalty and order in a world threatened by chaos, he is not the hero. For there is no regular hero either in this or in any of the other three plays; its true hero being England or Respublica after the fashion of the Morality Play, as pointed out in the last section. It is therefore truer to the nature of the separate plays that they should be given colorless regal titles than that they should be named after the seemingly most important characters or events.

Along with the Morality hero goes the assumption of divine interference. The theme of the play is the testing of England, already guilty and under a sort of curse, by French witchcraft. England is championed by a great and pious soldier, Talbot, and the witchcraft is directed principally at him. If the other chief men of England had all been like him, he could have resisted and saved England. But they are divided against each other, and through this division Talbot dies and the first stage in England's ruin and of the fulfillment of the curse is accomplished. Respublica has suffered the first terrible wounds.

As so often happens in literature the things which initially are the most troublesome prove to be the most enlightening. The Joan episodes, unpleasant and hence denied Shakespeare, are the clue to the whole plot. They are hinted at right in the front of the play. In the first scene Exeter, commenting on the funeral of Henry V, says:

> What! shall we curse the planets of mishap
> That plotted thus our glory's overthrow?
> Or shall we think the subtle-witted French
> Conjurers and sorcerers, that afraid of him
> By magic verses have contriv'd his end?

One cannot understand the bearing of these lines on the play without remembering how the influence of the stars and witchcraft fitted into the total Elizabethan conception of the universe. Though these two things were thought to be powerful in their effects and were dreaded, they did not work undirected. God was ultimately in control, and the divine part of man, his reason and the freedom of his will, need not yield to them. Further, God used both stars and evil spirits to forward his own ends. Joan, then, is not a mere piece of fortuitous witchcraft, not a mere freakish emissary of Satan, but a tool of the Almighty, as she herself (though unconsciously) declares in her words to Charles after her first appearance.

> Assign'd am I to be the English scourge.

Who but God has assigned her this duty? True, if this line were unsupported, we might hesitate to make this full inference. But combined with the various cosmic references and the piety of Talbot, it is certain. For not only the first scene of the play, but the second scene (where Joan first appears) begins with a reference to the heavens. The first passage was quoted above; the Dauphin Charles begins the second scene:

> Mars his true moving, even as in the heavens
> So in the earth, to this day is not known:
> Late did he shine upon the English side;
> Now we are victors; upon us he smiles.

Not only do these words contrast significantly with Bedford's opening speech about the "bad revolted stars"; they combine with it in presenting the whole world order with God, the unmoved mover, directing it. And the full context of witchcraft is implied when Talbot before Orleans, already harassed by Joan's supernatural power, exclaims of the French:

> Well, let them practice and converse with spirits:
> God is our fortress, in whose conquering name
> Let us resolve to scale their flinty bulwarks.

A modern, who needs much working up to pay any real heed to witchcraft, is apt not to notice such a passage and to pass on faintly disgusted with Talbot for being not only a butcher but a prig: an Elizabethan, granted a generally serious context, would find Talbot's defiance apt and noble.

What were the sins God sought to punish? There had been a number, but the preeminent one was the murder of Richard II, the shedding of the blood of God's deputy on earth. Henry IV had been punished by an uneasy reign but had not fully expiated the crime; Henry V, for his piety, had been allowed a brilliant reign. But the curse was there; and first England suffers through Henry V's early death and secondly she is tried by the witch-craft of Joan.

Into the struggle between Talbot and Joan, which is the main motive of the play, is introduced the theme of order and dissension. The first scene presents the funeral of Henry V and declares the disaster of his death. Dis-sension appears through the high words between the bad ambitious Beaufort, Bishop of Winchester, and Humphrey Duke of Gloucester, honest but hot-tempered, the regent of England. Bad news from France follows. But the case of England is not hopeless. Bedford sets off at once for France, Gloucester takes charge at home.

The next scene is before Orleans. The French are in a mood of facile triumph. They will relieve the town, still besieged by Salisbury and the English. Though ten to one they are beaten back with loss and confusion. That, the poet makes us feel, is the natural order, God's order, provided England is true to herself. Then Joan enters, a dazzling blonde, claiming her beauty to be from the Virgin—

> And, whereas I was black and swart before,
> With those clear rays which she infus'd on me
> That beauty am I bless'd with which you see—

but of course owing it to the Devil. She fascinates Charles and ends by imposing on the French a discipline and an order which by nature is not theirs. That this order is bogus, a devilish not a divine one, is evident by the single combat Charles the Dauphin has with Joan to test her pretensions. He is beaten; and for a man to yield to a woman was a fundamental upsetting of degree.

Then, before a background of dissension in England, the struggle between Talbot and Joan is worked out. There are three episodes: Orleans, Rouen, Bordeaux. Before Orleans Talbot's men melt before Joan's attack, and, though he is dauntless, she relieves the town. The French triumph. But now Bedford has arrived with Burgundian allies: there is a new union on the English side, and the town (quite unhistorically) is captured. Talbot has kept up his heart and with united supporters he triumphs. The pattern is repeated at Rouen. Through a trick Joan wins the town for the French. Again Talbot does not lose heart. He gets Burgundy to swear to capture the town or die. Bedford, brought in on a litter and near his death, insists on taking his share:

> Here will I sit before the walls of Roan[1]
> And will be partner of your weal or woe.

Union once more and it succeeds. The town is captured, and Talbot emerges more strongly than ever the symbol of true and virtuous order:

> Now will we take some order in the town,
> Placing therein some expert officers,
> And then depart to Paris to the king,
> For there young Henry with his nobles lie.

To which Burgundy, again showing the natural relation of French to English, replies,

> What wills Lord Talbot pleaseth Burgundy.

Talbot then goes on to more proprieties:

> But yet, before we go, let's not forget
> The noble Duke of Bedford late deceas'd
> But see his exequies fulfill'd in Roan.

But Joan had not yet ceased to be the English scourge,

---

[1] A monosyllable: the Elizabethan form of Rouen (now, alas, given up).

and Talbot was wrong in saying just before the above lines,

> I think her old familiar is asleep.

In the next scene, outside Rouen, Joan cheers the dispirited French leaders and says she has another plan: she will detach Burgundy from the English alliance. Then, in what must have been a most effective scene on the Elizabethan stage, the English forces pass across in triumph with colors spread, headed by Talbot, on their way to Paris. The Burgundians follow and Joan waylays them. She addresses to their Duke those commonplaces about avoiding civil war of which, ironically, England was even then in such desperate need, for between the episodes of Orleans and Rouen had come the quarrel between Lancastrians and Yorkists in the Temple Garden and Richard Plantagenet's resolve to claim the Duchy of York:

> See, see the pining malady of France;
> Behold the wounds, the most unnatural wounds,
> Which thou thyself hast given her woeful breast.
> O, turn thy edged sword another way;
> Strike those that hurt and hurt not those that help.
> One drop of blood drawn from thy country's bosom
> Should grieve thee more than streams of foreign gore.

Excellent advice when applied to England; but to France, where Massacres of St. Bartholomew were endemic, quite perverse. With a speed, familiar to readers of contemporary Elizabethan drama or of *Savonarola Brown,* Burgundy acquiesces and joins with the French. Joan, with a cynicism that anticipates the Bastard of Falconbridge, exclaims:

> Done like a Frenchman: turn, and turn again!

Meanwhile Talbot, ignorant of Burgundy's defection, arrives in Paris and does homage to Henry in the scene I have already pointed to [in an earlier passage, not printed

in this selection] as epitomizing the principle of degree
and the way a kingdom should be ordered. Henry is
crowned, and immediately after comes the news of
Burgundy's defection. Talbot leaves at once to renew the
wars. But the court he leaves, that should have been his
base and his certainty, shows itself divided and weak.
Yorkist and Lancastrian refer their quarrels to the king,
who quite fails to grasp the ugliness of the situation,
frivolously chooses a red rose for himself with the words,

> I see no reason, if I wear this rose,
> That anyone should therefore be suspicious
> I more incline to Somerset than York,

and sets out to return to England, leaving Somerset and
York in divided command of all the forces except the
few that accompany Talbot. English division is now
acutely contrasted with French reconciliation. Exeter pro-
nounces the choric comment that prepares for the
culminating catastrophe:

> No simple man that sees
> This jarring discord of nobility,
> This shouldering of each other in the court,
> This factious bandying of their favorites,
> But that it doth presage some ill event.
> 'Tis much when scepters are in children's hands,
> But more when envy breeds unkind division:
> There comes the ruin, there begins confusion.

From this there follows inevitably the final tragedy of
Talbot near Bordeaux. Twice he had resisted the machinations of Joan and triumphed; but then he was supported
by his own people. The third time, though he does all
he can, he perishes; for York and Somerset, to whom he
had sent for help, each refuses it for envy of the other.
Joan is not allowed to kill Talbot; that would be un-
seemly: he must die on heaps of French dead. After
his death she reports how his son had refused to fight her
("to be the pillage of a giglot wench") and insults over
his body. Lucy, who has come to learn the news, recites

the full list of Talbot's great titles; at which Joan exclaims:

> Here is a silly stately style indeed!
> The Turk, who two and fifty kingdoms hath,
> Writes not so tedious a style as this.
> Him that thou magnifi'st with all these titles
> Stinking and fly-blown lies here at our feet.

Joan, by God's permission and through the general collapse of order among the English nobility, has dealt England a great blow. Having dealt it, and ceasing to be God's tool, she loses her power. Her evil spirits desert her, and she is captured and burnt for the wicked woman she is. It is possible that we are meant to think that her evil spells are transferred to another Frenchwoman, Margaret of Anjou, who, at the end of the play, is allowed through the machinations of her would-be paramour, the unscrupulous Suffolk, to supplant the daughter of the Earl of Armagnac, already affianced, in the affections of Henry VI. On the ominous note of this royal perjury the play ends.

Such is the play's outline. There is no scene or episode not mentioned above that does not reinforce one or other of the main themes. Even the episode of Talbot and the Countess of Auvergne serves to exalt the hero as well as creating a legitimate diversion at a pause in the action.

Shakespeare took great trouble over his plot, but his emotions too were deeply stirred in his task. The gradual but sure stages in Talbot's destruction express the painful seriousness with which Shakespeare took the historical theme. He also took trouble over the characters, but he felt far less strongly about them. At least he made them consistent, even if he did not give them a great deal of life. For instance, Suffolk at his first appearance in the Temple Garden (II.iv) shows himself both diplomatic and unscrupulous. It is he who has brought the dispute between Somerset and York from the hall into the privacy of the garden:

> Within the Temple Hall we were too loud;
> The garden here is more convenient.

And, when asked his opinion on the legal point, he coolly
says,

> Faith, I have been a truant in the law
> And never yet could frame my will to it;
> And therefore frame the law unto my will.

York is the true anticipation of the

> dogged York, that reaches at the moon

of the second part. He is violently ambitious, yet not
rashly but obstinately and persistently: strong in all the
regal qualities but goodness of heart. Gloucester is simply
but sufficiently shown as the opposite of York: good-
hearted but free-spoken to a fault. The contrast of their
characters already prepares for the main motive of the
next play.

Talbot and Joan are the most alive, for they both have
a touch of breeziness, or hearty coarseness with which
Shakespeare liked to furnish his most successfully practical characters. Joan's remarks on Burgundy's change of
mind and on Talbot's dead body, quoted above, are examples. And this is Talbot's comment on Salisbury's dying
wounds received before Orleans:

> Hear, hear how dying Salisbury doth groan!
> It irks his heart he cannot be reveng'd.
> Frenchmen, I'll be a Salisbury to you:
> Pucelle or puzzle, Dolphin or dogfish,
> Your hearts I'll stamp out with my horse's heels
> And make a quagmire of your mingled brains.
> Convey me Salisbury into his tent.

In Henry VI's character Shakespeare shows little interest.
There is a strong religious feeling throughout the tetralogy
that culminates in *Richard III,* but it is religion applied to
the workings of history not the religious feelings in the
mind of a poor king and a saint. Shakespeare stops short

at the poor king, who is also pathetic; he omits the more interesting self-questionings of the same character in the *Mirror for Magistrates*.

For style, much of the play is a competent example of the dramatic norm of the period. As this:

> Crossing the sea from England into France,
> This fellow here with envious carping tongue
> Upbraided me about the rose I wear;
> Saying, the sanguine color of the leaves
> Did represent my master's blushing cheeks,
> When stubbornly he did repugn the truth
> About a certain question in the law
> Argu'd betwixt the Duke of York and him,
> With other vile and ignominious terms.
> In confutation of which rude reproach
> And in defense of my lord's worthiness
> I crave the benefit of law of arms.

But this is not the only way of writing. Once or twice the rhythm is unpleasantly lame, as when Joan says to Charles, about to try her in single combat,

> I am prepar'd. Here is my keen-edg'd sword,
> Deck'd with five flower-de-luces on each side,
> The which at Touraine, in Saint Katharine's churchyard,
> Out of a great deal of old iron I chose forth.

Such lameness is not so surprising when we refer the passage to its original in Holinshed:

> Then at the Dolphin's sending, by her assignment, from Saint Katharine's Church of Fierbois in Touraine (where she never had been and knew not) in a secret place there, among old iron, appointed she her sword to be sought out and brought her, that with five flower-delices was graven on both sides.

Shakespeare much later in his career was apt to be careless of rhythms when he paraphrased Holinshed. Besides, Holinshed is here reporting the French version of Joan's inspiration, and Shakespeare may be deliberately making

it ridiculous; just as, in general, he made the French talk
foolishly. Then sometimes there are outbursts of the turgid
or dulcet writing dear to the University Wits, to vary the
more sober norm of the play. The classical references,
profuse for a play on a historical theme, are in keeping
with these and form yet another link with *Titus Androni-
cus*. Here is Talbot's account of how the French treated
him in captivity:

> In open market-place produc'd they me,
> To be a public spectacle to all.
> Here, said they, is the terror of the French,
> The scarecrow that affrights our children so.
> Then broke I from the officers that led me
> And with my nails digg'd stones out of the ground
> To hurl at the beholders of my shame.
> My grisly countenance made others fly;
> None durst come near for fear of sudden death.
> In iron walls they deem'd me not secure.
> So great fear of my name 'mongst them was spread
> That they suppos'd I could rend bars of steel
> And spurn in pieces posts of adamant.

And for the dulcet style Suffolk's words to Margaret of
Anjou when he has captured her will do as illustration:

> Be not offended, nature's miracle,
> Thou are allotted to be ta'en by me:
> So doth the swan her downy cygnets save,
> Keeping them prisoner underneath her wings.
> Yet, if this servile usage once offend,
> Go and be free again as Suffolk's friend.
> O, stay! I have no power to let her pass;
> My hand would free her, but my heart says no.
> As plays the sun upon the glassy streams,
> Twinkling another counterfeited beam,
> So seems this gorgeous beauty to mine eyes.

When Shakespeare has to deal with his climax, the death
of Talbot, he wisely adds the formality of rhyme to the
heightened style of the University Wits. This is how Talbot describes his son's death:

Triumphant Death, smear'd with captivity,
Young Talbot's valor makes me smile at thee.
When he perceiv'd me shrink and on my knee,
His bloody sword he brandish'd over me,
And like a hungry lion did commence
Rough deeds of rage and stern impatience:
But when my angry guardant stood alone,
Tendering my ruin and assail'd of none,
Dizzy-eyed fury and great rage of heart
Suddenly made him from my side to start
Into the clustering battle of the French;
And in that sea of blood my boy did drench
His over-mounting spirit and there died,
My Icarus, my blossom, in his pride.

Shakespeare seems to have known that his power over
words did not match the grandeur of conception contained
in Talbot's death. So he resorted to the conventional, the
formal, the stylized, as the best way out.

But in compensation, bits of imaginative writing show
themselves at intervals throughout the play; and as much
in the less dignified scenes as in the rest. That they are
thus scattered is a strong argument for the whole play
being Shakespeare's. Thus Reignier, commenting on English valor, uses the metaphor of the artificial figure of a
man striking the hours of a clock with a hammer, as
Shakespeare was to use it again with superb effect in
Richard III:

I think by some odd gimmers or device
Their arms are set like clocks, still to strike on;
Else ne'er could they hold out so as they do.

Again, Talbot, deserted by his men in front of Orleans,
exclaims,

My thoughts are whirled like a potter's wheel.

Shakespeare knows exactly what to make the servingmen
of Gloucester and Winchester say, when they quarrel:

First Serv. Nay, if we be forbidden stones, we'll fall to it
  with our teeth.
Second Serv. Do what ye dare, we are as resolute.

Talbot, offering terms to the French commanders in Bordeaux, gets beyond good melodrama and touches true
grandeur:

> But, if you frown upon this proffer'd peace,
> You tempt the fury of my three attendants,
> Lean famine, quartering steel, and climbing fire;
> Who in a moment even with the earth
> Shall lay your stately and air-braving towers,
> If you forsake the offer of their love.

But it is rare for Shakespeare's execution to be thus equal
to his theme; and the chief virtue of the play must reside
in the vehement energy with which Shakespeare both
shaped this single play and conceived it as an organic
part of a vast design.

J. P. BROCKBANK

from *The Frame of Disorder—"Henry VI"*

The four plays about the Wars of the Roses were
staged fully and in sequence, probably for the first time,
in 1953. The experience was arresting and moving, tes-
tifying to the continuity of our own preoccupations with
those of Tudor England; here, it seemed, was yet another
historical instance of anarchy owed to innocence and
order won by atrocity. The three parts of *Henry VI* express the plight of individuals caught up in a cataclysmic
movement of events for which responsibility is communal
and historical, not personal and immediate, and they
reveal the genesis out of prolonged violence of two figures representing the ultimate predicament of man as a
political animal—Henry and Richard, martyr and machiavel. But one would not wish to overstress whatever
analogues there may be between the fifteenth century and
the twentieth, since these might be proved quite as striking for ages other than our own. If we are now more
sympathetically disposed toward Shakespeare's history
plays than were the readers and audiences of seventy
years ago, it is largely because we have more flexible ideas
about the many possible forms that history might take.

From "The Frame of Disorder—*Henry VI*," by J. P. Brockbank, in
Stratford-upon-Avon Studies 3: Early Shakespeare, eds. John Russell
Brown and Bernard Harris. London: Edward Arnold (Publishers) Ltd.,
1961. Reprinted by permission of the publishers. Additional excerpts from
this book appear in the Signet Classic editions of *2 Henry VI* and *3 Henry
VI*.

We are less dominated by the Positivist view that the truth is co-extensive with, and not merely consistent with, the facts. Contemporaries of Boswell-Stone were reluctant to take seriously a vision of the past that made free with the data for purposes they took to be simply dramatic. Following the lead of Richard Simpson, critics began to read Shakespeare's histories as documents of Tudor England, addressed primarily to contemporary problems and not fundamentally curious about the pastness of the past.[1] Now we are better placed to see them from the point of view represented, for instance, by R. G. Collingwood's *The Idea of History* and Herbert Butterfield's *Christianity and History,* putting a less exclusive stress on facts, and looking harder at the myths and hypotheses used to interpret them—at ideas of providence, historical process, personal responsibility and the role of the hero. These are precisely the ideas that the playwright is fitted to explore and clarify, and Shakespeare's treatment of them is the most searching our literature has to offer. For Shakespeare was peculiarly sensitive to the subtle analogues between the world and the stage, between the shape of events and the shape of a play, between the relationship of historical process to individuals and that of the playwright to his characters. He tried from the beginning to meet the urgent and practical problem of finding dramatic forms and conventions that would express whatever coherence and order could be found in the "plots" of chronicle history. Where narrative and play are incompatible, it may be the record and it may be the art that is defective as an image of human life, and in the plays framed from English and Roman history it is possible to trace subtle modulations of spectacle, structure and dialogue as they seek to express and elucidate the full potential of the source material. A full account would take in *The Tempest,* which is the last of Shakespeare's plays to be made out of historical documents and which has much to do with the rule of providence over the po-

[1] Richard Simpson, "The Politics of Shakespeare's History Plays," in *Trans. New Sh. Soc.* (1874). A similar approach is made by L. B. Campbell.

litical activities of man. But from these early plays alone there is much to be learned about the vision and technique of historical drama, and these are the plays that are submitted most rigorously to the test of allegiance to historical record.

Part 1 and the Pageantry of Dissension

We might begin by taking a famous passage of Nashe as the earliest surviving critical comment on *Part 1*.[2]

How would it have joyed brave *Talbot* (the terror of the French) to think that after he had lyne two hundred yeares in his Tombe, hee should triumphe againe on the Stage, and have his bones new embalmed with the teares of ten thousand spectators at least, (at severall times) who, in the Tragedian that represents his person, imagine they behold him fresh bleeding.

This, primarily, is the ritual experience Shakespeare sought and won. He transposed the past of the tombs, the "rusty brass" and the "worm-eaten books" into living spectacle. Whatever else must be said about all three plays, they keep this quality of epic mime and with it an elementary power to move large audiences. There is, too, something in Nashe's glance at those early performances that chimes with Coleridge's observation that "in order that a drama may be properly historical, it is necessary that it should be the history of the people to whom it is addressed."[3] Shakespeare's early histories are addressed primarily to the audience's heroic sense of community, to its readiness to belong to an England represented by its court and its army, to its eagerness to enjoy a public show celebrating the continuing history of its prestige and power. This does not mean, however, that we must surrender these early plays to Joyce's remark that Shakespeare's "pageants, the histories, sail full-bellied on a tide

2 Quoted in E. K. Chambers, *Shakespeare* (1930), II, p. 188.
3 T. M. Raysor (ed.), *Coleridge's Shakespeare Criticism* (1930) I, p. 138.

of Mafeking enthusiasm." In the more mature plays of
Henry IV the heroic sense of community will be chal-
lenged by the unheroic—by that range of allegiances
which binds us less to authority and the King than to each
other and to Falstaff; and the death of Hotspur is a more
complicated theatrical experience than that of Talbot in
Nashe's description. But the early histories too express
stresses and ironies, complexities and intricate perspec-
tives beyond the reach of the condescensions usually
allowed them.

Even *Part 1* has its share. If this is a play more moving
to watch than to read it is because it makes the historical
facts eloquent through the language of pageantry. In a
way that Nashe does not sufficiently suggest, Shakespeare
exploits the poignant contrast between the past nostal-
gically apprehended through its monuments, and the past
keenly re-enacted in the present—between the past "en-
tombed" "and fresh-bleeding." The effect, which testifies
to the continuity of stage techniques with those of the
Tournament and the civic pageant, is felt immediately in
the first scene (where the mood of a cathedral entomb-
ment is mocked by the energies of the brawl), in the
scene of Bedford's death (III.ii), and, most distinctly, in
the death of Talbot (IV.vii). These are among the several episodes of *Henry VI* that are presented both as
"events"—as if they actually happened, the figures caught
up in them alive and free, and as "occasions"—hap-
penings that have some symbolic significance, or are (in
retrospect) "inevitable" turning-points in the history.
Thus the scene of Talbot's and Lisle's death would, if perfectly executed, present the chronicled event with con-
vincing documentary detail, in a style befitting the occasion—the fire of English chivalry glowing brightest before
it expires. The context ensures that Talbot stands at his
death for the martial glory of England, and Bordeaux for
the dominion of France. When the English and French
nobles meet over his corpse (IV.vii), the retrospective,
reflective mood and the instant, practical mood are sustained side by side; the first calling to mind the image of a
memorial tomb seen in the remote perspective of a later

time, and the second recalling us to the hard realities of
the battlefield. Talbot is discovered dead with his son "en-
hearsed in his arms" (IV.vii.45), resembling a figure on
a monument. Lucy's long intonement of Talbot's titles
was taken at first or second hand from the inscription on
Talbot's actual tomb at Rouen, and it retains its lapidary
formality.[4] Joan's lines,

> Him that thou magnifiest with all these titles
> Stinking and fly-blown lies here at our feet.
>
> (IV.vii.75)

have been mocked for their documentary impropriety
(fly-blown in two minutes!) but they serve to accent the
recollection in the spectacle of a Tudor tomb. Beneath
the effigy of the complete man in, as it were, painted
marble finery, lies the image of the rotten corpse. Joan's
jeer mediates between the mutability threnody and the
return to the exigencies of battle; the action gets under
way again—there is a body to dispose of.

While there are other opportunities to arrest the flux
of events, they are not all of this kind. The changes in
pace and shifts of perspective owe as much to the chronicle as to the techniques of pageantry. The essential events
and the processes and energies that shape and direct them
are transmitted into the spectacle with a high sense of
responsibility to the chronicle vision.

The three parts of *Henry VI* coincide with three distinct
phases of the history and show that Shakespeare did what
he could to tease a form for each of the plays out of the
given material. The first phase of Holinshed's version[5]
reports about four hundred incidents in the French cam-
paign, some perfunctorily and some with full solemnity.
The siege of Orleans is the most conspicuous in both
chronicle and play. Holinshed finds occasion to deploy his
epic clichés, with the "Englishmen" behaving themselves

---

[4] See J. Pearce, "An Earlier Talbot Epitaph," *Modern Language
Notes* (1944), p. 327.

[5] Pp. 585–625 in the 1587 ed. These are the "first phase" as they
supply almost all the material of *Part 1*. *Part 2* uses pp. 622–43, and
Part 3 pp. 643–93.

"right valiantlie under the conduct of their couragious capteine" to keep and enlarge "that which Henrie the fift had by his magnanimite & puissance atchived" (*Hol.* [1587/1808], p. 161). But the accent changes to somber historical prophecy, marking the ineluctable, impersonal historical law:

> But all helped not. For who can hold that which will awaie: In so much that some cities by fraudulent practises, othersome by martial prowesse were recovered by the French, to the great discouragement of the English and the appalling of their spirits; whose hope was now dashed partlie by their great losses and discomfitures (as after you shall heare) but cheeflie by the death of the late deceassed Henrie their victorious king.

These opening pages license a chauvinistic battle-play framing an historical morality about the evil consequences of civil dissension. Here is Holinshed on the loss of a group of towns in 1451:

> Everie daie was looking for aid, but none came. And whie? Even bicause the divelish division that reigned in England, so incombred the heads of the noble men there, that the honor of the realme was cleerelie forgotten. (*Hol.*, p. 228)

The chronicled sources of disaster are more nakedly sprung in the play: the loss of the puissant and magnanimous Henry V, the hostile stars, the hard fortunes of war, the perverse skill of the French, the steady eclipse of English chivalry with the deaths of its aging heroes, and the corrosive quarrels and dynastic rivalries of the nobles at home. All this is manifest in the mere pantomime of *Part 1*—its force would be felt by the stone-deaf, and the routine of the play's rhetoric does much to accent and little to qualify, explore or challenge the basic simplicities of the history.

The originality of Shakespeare's accomplishments is in the shedding of all literary artifice except that which serves to express the temper and structure of the history.

The first scene, for instance, establishes at once that
double perspective which controls the mood of the chronicle—the sense of being close to the event together with
a sense of knowing its consequences. The messenger's long
review of the calamities of thirty future years, spoken in
the memorial presence of the dead Henry V, is a precise
dramatic expression of the narrative's parenthesis, "as
after you shall heare," of which many repetitions catch
the effect of a remorseless historical law expounded by
an omniscient commentator.

The symmetrical sallies and counter-sallies of the next
hour of the pantomime express the fickle movement of
Mars, so often moralized by Holinshed: "thus did things
waver in doubtful balance betwixt the two nations English and French"; "thus oftentimes varied the chance of
doubtful war"; "thus flowed the victory, sometimes on the
one party, and sometimes on the other" (*Hol.*, pp. 172,
180, 192). So speaks the dramatic Dauphin:

> Mars his true moving, even as in the heavens
> So in the earth, to this day is not known:
> Late did he shine upon the English side;
> Now we are victors; upon us he smiles.
>
> (I.ii.1)

The literary commonplace carries the chronicle moral in
a naïve rhetoric transparent enough to let the raw facts
tell.

It is French cunning that most often conspires with
Mars to confound the English. The sniping of Salisbury at
Orleans exemplifies it in an arresting stage effect ready-
made in Holinshed for upper stage (tarras) performance.
But as Holinshed's data is otherwise scanty and undra-
matic, Shakespeare amplifies it by making the French instead of the English employ "counterfeit husbandmen" to
capture Rouen (*Stone*, pp. 205–07). He betrays the
chronicle detail in order to enforce one of its generaliza-
tions, for while on one occasion defending the use of fraud
in lawful war, Holinshed habitually prefers honest violence—an impression strengthened in the play by the

rival characterizations of Joan and Talbot. Talbot's stratagem at Auvergne (II.iii) is not subtle-witted but represents the triumph of soldierly resourcefulness over French
and female craft.

While "martiall feates, and daily skirmishes" continue
in France, the play returns in four scenes to England and
conveys the essential Holinshed by keeping the civil
causes coincident with the military effects. Thus the
dramatic concurrence of the siege of Orleans and the
brawl outside the Tower of London (I.iii) directly ex-
presses the chronicle point, "Through dissention at home,
all lost abroad" (*Hol.*, p. 228). The Gloster-Winchester
feud is elaborately chronicled and patience and some
skill go into Shakespeare's abbreviation of it. More important than his management of the intricate detail, however, is the strategic liberty taken with the facts in order
to reduce the formal reconciliation elaborately mounted
in the chronicle to a repetition of the earlier squabble, but
this time concluded with a reluctant, casual handshake;
the Mayor, the muttered asides, and the servants off to the
surgeon's and the tavern, demote the dignity of the event
(*Hol.*, p. 146).[6] That quarrel thus becomes representative
of those which Holinshed ascribes to "privie malice and
inward grudge," while the dynastic rivalry assumes by
contrast a status appropriate to its remoter origin and
more terrible consequence.

It is in his presentation of the struggle between Lancaster and York that Shakespeare does most to transcend
the temper and enrich the data of the chronicle. For in
the early pages of Holinshed the struggle is nowhere
clearly epitomized. There are only allusions to things that
will "hereafter more manifestlie appeare"; Henry, for instance, creates Plantagenet Duke of York, "not foreseeing
that this preferment should be his destruction, nor that
his seed should of his generation be the extreame end and
finall conclusion" (*Hol.*, p. 155; *Stone,* p. 223). Hence
Shakespeare's invention of four scenes which, through the
heraldic formality of their language, reveal the hidden

---

6 Here it is Bedford who formally rebukes the quarrelsome lords;
the play's homely figure of the mayor is borrowed from Fabyan.

keenness and permanence of the dynastic conflict. The only distinguished one—the Temple scene—is much in the manner of *Richard II;* there is the same tension between ceremony and spleen:

> And that I'll prove on better men than Somerset,
> Were growing time once ripen'd to my will.
>
> (II.iv.98)

But the note is caught again in the scene of Mortimer's death:

> Here dies the dusky torch of Mortimer,
> Choked with ambition of the meaner sort.
>
> (II.v.122)

The two scenes between Vernon and Basset (III.iv and IV.i) extend the Roses dispute from the masters to the "servants"; but unlike those other servants who "enter with bloody pates" (III.i.85 SD) in pursuit of Winchester's and Gloster's causes, these conduct their quarrel according to "the law of arms." Ceremony and savagery are equally characteristic of chronicle taste, and in *Part 1* a full range of types of dissension is displayed by the mutations of the spectacle.

The labored and repetitious data of the chronicle are clarified without undue simplification, with the audience required to dwell at leisure on episodes of momentous and lasting significance to the course of history. The rhythm between pattern and process is maintained; the play like the history must be both reflected upon and lived through, its moral shape apprehended but its clamor and hurly-burly wracking the nerves. But not all the chronicle material is adroitly and happily assimilated. Shakespeare's embarrassment as heir to the facts and judgments of Holinshed is disconcertingly evident in his treatment of Joan. Holinshed presents two versions; a "French" one, stated at length but unsympathetically, "that this Jone (forsooth) was a damsell divine" (*Hol.,* p. 171; *Stone,* pp. 210–12); and an "English" one, owed to Monstrelet, that she was "a damnable sorcerer suborned by Satan" (*Hol.*, p. 172). Shakespeare pursues the chronicle by making her a manifestly evil angel of light, and as the trick of turning devil into seeming angel was a Morality Play commonplace, a technique of presentation lay to hand.[7] But the figure was much easier to accept under the old allegoric conventions of the Morality Play that Shakespeare has all but discarded, than under the new historical documentary ones he was forging. In the early scenes the nice and nasty views about Joan are credibly distributed between the French and English,[8] but after allowing her to voice an authentic French patriotism (winning Burgundy back to her cause) Shakespeare capitulates and throws his French Daniel to the English lions, "Done like a Frenchman: turne and turne againe" (III.iii.85). Shakespeare—as an examination of the detail would show—does nothing to mask and much to stress the tension between the rival images of "Puzel" and "Pussel," the "high-minded strumpet" and "the holy prophetess." Late in the play she is made to speak a searching indictment of English hypocrisy (V.iv. 36ff.) whose barbs are not removed by the spectacle of her converse with evil spirits.

The play ends with the patching of a false peace which holds no promise of a renewed civil order, and whose terms, born out of a silly flirtation, prefigure the final loss of France. None of the many reconciliations have any quality of goodwill, Shakespeare taking his tone again from Holinshed:

> But what cause soever hindered their accord and unitie
> . . . certeine it is, that the onelie and principal cause was,
> for that the God of peace and love was not among them,
> without whom no discord is quenched, no knot of con-
> cord fastened, no bond of peace confirmed, no distracted

---

[7] E.g., John Bale, *The Temptation of our Lord* (see *Works*, ed. Farmer, p. 155), and *The Conflict of Conscience* (see Hazlitt-Dodsley, Vol. VI, p. 35).
[8] The only mocking lines spoken of Joan by the French are Alençon's at I.ii.119; the English messenger calls her "holy prophetess" at I.iv.102.

minds reconciled, no true freendship mainteined. (*Hol.*, p. 183)

Suffolk's courtship of Margaret (V.iii) prefaces a false peace with a false love. To parody the absurdities of political romance Shakespeare allows Suffolk the style of a professional philanderer (one thinks of de Simier's wooing of Elizabeth for Alençon) and compiles for him "A volume of enticing lines" more felicitous than Lacy's in *Friar Bacon and Friar Bungay;* but in Greene's play the courtship is an engaging frolic merely, while here the treacheries exercised in the politics of flirtation are as sinister as they are amusing—the betrayal of trust must have evil consequences in the harsh chronicle setting.

Holinshed grieves that "the God of peace and love" was not among the jarring nobles; but in a sense he was —in the unfortunate person of King Henry—and Shakespeare is well aware of the irony. Henry is "too virtuous to rule the realm of England," like Elidure, the comically naïve King in the early chronicle-morality *Nobody and Somebody,*[9] but Shakespeare makes the point unsmilingly. In the *Henry VI* plays, virtue, through varying degrees of culpable innocence, connives in its own destruction. Had they been performed in the reign of Henry VII, when the canonization of "Holy Harry" was still a point of debate and his martyrdom a theme for civic spectacle, those who thought the King an innocent might have appealed to the first two plays, and those who took him for a saint, to the last. For as the plays advance, the paradoxical plight of moral man under the rule of historical and political processes grows more disturbing until it reaches something like a tragic solution.

---

9 This play (edited by Richard Simpson for the Shakespeare Society) treats the ups and downs of Elidure's reign with challenging irreverence. The extant edition is of 1606, but the original may antedate *Henry VI.*

Suggested References

The number of possible references is vast and grows alarmingly. (The *Shakespeare Quarterly* devotes a substantial part of one issue each year to a list of the previous year's work, and *Shakespeare Survey*—an annual publication—includes a substantial review of recent scholarship, as well as an occasional essay surveying a few decades of scholarship on a chosen topic.) Though no works are indispensable, those listed below have been found helpful.

1. Shakespeare's Times

Byrne, M. St. Clare. *Elizabethan Life in Town and Country*. Rev. ed. New York: Barnes & Noble, Inc., 1961. Chapters on manners, beliefs, education, etc., with illustrations.

Craig, Hardin. *The Enchanted Glass: the Elizabethan Mind in Literature*. New York and London: Oxford University Press, 1936. The Elizabethan intellectual climate.

Joseph, B. L. *Shakespeare's Eden: The Commonwealth of England 1558–1629*. New York: Barnes & Noble, Inc., 1971. An account of the social, political, economic, and cultural life of England.

Nicoll, Allardyce (ed.). *The Elizabethans*. London: Cambridge University Press, 1957. An anthology of Elizabethan writings, especially valuable for its illustrations from paintings, title pages, etc.

Shakespeare's England. 2 vols. Oxford: The Clarendon Press, 1916. A large collection of scholarly essays on a wide variety of topics (e.g., astrology, costume, gardening, horsemanship), with special attention to Shakespeare's references to these topics.

Tillyard, E. M. W. *The Elizabethan World Picture*. London: Chatto & Windus, 1943; New York: The Macmillan Company, 1944. A brief account of some Elizabethan ideas of the universe.

Wilson, John Dover (ed.). *Life in Shakespeare's England.* 2nd ed. New York: The Macmillan Company, 1913. An anthology of Elizabethan writings on the countryside, superstition, education, the court, etc.

2. Shakespeare

Barnet, Sylvan. *A Short Guide to Shakespeare.* New York: Harcourt Brace Jovanovich, Inc., 1974. An introduction to all of the works and to the traditions behind them.

Bentley, Gerald E. *Shakespeare: A Biographical Handbook.* New Haven, Conn.: Yale University Press, 1961. The facts about Shakespeare, with virtually no conjecture intermingled.

Bradby, Anne (ed.). *Shakespeare Criticism, 1919–1935.* London: Oxford University Press, 1936. A small anthology of excellent essays on the plays.

Bush, Geoffrey. *Shakespeare and the Natural Condition.* Cambridge, Mass.: Harvard University Press; London: Oxford University Press, 1956. A short, sensitive account of Shakespeare's view of "Nature," touching most of the works.

Chambers, E. K. *William Shakespeare: A Study of Facts and Problems.* 2 vols. London: Oxford University Press, 1930. An invaluable, detailed reference work; not for the casual reader.

Chute, Marchette. *Shakespeare of London.* New York: E. P. Dutton & Co., Inc., 1949. A readable biography fused with portraits of Stratford and London life.

Clemen, Wolfgang H. *The Development of Shakespeare's Imagery.* Cambridge, Mass.: Harvard University Press, 1951. (Originally published in German, 1936.) A temperate account of a subject often abused.

Craig, Hardin. *An Interpretation of Shakespeare.* Columbia, Mo.: Lucas Brothers, 1948. A scholar's book designed for the layman. Comments on all the works.

Dean, Leonard F. (ed.). *Shakespeare: Modern Essays in Criticism.* New York: Oxford University Press, 1957. Mostly mid-twentieth-century critical studies, covering Shakespeare's artistry.

Granville-Barker, Harley. *Prefaces to Shakespeare.* 2 vols. Princeton, N.J.: Princeton University Press, 1946–47. Essays on ten plays by a scholarly man of the theater.

Harbage, Alfred. *As They Liked It.* New York: The Macmillan Company, 1947. A sensitive, long essay on Shakespeare, morality, and the audience's expectations.

————*William Shakespeare: A Reader's Guide.* New York: Farrar, Straus, 1963. Extensive comments, scene by scene, on fourteen plays.

Ridler, Anne Bradby (ed.). *Shakespeare Criticism, 1935–1960.* New York and London: Oxford University Press, 1963. An excellent continuation of the anthology edited earlier by Miss Bradby (see above).

Schoenbaum, S. *Shakespeare's Lives.* Oxford: Clarendon Press, 1970. A review of the evidence, and an examination of many biographies, including those by Baconians and other

Smith, D. Nichol (ed.). *Shakespeare Criticism.* New York: Oxford University Press, 1916. A selection of criticism from 1623 to 1840, ranging from Ben Jonson to Thomas Carlyle.

Spencer, Theodore. *Shakespeare and the Nature of Man.* New York: The Macmillan Company, 1942. Shakespeare's plays in relation to Elizabethan thought.

Stoll, Elmer Edgar. *Shakespeare and Other Masters.* Cambridge, Mass.: Harvard University Press; London: Oxford University Press, 1040. Essays on tragedy, comedy, and aspects of dramaturgy, with special reference to some of Shakespeare's plays.

Traversi, D. A. *An Approach to Shakespeare.* Rev. ed. New York: Doubleday & Co., Inc., 1956. An analysis of the plays, beginning with words, images, and themes, rather than with characters.

Van Doren, Mark. *Shakespeare.* New York: Henry Holt & Company, Inc., 1939. Brief, perceptive readings of all of the plays.

Whitaker, Virgil K. *Shakespeare's Use of Learning.* San Marino, Calif.: Huntington Library, 1953. A study of the relation of Shakespeare's reading to his development as a dramatist.

3. Shakespeare's Theater

Adams, John Cranford. *The Globe Playhouse.* Rev. ed. New York: Barnes & Noble, Inc., 1961. A detailed conjecture about the physical characteristics of the theater Shakespeare often wrote for.

Beckerman, Bernard. *Shakespeare at the Globe, 1599–1609.* New York: The Macmillan Company, 1962. On the playhouse and on Elizabethan dramaturgy, acting, and staging.

Chambers, E. K. *The Elizabethan Stage.* 4 vols. New York: Oxford University Press, 1923. Reprinted with corrections, 1945. An invaluable reference work on theaters, theatrical companies, and staging at court.

Gurr, Andrew. *The Shakespearean Stage 1574–1642.* Cambridge: Cambridge University Press, 1970. On the acting companies, the actors, the playhouses, the stages, and the audiences.

Harbage, Alfred. *Shakespeare's Audience.* New York: Columbia University Press; London: Oxford University Press, 1941. A study of the size and nature of the theatrical public.

Hodges, C. Walter. *The Globe Restored.* London: Ernest Benn, Ltd., 1953; New York: Coward-McCann, Inc., 1954. A well-illustrated and readable attempt to reconstruct the Globe Theatre.

Kernodle, George R. *From Art to Theatre: Form and Convention in the Renaissance.* Chicago: University of Chicago Press, 1944. Pioneering and stimulating work on the symbolic and cultural meanings of theater construction.

Nagler, A. M. *Shakespeare's Stage.* Tr. by Ralph Manheim. New Haven, Conn.: Yale University Press, 1958. An excellent brief introduction to the physical aspect of the playhouse.

Smith, Irwin. *Shakespeare's Globe Playhouse.* New York: Charles Scribner's Sons, 1957. Chiefly indebted to J. C. Adams' controversial book, with additional material and scale drawings for model-builders.

Venezky, Alice S. *Pageantry on the Shakespearean Stage.* New York: Twayne Publishers, Inc., 1951. An examination of spectacle in Elizabethan drama.

4. Miscellaneous Reference Works

Abbott, E. A. *A Shakespearean Grammar*. New edition. New York: The Macmillan Company, 1877. An examination of differences between Elizabethan and modern grammar.

Bartlett, John. *A New and Complete Concordance . . . to . . . Shakespeare*. New York: The Macmillan Company, 1894. An index to most of Shakespeare's words.

Berman, Ronald. *A Reader's Guide to Shakespeare's Plays*. Chicago: Scott, Foresman and Company, 1965. A short bibliography of the chief articles and books on each play.

Bullough, Geoffrey. *Narrative and Dramatic Sources of Shakespeare*. 5 vols. Vols. 6 and 7 in preparation. New York: Columbia University Press; London: Routledge & Kegan Paul, Ltd., 1957–. A collection of many of the books Shakespeare drew upon.

Campbell, Oscar James, and Edward G. Quinn. *The Reader's Encyclopedia of Shakespeare*. New York: Thomas Y. Crowell Co., 1966. More than 2,700 entries, from a few sentences to a few pages on everything related to Shakespeare.

Greg, W. W. *The Shakespeare First Folio*. New York and London: Oxford University Press, 1955. A detailed yet readable history of the first collection (1623) of Shakespeare's plays.

Kökeritz, Helge. *Shakespeare's Names*. New Haven, Conn.: Yale University Press, 1959; London: Oxford University Press, 1960. A guide to the pronunciation of some 1,800 names appearing in Shakespeare.

———. *Shakespeare's Pronunciation*. New Haven, Conn.: Yale University Press; London: Oxford University Press, 1953. Contains much information about puns and rhymes.

Linthicum, Marie C. *Costume in the Drama of Shakespeare and His Contemporaries*. New York and London: Oxford University Press, 1936. On the fabrics and dress of the age, and references to them in the plays.

Muir, Kenneth. *Shakespeare's Sources*. London: Methuen & Co., Ltd., 1957. Vol. 2 in preparation. The first volume, on the comedies and tragedies, attempts to as-

certain what books were Shakespeare's sources, and
what use he made of them.

Onions, C. T. *A Shakespeare Glossary*. London: Oxford University Press, 1911; 2nd ed., rev., with en-
larged addenda, 1953. Definitions of words (or senses
of words) now obsolete.

Partridge, Eric. *Shakespeare's Bawdy*. Rev. ed. New York:
E. P. Dutton & Co., Inc.; London: Routledge & Kegan
Paul, Ltd., 1955. A glossary of bawdy words and
phrases.

Shakespeare Quarterly. See headnote to Suggested References.

Shakespeare Survey. See headnote to Suggested References.

Smith, Gordon Ross. *A Classified Shakespeare Bibliography 1936–1958*. University Park, Pa.: Pennsylvania
State University Press, 1963. A list of some 20,000
items on Shakespeare.

Spevack, Marvin. *The Harvard Concordance to Shakespeare*. Cambridge, Mass.: Harvard University Press,
1973. An index to Shakespeare's words.

Wells, Stanley, ed. *Shakespeare: Select Bibliographies*. London: Oxford University Press, 1973. Seventeen essays
surveying scholarship and criticism of Shakespeare's life,
work, and theater.

5. *Henry VI, Part One*

Alexander, Peter. *Shakespeare's Henry VI and Richard
III*. Intr. by Alfred W. Pollard. Cambridge: The
University Press, 1929.

Brockbank, J. P. "The Frame of Disorder—'Henry VI,' "
Shakespeare Institute Studies: Early Shakespeare, eds.
John Russell Brown and Bernard Harris. London: Edward Arnold, Ltd., 1961; New York: Schocken Books,
1966. Reprinted in part on pages 205–15.

Cairncross, Andrew S. (ed.). *The Arden Shakespeare:
The First Part of King Henry VI*. London: Methuen
& Co., Ltd.; Cambridge, Mass.: Harvard University
Press, 1962.

Campbell, Lily B. *Shakespeare's "Histories": Mirrors of
Elizabethan Policy*. San Marino, Calif.: The Hunting-

ton Library; London: Cambridge University Press, 1947.

Clemen, Wolfgang H. "Anticipation and Foreboding in Shakespeare's Early Histories," *Shakespeare Survey 6,* ed. Allardyce Nicoll. Cambridge: The University Press, 1953.

Gaw, Allison. *The Origin and Development of 1 Henry VI in Relation to Shakespeare, Marlowe, Peele, and Greene.* Los Angeles: University of Southern California, 1926.

Jackson, Sir Barry. "On Producing *Henry VI,*" *Shakespeare Survey 6,* ed. Allardyce Nicoll. Cambridge: The University Press, 1953. Reprinted in the Signet Classic edition of *2 Henry VI.*

Jorgensen, Paul A. *Shakespeare's Military World.* Berkeley: University of California Press, 1956.

Kirschbaum, Leo. "The Authorship of *1 Henry VI,*" *PMLA,* LXVII (1952), 809–822.

Ornstein, Robert. *A Kingdom for a Stage.* Cambridge, Mass.: Harvard University Press, 1972.

Price, Hereward T. *Construction in Shakespeare,* Ann Arbor, Mich.: University of Michigan Press, 1951.

Reese, Max Meredith. *The Cease of Majesty: A Study of Shakespeare's History Plays.* London: Edward Arnold, Ltd., 1961; New York: St. Martin's Press, Inc., 1962.

Ribner, Irving. *The English History Play in the Age of Shakespeare.* Princeton, N.J.: Princeton University Press; London: Oxford University Press, 1957.

Riggs, David. *Shakespeare's Heroical Histories: "Henry VI" and Its Literary Tradition.* Cambridge, Mass.: Harvard University Press, 1971.

Talbert, Ernest William. *Elizabethan Drama and Shakespeare's Early Plays: An Essay in Historical Criticism.* Chapel Hill, N. C.: The University of North Carolina Press, 1963.

Tillyard, E. M. W. *Shakespeare's History Plays.* London: Chatto and Windus, 1944; New York: Collier Books, 1962. Reprinted in part on pages 190–204.

Wilson, John Dover (ed.). *The New Cambridge Shakespeare: The First Part of King Henry VI.* Cambridge: The University Press, 1952.

THE SIGNET CLASSIC SHAKESPEARE

With the publication of Shakespeare's Narrative Poems, the Signet Classic Shakespeare is now complete. The 40 volumes include not only the Narrative Poems (introduction by William Empson), and the 37 canonical plays, but also the Sonnets (introduction by W. H. Auden) and The Two Noble Kinsmen (edited by Clifford Leech), a play which most modern scholars think is at least partly by Shakespeare.

☐ **ALL'S WELL THAT ENDS WELL,** Sylvan Barnet, ed.
(#CD296—50¢)

☐ **ANTONY AND CLEOPATRA,** Barbara Everett, ed.
(#CQ741—95¢)

☐ **AS YOU LIKE IT,** Albert Gilman, ed.   (#CQ933—95¢)

☐ **THE COMEDY OF ERRORS,** Harry Levin
(#CY960—$1.25)

☐ **CORIOLANUS,** Reuben Brower, ed.   (#CQ806—95¢)

☐ **CYMBELINE,** Richard Hosley, ed.   (#CQ763—95¢)

☐ **HAMLET,** Edward Hubler, ed.   (#CY1022—$1.25)

☐ **HENRY IV, Part I,** Maynard Mack, ed. (#CY948—$1.25)

☐ **HENRY IV, Part II,** Norman H. Holland, ed.
(#CQ856—95¢)

☐ **HENRY VI, Part II,** Arthur Freeman, ed., Boston.
(#CY995—$1.25)

C

- ☐ **HENRY VI, Part III**, Milton Crane, ed. (#CD336—50¢)
- ☐ **JULIUS CAESAR**, William and Barbara Rosen, eds. (#CY983—$1.25)
- ☐ **MACBETH**, Sylvan Barnet, ed. (#CY974—$1.25)
- ☐ **MEASURE FOR MEASURE**, S. Nagarajan, ed. (#CQ861—95¢)
- ☐ **THE MERCHANT OF VENICE**, Kenneth O. Myrick, ed. (#CY1017—$1.25)
- ☐ **THE MERRY WIVES OF WINDSOR**, William Green, ed. (#CD318—50¢)
- ☐ **A MIDSUMMER NIGHT'S DREAM**, Wolfgang Clemen, ed. (#CY973—$1.25)
- ☐ **MUCH ADO ABOUT NOTHING**, David Stevenson, ed. (#CQ830—95¢)
- ☐ **RICHARD II**, Kenneth Muir, ed. (#CQ808—95¢)
- ☐ **RICHARD III**, Mark Eccles, ed. (#CQ831—95¢)
- ☐ **ROMEO AND JULIET**, Joseph Bryant, ed. (#CY968—$1.25)
- ☐ **THE TAMING OF THE SHREW**, Robert Heilman, ed. (#CQ792—95¢)
- ☐ **THE TEMPEST**, Robert Langbaum, ed. (#CY994—$1.25)
- ☐ **TIMON OF ATHENS**, Maurice Charney, ed. (#CD289—50¢)
- ☐ **TROILUS AND CRESSIDA**, Daniel Seltzer, ed. (#CQ935—95¢)
- ☐ **TWELFTH NIGHT**, Herschel Clay Baker, ed. (#CQ748—95¢)
- ☐ **THE TWO GENTLEMEN OF VERONA**, Bertrand Evans, ed. (#CQ805—95¢)

THE NEW AMERICAN LIBRARY, INC.,
P.O. Box 999, Bergenfield, New Jersey 07621

Please send me the SIGNET CLASSIC BOOKS I have checked above. I am enclosing $_____(check or money order—no currency or C.O.D.'s). Please include the list price plus 35¢ a copy to cover handling and mailing costs. (Prices and numbers are subject to change without notice.)

Name_____

Address_____

City_____State_____Zip Code_____

Allow at least 4 weeks for delivery